DIABLO LAKE: PROTECTED

LAUREN DANE

carina
press

carina press®

Recycling programs
for this product may
not exist in your area.

ISBN-13: 978-1-335-50810-2

Diablo Lake: Protected

First published in 2017. This edition published in 2023.

Copyright © 2017 by Lauren Dane

For questions and comments about the quality of this book, please contact us at CustomerService@Harlequin.com.

Carina Press
22 Adelaide St. West, 41st Floor
Toronto, Ontario M5H 4E3, Canada
www.CarinaPress.com

Printed in U.S.A.

To everyone who loves paranormal romance
enough to bring it back—thank you!

DIABLO LAKE: PROTECTED

Chapter One

Aimee pulled her car into a spot at the rear of the mercantile. She'd walk over to Katie Faith's house from there because her driveway was currently housing construction stuff they were using on some remodeling going on.

The breeze on the back of her neck was unfamiliar, but she sort of liked it. She loved the soft fuzz at the base of her skull.

She headed across the lawns, pausing to breathe in the life her best friend had brought with her when she'd moved in. Roses burst forth over every planter box. They climbed up trellises and spilled across the edges of all the walks.

In December, this sight would be totally unreal in any other place but Diablo Lake. In Diablo Lake, roses in December meant a witch lived there and gave the earth her power.

A bunch of gorgeous men stood outside her best friend's place, all sweaty from building things. She paused to take it in, because life presented you blessings and it was disrespectful not to enjoy and appreciate them.

Hot werewolves with tools. It should be a calendar. Aimee made a mental note because, come to think of it, what a fantastic fundraiser idea for the organization she worked for.

She hummed her delight at the thought, and being werewolves with super hearing, the group of 'em all looked in her direction. They hadn't been alarmed, which meant they'd recognized her scent and most likely her magic.

"Hey, y'all," she called out, pretending she'd been thinking about cobbler instead of pecs and abs glistening in the sun.

Jace, Katie Faith's husband and most assuredly a gorgeous werewolf, paused, his eyes widening and his smile of welcome dropping into surprise. "You cut your hair."

Suddenly she went very shy and sort of embarrassed before reminding herself that hair grew back.

"I like it." Damon, one of Jace's brothers, stepped a little closer. "It's got blue in it. I didn't see it at first because your hair is already dark. Saucy. Diablo Lake definitely needs more saucy."

Saucy she could do.

Moment of panic passed, she said, "Thanks. I just thought a change would be nice and since the wedding is over and I don't have to worry about pictures, I figured why not do something big?"

Katie Faith came out onto the porch. "Did I hear Aimee out here?" Then she gasped, rushing over to get up in Aimee's space to get a look at her new haircut.

"It's fantastic. Flirty. So sexy. Mysterious even. My God, why do you have such perfect features for short hair?"

Aimee, used to the way her best friend talked, understood it was all compliments and let herself be drawn into the house as she said her goodbyes to the others over her shoulder.

Once they were out of immediate earshot—though if they'd wanted to, the wolves could easily overhear though it was considered good manners to attempt not to eavesdrop—Aimee grabbed Katie Faith's hand.

"Spill this story." Katie Faith pointed at Aimee's head with her free hand. "This is a reaction haircut. With some get-me-over-something colored tips."

"This calls for liquor."

Katie Faith nodded and led the way. In the large and old-school kitchen, her friend poured them each a shot of tequila and then she clinked her glass to Aimee's. "All right. Let's hear it."

"So, Bob called me yesterday. Totally out of the blue."

Three years before she'd met Bob through her job as a rural social worker. He worked for one of the agencies the grant that funded her job came from.

They'd been on and off over those years. Meeting when she went to Knoxville to check in with some of her clients and at the main office of the social service agency she worked for.

Katie Faith's "bullshit" eyebrow rose. "Did he, now? In a booty-call way?"

Aimee got up to paw around through the cabinets until she found some chips and came back over.

"Well, it was weird. You know, he and I finally and truly broke things off more than six months back now. I haven't seen him or spoken to him since. And, well, I know this sounds mean, but I really don't miss him. It was fun while it lasted, but it was never going anywhere permanent."

Even if they had both wanted to get more serious, there was still the problem of him not being from Diablo Lake. Bringing a human into town was a big deal. Marrying them into the community took dedication and a real match.

That was never what it had been with Bob.

"So," Aimee continued, "he told me he wanted to meet up because he'd been thinking about me and I was like, 'Dude, no, really it's okay. I've moved on, I'm not mad but I'm done.' So then he's like, 'Please can you just meet me? Just a few minutes.'"

She tore open the bag and stuffed her face in between the next two shots.

Katie Faith leaned back in her chair and gave her an appraising look before shaking her head slowly. "Oh, Aimee-girl, you're going to kill me with this story, aren't you? Last time you took this many shots of liquor in a short period of time it was the night I got left at the altar."

Aimee snorted, remembering that gawdawful scene when Darrell Pembry left her best friend waiting at the church to run off with another woman. "Well, this isn't as horrible as that, at least. However, you don't even know half. Just wait for it." She waved a hand. "So it was Friday and that's when I go down to Knoxville anyway. I agreed to meet him for coffee. Because, girl, no one gets between me and lunch and if it was going to go badly, I didn't want to mess up a meal."

They bumped fists. "So say we all," Katie Faith intoned, which made her laugh.

"I get there and he's sitting at a table already. I go over and he gives me the gracious-ex cheek kiss and hug and I'm like, he was a pretty good guy, I hope this can be cordial but I'm not feeling any tinglies at all. Not a one."

And at one time, they'd really had them.

"And then." She took a bracing breath because even remembering, it filled her with so much emotion. "Sweet, sweet baby Jesus. The man tells me several things. First, he's married. Has been for *fifteen* years." Nausea rose again at the feeling of betrayal that'd washed over her.

"Get out!" Katie Faith yelled it so loud Jace pounded into the room, looking alarmed. She winced at the sight and gave him a sheepish smile. "Sorry, honey. Aimee just told me something totally awful."

Jace turned his gaze Aimee's way, staring carefully. "Do you need us to teach someone a lesson for you?"

Aww, he'd just offered to beat a boy up for getting fresh like a real big brother would.

"As much pleasure as that would give me, I'm good. Thanks though," Aimee told him.

He nodded once before walking from the room, telling everyone to get back to work.

"But wait, there's more." Aimee thanked Katie Faith for the shot she poured. "Hoo, I'm going to be so drunk. I'm going to say something unwise and probably be hungover tomorrow. I'm making bad choices. Ugh. Bob also told me he has five children. Five." That still made her want to run him over with her car.

"I'm going to Knoxville right now to punch him right in the butthole!" Katie Faith snarled.

Thank God for friends. "That's a really good one. I'll tuck that aside for future use," Aimee told her.

"Honey, I'm so sorry. What a maggot-eating shitlord. What did you say when he told you this?"

"You're on fire tonight. I need to write that one down and you know how much I love *shitlord* as an insult. Bob is a *total* maggot-eating shitlord. So when he busted out that he had kids and a wife I said, 'What the fuck

did you just say?' And I may have said it loud enough
to get a look from a woman nearby. Then I said to her,
'He just told me he's married and has five kids. After
dating me for nearly three years.'"

Katie Faith hooted with laughter. "Did you really? I
am so bummed I missed that part."

"She said, 'You go 'head on, honey, that deserves all
the bad words.' Then she told him she hoped his pecker
fell off. It was a pretty righteous moment. Anyway I
was like, 'Why did you tell me this now? We broke up
six months ago, I haven't thought of you in about five
and a half months. How could you involve me in something so shady?' And *then* he says he's also got a porn-
addiction problem so he has to come to me as one of
his steps to make amends. I tossed my still very warm
drink at him and stormed out. Then I spent too much
money on some boots and cut all my hair off and got
blue tips because I'm a cliché."

Katie Faith shook her head. "You're not a cliché at
all. That blue looks so cute. I'm surprised you didn't
call me for bail money. I might need it after that. What
are you going to do? We can borrow Jace's truck, load
it with our friends and hunt him down. I have extra
baseball bats."

This was why she'd come to see her friend. Aimee
laughed, wiping away an embarrassed tear. "I was already done with him, you know? I would *never* have
been with him if I'd known he was married. So I don't
feel guilty. Not that way. But he *used* me. Made me into
the other woman. I really hate that. And I hate that he
told me all that to make himself feel better. It only made
me feel worse! I'm probably going to take a five-hour
shower now. I feel so bad for his wife and kids. How
could I not have seen?"

She'd asked herself that very question over and over. But the place he'd met her was an apartment. One she thought was his and there was no way a family of seven lived there. It was a one-bedroom condo a single man lived in. Ugh.

"He had a single guy apartment. I wonder if it's his or if he borrowed it when I came to see him?"

"Like one of those fuck pads the guys in the movies get." Katie Faith nodded and Aimee settled in. When her friend got liquored up she said the best, weirdest stuff. "Remember that one we saw? The guy from *The Lord of the Rings* movies was in it. He was a Cheaty McCheat-erson and he and his douche-canoe friends all shared this condo where they took their side action back."

Aimee nodded. "That guy's hot. But that one had murder in it. Ew. No. I hope I wasn't using the murder-my-mistress sheets."

"That would be a cliché for sure." Katie Faith gave a dramatic sigh. "He's a pig. Good riddance. Thank God you used condoms. Your hair looks totally adorable and lastly, you didn't see because he's a cheater who crafted a life on the side meant to fool everyone in what was most definitely not a murder fuck pad."

With one last sigh, Aimee said, "So, that was my day. How was yours?"

Katie Faith, still frowning, hugged her tight before getting up. "We need to eat something. My dad brought soup to the Counter at closing time tonight. Since my mom has been keeping him at home to avoid all the drama in town, he's been cooking like crazy. Not that I'm complaining, mind you."

She puttered around the kitchen—one of the rooms they'd remodel come spring—getting the soup heated as Aimee let out some more of her guilt and anxiety.

But now the situation in town—heightened tensions between the shifters—came into focus once more.

A different sort of anxiety.

Katie Faith's father had suffered a heart attack that'd nearly taken his life just four months before. Her family had needed her for support and to run the soda fountain and it had brought Aimee's best friend home, had given Katie Faith real true love and had come at a time to be a match to dry grass.

The wolves' constant back-and-forth had dragged the witches into the fray. Which had involved Katie Faith and, in turn, had only made her father's health more precarious, and her normally really easygoing mother actually got into a public brawl just the month before.

The town was a magical place. Literally. But the more drama and anger that was dredged up, the harder the land had to work to connect with the magic of all the witches. Everyone was at odds and it was exhausting.

"Dude, this is bananas. Like every last bit of today has been absolutely ridiculous and all this town stuff is bonkers. I stopped by to see your dad yesterday on my way home. He's looking better, but his energy is a little frantic."

All her life, Aimee's magic had been the nurturing type. She wanted to make things better for people and animals. And plants too.

She was a green witch. Happy to bring life wherever she went. It meant she was able to use those gifts in dealing with clients because she was empathic. Avery, Katie Faith's dad, was anxious for his family. Resentful that he'd been weakened and guilty because he felt he didn't do his job.

Aimee helped relieve some of his stress, talked him into a better place where he could more easily see he was doing so much more than he'd thought to protect his family.

"My mom told me you hung out with him for an hour having tea and listening to his country music. Thanks for that." Katie Faith had her own frantic energy, as she'd been at the center of a lot of the mess in town. Though here, in this big solid house, it was calmer. More steady.

"Your dad is great and he made hummingbird cake, so naturally I had to stay for tea." He'd started to loosen up, let go of the negative energy he'd been clinging to. "I encouraged your mom to get him away from town more often. I talked to Wade and he told me he's going to be traveling for work and he needs a house sitter to hang with the animals, deal with the gardens, all that stuff. I suggested he call your mom so that'll happen soon too."

Wade was Aimee's brother. He'd left Diablo Lake to settle in Asheville after college. He did employee training seminars on tech support so he traveled several times a year. His place was near enough, but far enough away that Katie Faith's parents could go and not feel guilty but be out of the drama.

"What a big old Softie Softerson you are." Katie Faith put a bowl of mushroom soup in front of her.

"Am not. I'm heartless and cruel. Oh, and I'm a strumpet."

Katie Faith snickered. "A strumpet? I was thinking more a floozie with loose morals."

Aimee nodded as she thought that over while she ate her soup. "I'll have to consider that."

"I couldn't talk them out of the Consort meeting though," Katie Faith said of the group of witches in Diablo Lake and their regular meeting. "I tried but my mom said she wasn't going anywhere until she got her say. So."

Jace wandered in, grabbed beers and left once more, pretending he hadn't been checking on them.

"He's so cute to pretend we don't know he's listening to all this," Katie Faith told her with an eye roll.

A while back her friend had told her of how nosy and bossy and in-your-business wolves were, and the more Aimee hung around them, the better she understood what she'd meant.

But at the heart of it with Jace was his wanting to protect Katie Faith's well-being. And as Aimee cared about that too, she gave him some leeway.

If only the same could be said of *all* the wolves in town. The constant tussling over power had always been part of life. But lately it had been much more personal and hateful as some old grievances had resurfaced.

The witches had been pulled into the whole mess and they'd all had it. All that negative energy would degrade the heart of power all those who lived in Diablo Lake were protected by.

That heart of power the witches had taken an oath to protect, back in the very beginning of their peculiar little town in the middle-of-nowhere Tennessee, also happened to feed their magical power. The earth fed their magic so they were being impacted on multiple levels.

The Consort, run by the elder witches in town, had called a meeting to discuss the situation the following week.

"At least it's not before eight in the morning." Aimee didn't much mind getting up early. But on a Saturday when she'd had the week she had?

Katie Faith curled her lip at the very idea of getting up that early, though she'd do it if she had to. As her friend was a nightmare of a human being before she had coffee, Aimee was relieved on that front as well.

"Why don't you stay over? You can sleep in the spare room. We can watch something scary, even." Katie Faith's hopeful expression made her feel so much better.

"Thank you. But I'm feeling better now. I mean, I wasn't bummed we weren't together and now it makes me even more glad. I just feel dirty, and not the good way. I'll walk home."

"No, you won't. There are a jillion wolves here, and one of them hasn't been doing tequila shots so they can drive you home. But you don't have to go just yet, right? I feel like I haven't seen you in forever."

"You got married a week ago. I've seen you three days this week so far. I think we're okay." Aimee rolled her eyes, glad to have a friend like Katie Faith.

"Being married has been pretty cool."

"So you two still bang and stuff? Now that the thrill is gone?" Aimee teased.

"It's a chore, but we make it work. I mean, someone has to do Jace, it may as well be me."

"Glad you make the sacrifice."

Chapter Two

Macrae Pembry, better known as Mac, shut his computer down, readying to leave after a long day trying to get the Pembry Wolves back on track as a business.

His dad had called him away from London to come home. Come back to Diablo Lake because the family needed him.

Because of course he'd come when called.

The town was on the verge of blowing up and, as it had been for years, his brother's stupid bullshit was at the center of it all. He hadn't expected the hot mess of complicated inter-pack politics he'd discovered upon his return. His mother seemed on the verge of a breakdown, her behavior more and more erratic, and his father and brother were on the outs with the witches.

As much as he wanted to wade in, set stuff on fire and kick the butts of everyone involved, control was what he needed. A wolf in control could run a pack. A wolf without it just made things worse.

He'd need to reach down and use every bit of his training to do this without ripping things apart further.

"Thank God you're finally done. I was thinking I'd have to stay here, pretending to work for another hour at least."

Mac looked toward his cousin Huston, who'd become his assistant when he'd come back home.

"God forbid you actually work hard." He stood, stretching his back, satisfied by the cracking of his spine as he did. It'd been too long since he'd been on a run. If he didn't get out at least every few days, he began to get antsy.

Things in Diablo Lake were tense enough without his energy adding to it. But for that night he planned dinner, beer and television and bed before ten.

That was as sexy as it got for him in the two months he'd been home after spending years in the army and then in college, preparing to come back strong enough to lead his pack.

Though he hadn't imagined the pack would be in such a damned mess when it was time. Or that he might have to push his father out, even when they both knew he was better to run things than his dumbass brother Darrell.

"I'm up for a pizza and some beer, your treat," Huston said.

As Mac lived in his cousin's house now, which saved him from having to bunk at his parents' or with one of his siblings, he figured he could swing that.

He nodded. "Lots of beer."

They headed out of the small building the pack owned just north of city hall. It perched right on the edge of Dooley and Pembry territory. A poke in the eye, his grandfather had said when he bought it.

The last thing Diablo Lake needed just then was anything that provoked pokes in the eye. Then again, it had probably been the last thing needed at the time as well.

Sometimes werewolves could be total assholes.

Case in point, it was taking everything in him and a few others in the pack to keep his mother and brother from starting a damned war over some fucked-up bullshit from the past and his daddy's overinflated ego.

Not for the first time, he thought about what his life could have been if he'd stayed away. But there was no staying away from Diablo Lake for him. He had a role to play, one his uncle reminded him of when he'd called to get Mac home once more.

The Red Roof Inn sat on Diablo Lake Avenue, the main street that bisected what was their tiny downtown business district. A grocery store that still closed on Sundays and after nine every night was at the far end of town. Two bars including Pete's, a windowless haunt full of the type of guys Mac had spent his time avoiding while he'd been in the military and the kind of place that still had pickled eggs in a jar on the back counter. Salt & Pepper, a diner, and the Counter, a soda fountain and sandwich place, also made up that business core.

The RRI had only opened up two years before. A local brewpub that also made pizza, burgers and wings, it was run by two witches who'd gotten themselves trained and educated and had returned home to put that knowledge to good use for everyone in town.

The younger generation of adults in town flocked here and left all their beefs at the door or risked being barred. This was *their* place.

He pushed the door open and a rush of magic hit him, welcomed him. Reminded him why he'd always planned to come back to Diablo Lake.

Inside there were witches, of course, and shifters from all walks of life and parts of town. Dooleys and

Pembrys made up the wolves while Cuthberts and Ruizes were there among other cat shifters, though they mostly kept to themselves, as cats tended to do.

Lots of pretty women laughed as they sat at the bar or at the booths and tables throughout and he was even more glad he'd come that night. Perhaps some of that tension knotting his shoulders could be lessened if he found solace and naked cardio with some female company.

Across the room, a table full of cousins and friends waved them over with a hail of their names. This was another thing he'd found himself missing when he'd been away. The camaraderie he experienced, the belonging, was like nothing else.

"We just ordered a few pizzas. Pitchers will be here shortly too," Everett, Huston's older brother, told them once they got settled.

Growing up, Mac had spent more time with his aunt and uncle than he had with his mother and father. Darrell was the favorite and no matter what anyone else did, it never mattered.

Because his uncle had challenged Mac's father and lost, that he'd given a place in his household to Mac had simply been part of how pack and family structure worked. His aunt and uncle understood what it meant to give comfort and a place of stability and safety to the next generation of pack leadership.

Hard to believe Huston and Everett's dad had been raised in the same house as Dwayne. They might have been brothers, but the two couldn't have been more different.

His uncle had the heart and soul of a leader, and always would. He'd instilled a great deal of important values in Mac. But he wasn't as physically strong, or as viciously needy to be in charge as his brother, Mac's dad. And it was their way to respect and extol the virtues of physical strength.

And yet, sometimes it netted stupid assholes in charge, or in line to be in charge, like his brother Darrell.

Irritated, he needed to move a little, burn off some energy.

With so many of them at the table, they'd be out of beer before it even settled on the table long enough to leave a ring around the glasses. "I'm going to order an extra pitcher or two," he told Huston as he stood. "I'll be right back."

He ambled over to the bar, looking around the room, still in the process of coming home. People had changed in many ways, but underneath the beards and whatnot, they were the same in all the ones that counted.

As he waited for the bartender to make her way down to him, he stepped back and nearly clotheslined someone when he reached out to drop some cash in the tip jar.

"Oh crap! You okay?" He grabbed the woman, keeping her upright, and all that delightful, sexy magic she carried washed through him. His scalp tingled, his own magic reared up to touch hers. And his dick was so hard it hurt.

"Whoa!" Her eyes wide for a moment, still startled, Aimee Benton stood so very close to him he had an urge to rub himself against her.

Damn it all, the woman was fucking gorgeous. She smelled really good and she'd grown into her beauty in all the best ways.

"Sorry about that," he said, shoving his hands into his pockets instead of reaching out to touch her hair.

It'd been nearly to her butt just a few days before when he'd checked her ass out at the grocery store. As he did every time he saw her. "You all right?"

"I nearly got laid out by a once-star tight end. Not too many people can say they avoided it." Her mouth quirked up.

She'd remembered. *Huh.* Stupid to be flattered, but he was anyway.

"Lucky for you the army helped me hone my speed with some control," he teased.

She paused a moment, her tongue sliding over her bottom lip and he came so close to actually whimpering, he had to fight a blush.

Jesus. Like a fourteen-year-old first-transformed wolf.

"Looks like it worked out for you, as you didn't knock me on my ass," she said at last.

The bartender came to take their orders and he needed to get back to the table and his friends and family, but damn if he didn't want just a little bit more of her.

"I like the hair." He tipped his chin.

A flush of pleasure worked up her neck and he fought the desire to brush his lips against the skin at the nape where he knew she'd be downy soft and fragrant with power.

"Yeah? Thanks. It's a big change. But sometimes that's what you need, right?"

He nodded, trying not to stare at her mouth. Or her tits as they pressed against the soft cotton of the long-sleeved shirt she had on.

Or the freckles dancing across the bridge of her nose.

Her blush had brought her scent to his senses like a caress and he sucked in deep, wanting all of it and more.

She gulped and the predator in him stepped closer before the man could even think about it. She wasn't alarmed though. The kick in her pulse and the catch of her breath were from pleasure, not fear.

"I should, uh…" she said, her gaze locked with his as they continued to stand there as the world seemed to fade into the background. He shifted, shielding her with his body so the crowd couldn't jostle her, and she smiled her thanks.

Somewhere in the background he heard her name being called and she broke her attention away to glance back over her shoulder.

"I have to go. Have a good night," she said, grabbing the bottles after handing over her money. She dashed away through the crowd at the bar so he made his way back to the table with two extra pitchers.

Once he got a slice of pizza and filled his glass, he leaned back, scanning the room until he found her sitting with her friends. At one point she tipped her head back as she laughed at something Katie Faith said, the two thick-as-thieves, sitting at the same table with several witches and more than a few Dooley wolves.

He chafed at that.

He wanted… Well, he wasn't quite past the stage where he'd been consumed with thoughts of having sex—a lot of sex—with her.

Even as he stared at her, he saw the division in the room. The only witches with Pembry wolves were those who were already married in and their close relations.

His father had allowed this alienation to take root and it had to be dug out. It was outrageously dangerous to do anything else. Let this bubbling tension erupt into full-blown aggression between packs and they risked the loss of the magic that kept the whole area—and those living there—safe. Many would move away but there were very few places like Diablo Lake, and none more special than his hometown.

"Stop staring at her like that. She's going to think you're scary and you're going to creep her out," Huston said, breaking into Mac's thoughts.

Defensive, he flipped his cousin off. "I wasn't being creepy. I was just thinking about the state of things in town. The alienation is beginning to feel normal. We can't allow that to continue."

"And you thought all that while you were staring at Aimee like you were starving and she was your steak dinner," Huston added.

Mac snorted a laugh. "Looking at a beautiful witch helps my concentration on my Machiavellian plans."

"She's single."

And the best friend of the witch who'd just married his archrival. Or whatever his mother liked to fuss about at any given time when it came to her never-ending hate-on for Jace Dooley and his long-dead father.

"I've been back two months, let's just take this one step at a time. Let me deal with all this shifter business and then maybe I can consider dating."

"Ha! Good luck with that. You just gonna beat off forever? Because there's a big mess to clean up and I don't know how long it'll take." Everett shoved a huge slice of pizza into his face.

"I hardly think jerking off forever and dating are the only choices I have." Mac didn't rise to the bait. If he did, his cousins would only fuck with him worse. "Maybe for losers like you, though." He shrugged and then ducked to avoid the lazy backhand Everett aimed in his direction.

"Darrell came in today and got mad when we didn't give his car repairs to him for free," Everett said.

"As you now run the place with Jace Dooley, I imagine he'd be far more likely to be charged twice as much," Mac told his cousin.

"Your brother is a turd." Huston shrugged.

"I'm sick of him strutting around town like a peacock. Stirring the pot every time he can. It's a waste of time. Worse, it's bad for everyone." Everett blew out a long breath.

There was only so much he could say in public. It wasn't the time or the place to start talking family and pack business.

Mac nodded once to let his cousins know he heard, understood and they'd talk about it soon.

"I don't think I've seen you look twice at a witch before," Huston said quietly once the table had moved on to a new topic.

"I look twice when someone catches my eye. Lots of witches do and have."

"Which must be why you're so defensive."

"Are you *trying* to provoke me into being grumpy?" he asked Huston.

Everett thought that was hilarious. "It's like you just met him. He's a dick who gets on everyone's nerves."

"Yeah, well, I'm no Darrell." Huston flipped his brother off.

They all laughed and Mac didn't even feel bad. His brother had created the situation and he had to clean it up.

And he'd have to clean it up while fending off his

parents, who had spoiled Darrell to the point of utter uselessness.

But he didn't have to think about it that night. He had pizza and beer and company. He'd enjoy those and think about pack business the next day.

Chapter Three

Aimee had spent the afternoon at an assisted-living facility, stopping in to visit with her clients. The facility was run by witches—though they couldn't be out about that fact in the regular world—and most of the elderly living there were gifted in some sense.

There were more witches and shifters than those who lived in Diablo Lake, of course. There were other towns similar to theirs, places paranormals, or the gifted, sought one another—and safety in numbers—to create a community.

Mainly though, they lived in cities like everyone else, limiting their true nature to keep themselves hidden and safe.

But when they got very sick or needed to be placed in elder or hospice care, the human options were not very good for the gifted.

Shifters needed the opportunity to change forms. That magic was integral to their very lives so their placement had to be near some sort of wilderness that afforded them privacy to run as wolves regularly.

Witches needed to continue to nurture their power or it got weak and in doing so, made the witch weak. Magic was as necessary to their vitality as a healthy circulatory system. Part of what Aimee did regularly with home visits was garden or work kitchen magic with witches all over the area.

A quiet connection shared with someone was part of the thread that held a good life together. Her dad had told her that when she'd been a little girl. He'd been drawn to law enforcement by his talents too. He spent a lot of time in his truck just driving all over the huge— and at times difficult and nearly impassibly remote— territory that made up Diablo Lake. To check in. To keep his attention on the heart of their community, to be that thread to those of their kind.

Places like Maple River—the facility she was in just then—existed all over the world, created and run by their own. Holding together good lives for those who were on the slow and steady path to leaving this world.

Their elders were the heart of their community. The institutional memory. Mostly, if at all possible, families or those close to the elderly witch or shifter would take them in. Even if outside assistance was necessary.

But that wasn't always possible. Sometimes there was no family, or no one who could take on that sort of commitment for a host of reasons. And in those cases, they were fortunate enough to have enough beds and slots for their elders in facilities like this one.

Truth was, Aimee only hoped she'd be half as amazing as the clients she dealt with daily. The things she learned, the stories they shared with her, the spells and recipes, were just part of the myriad ways they enriched her life.

Even the tough ones taught her things.

Right at the moment, her tough one was simply a

mean-spirited old cuss who hated that he was getting old and would be dying sooner than later.

He didn't like women. Unless they were serving him in some way, as he informed her the first day she met him. In that same conversation he also let her know of his dislike for do-gooders.

He didn't like a lot of things and most people. But for some twisted reason, Aimee wanted to reach him. Wanted to be there so he knew he wasn't alone. He made it really hard so half the time she did it out of sheer will, so he wouldn't win his attempts to make everyone hate him.

It had taken six months just to get him to acknowledge her presence at all half the time.

Right then he sat at a table in the common room working on a jigsaw puzzle. The one thing, after over a year of trying, he'd actually accepted from her were the puzzles and word-hunt books she brought and pretended they were for everyone—even though no one else touched them because they didn't like him either and he was less grouchy when he had things to do.

She made sure her smile was off her features as she cruised his way. He'd balk if she was friendly. Aimee paused to say her goodbye to a few people here and there, one last connection with them and a way to gentle him to her approach.

"Mr. Hatcher," she said as she looked over the puzzle.

He harrumphed.

"The medication you need has been approved. I left it at the nurse's desk." The treatment for the seizures he'd developed over the last three years was not only ridiculously expensive but experimental because he was a witch, and their physiology reacted slightly differently to some medications than humans' did. They had to run their own trials, outside the notice of human authorities.

"Pay special attention to any side effects and let the nurse know, or call me, if you have questions or need help. I'll check in over the next few days to see how it's working."

He harrumphed again.

She resisted the urge to touch him, though she sensed he needed a hug. His loneliness seemed to call out to her so much more loudly than his attitude.

"Have a good evening, Mr. Hatcher. Blessed be."

She didn't smile until she turned away.

On the drive back home, she listened to a new audio-book. Winter had come and the deeper she drove into the mountains, the more treacherous driving conditions were.

However, her tires were spelled by her mother to keep traction, which got her home safely every time. Some parts of the year meant the roads were closed, but like the tires, she had spells to get around those sorts of impediments as well.

At the end of her nearly two-hour trip home, all she wanted was dinner and a glass of wine to enjoy while she watched her reality shows and pretended to feel guilty.

But she had no food. Damn it.

She could eat cereal, she was sure she had some of that. She could even go to Katie Faith's or her parents' place to give puppy-dog eyes and get fed.

But really, she just wanted to put on pajamas and veg out on her own.

So she stopped at the market on her way home, narrowly avoiding getting her bumper clipped by Bonita Pembry, who needed to have had her car taken from her at least a decade ago.

Making a mental note to talk with Bonita's kids once more about taking her keys away, she hitched her bag up on her shoulder and headed inside.

The air hung heavy with tension as the doors slid open and she briefly wished she'd stopped back in Wolcott for groceries instead. Of late, at least half the time she went into a public space where they all gathered, this was the result.

As an empathic witch, her filters helped keep all that out, stopped the basic seepage of negative energy into her life that could make her sick and deplete her magic.

That night, as she pushed her buggy—and of course it was the one with the screwy wobbly front wheel—she just wanted to get her groceries and get out.

Halfway down the first aisle to get bread she nearly got bowled over by two wolves arguing about something or other. Normal big men were bad enough, but werewolves tended to all be supersized so as they barreled past she had to grab the shelf to keep from losing her feet.

"Hey!"

They waved a hand over their shoulders and called back an apology, but for goodness' sake they didn't even look to see if she was okay.

It came over her then. She just didn't want to deal with more bullshit politics between wolves that day. Her filters were paper thin and she was exhausted past the point of caring who she offended. Really bad ingredients in a recipe for possible disaster. The last place she wanted to be was anywhere public. She decided to forage in her pantry, or maybe give in and eat that old diet frozen meal she'd been avoiding for months. She was going home.

Once she returned the buggy and then got back outside, things were a little better and she could get her
breath a lot easier. She was in the process of stepping
off the raised walk at the store's entry to walk across
the lot to where she'd parked when the arguing wolves
barreled out the doors behind her in a tangle of fists
and really foul language.

Everything seemed to slow down as they headed
straight for her. She had a moment to make her muscles
obey to move, but surprise and the speed of the fighting shifters got the best of her.

Suddenly she was plucked up and spun out of the
way, thrust several feet away from the melee.

"You okay? Stay there." Mac Pembry gave her one
last, quick look before he turned his attention back to
the fight and snapped out a command to stop that not
only brought the fight to a halt, but ended Aimee's shaking as well.

Huh.

Something in her magic responded to his. Clicked
into place. She thought about it, picked it over a little in
her head as she realized how unique the experience was.

But when the jangly bits of fear left her she got
pissed. What the hell did the wolves in this town think
they were doing? This was beyond irresponsible! They
were so much bigger than everyone else. Had much
more strength and if *they* couldn't use it safely—like
witches had to use their power—the rest of the town
could easily get caught in the crossfire.

And for what? Dick measuring?

Anger, cold and hard, gave Mac the focus he needed.
As he stalked over, he took in and weighed each option,

each potential problem or weakness. The power of the pack seemed to flow until it roared in his ears.

This was what it meant to be Prime, or next in line to run the Pembry werewolf pack. The power of his wolves, their magic included, wouldn't transfer to just anyone. It was their faith and fealty to the Prime and the very top leader, the Patron, that made those wolves so much stronger. It's what enabled them to keep power and hold it.

His wolf snarled as Mac reached in to jab the biggest guy, a Dooley, in the face hard enough to send him stumbling back a few feet. Mac turned to grab the other wolf—one of his—and held him there by the hair.

Everything seemed to slow as he asserted control and every wolf there, Dooleys included, was affected. No one held his gaze, or even tried to. That wild part of his soul paced and prowled, hungry to make a point.

He kept his voice low, but insistent. "I know you have better things to be doing right now than bringing shame to your family acting this way in public. The cops have been called, you can bet on that. Carl's mad enough at us as it is and I am sick and fucking tired of you shitheads embarrassing all the rest of us shifters."

He shoved the Pembry wolf he'd been holding. Couldn't have been old enough to drink more than a year or two. The other one looked just as young and stupid. "Act like you got some sense."

Werewolves and cat shifters had rules, laws that'd been passed down generation after generation in town. They were stronger and faster and most often larger than the witches who didn't heal as quickly either. This was the sort of thing that could make witches fear them even more.

"You're not my Patron," one of the wolves who'd gathered to watch called out.

Ronnie, one of his brother Darrell's idiot fanboys, didn't know what hit him, even as his back made contact with a brick wall.

No damned discipline in this pack. Jesus.

"You got anything else to say?" Mac's voice held nothing but cold contempt. Ronnie, perhaps too stunned, kept his mouth shut and then lowered his gaze.

Mac told the two who'd been fighting to make their apologies to Aimee, whose color had come back from the pallor that'd made him so pissed to start with. She'd been shaken and he didn't like that one bit.

They told her how sorry they were and that it would never happen again.

Her normally pleasant demeanor had gone wary and no-small-amount stony. She nodded at them and made a shooing motion with her hand. They looked to him for permission, which he gave and they ran off. He glared at the rest, all the bystanders, who scrambled quick enough to keep him from punching anyone else.

Once he was satisfied the problem had been solved for the moment, he focused on her features, carefully taking her in. "Are you really all right?" He kept his voice quiet, knowing she'd had a scare.

Instead of bursting into tears, she propped a hand on her hip and cocked it with a glare his way. "Luckily, yes. I may have scared a few new gray hairs into existence though. This is a problem. What are you going to do about it?"

Well. That had been unexpectedly hot.

The chief of police—also Aimee's dad—rushed over,

the battle between cop and daddy clear on his features. "What the Sam hell is going on here?"

Aimee waved the hand not on her hip. "The usual. Wolves beating one another up in public. It's a weekly occurrence and I know I'm not the only one *who is really tired* of it." She sent a fake sweet smile Mac's way.

She had a viciously sharp tongue. Who knew that'd suddenly be his favorite flavor?

"There was a Dooley wolf in that fight too, if I recall," Mac said.

"Notice I didn't even mention Pembry. *You* made it about that. And I'm not surprised." The prim sniff of outrage at the end was the perfect capper.

Carl, the cop and aforementioned dad of the woman he'd just been imagining naked, spoke and sent that little fantasy away. "I'm not in any sort of mood for excuses, Mac. This is getting worse by the day, and don't feed me any bullcrap about this being Katie Faith's fault, 'cause you know that's not true." He gave his best stern-cop face. It worked. Carl wasn't shifter big, but he was big enough and certainly a powerful enough witch that he could handle himself just fine. He could be scary when he needed to be.

Damn his father for making such a mess. Inept leadership, favoritism and laziness had taken over as a work ethic in the years he'd been gone.

Mac took a deep breath. "I'm doing my best, sir, to get things under control. I surely don't blame Katie Faith for anything of the sort. But even without that, there's been some upheaval. Shifters are just working out their issues. Cats do it too."

"The cats keep their interpersonal bullshit away from the grocery store. Because of that, the cats aren't my problem right now. The wolves are. And they have been. *What are y'all gonna do about it?* I'm down an officer as it is and I'm sick and tired of cleaning up after you. This stuff takes up half my time at this point."

"That's not your business, Carl. That's pack business. We'll handle it."

Carl curled his lip. "If I was holding my breath waiting for that promise to come true, I'd have been dead long ago. Every time your pack *business* spills out into *my* streets y'all make it my problem. You make it the problem of the witches in this town too. So I'm going to advise you to handle this for real or others will. You hear me?"

Aimee moved to stand next to her father, lending him her magic. Understanding why Mac was being so aggressively defensive but not allowing him to intimidate her father. Or through them, the witches.

Mac stared at her, frozen for long seconds. Fascinated, Aimee watched him breathe in, sucking the air all around him over his palate. He shook his head slowly and then rolled his shoulders.

"I'm working on it. I truly am. Now if you're all right, Aimee, I need to get to dealing with some of that business we were just discussing." Mac stepped back, not turning from either of them until he'd gotten a bit more space.

For a jerkface werewolf, he had a great butt. Like seriously fantastic.

"Why don't you come on over to the house and tell me what happened," her dad said as he guided her to her car.

She'd long since given up on her dinner and televi-

sion so she might as well let her mom feed her. And it
wasn't like her dad was going to give her another choice
anyway.

"I'll see you there shortly," she told him.

From her parents' driveway, she texted Katie Faith to
let her know what happened. Because she was with Jace
now, it meant she was in charge of the Dooley wolves
too. And one of those morons at the fight was a Dooley.

Her mother came out to the porch and motioned her
inside. Not one to disobey a command given by Trula
Faye Benton, Aimee heaved herself out of her car.

"I'm so hungry," she said and hoped she sounded
pitiful enough to get something with gravy on it.

"Come on in, baby. I've got a pot of beans on the
stove and some ham if you want me to fry you some up."

Sighing happily, she accepted the hug and headed to
the kitchen. "That sounds so good."

Her mom bustled around as Aimee told her the details of what had happened and by the time she was
done, she had a plate of food and some tea so it really
didn't seem as annoying.

Her dad came in, and before Aimee even got to her
third piece of corn bread, Katie Faith had shown up,
pissed off and worried.

Once she'd gotten a meal into her and had told the
story a few times, she began to feel a little more like
herself.

And then she felt bad. "I snapped at Mac Pembry.
He was just trying to help me."

"I imagine it's pretty scary to have two full-sized
werewolf males in their prime barreling toward you.

Must have been a whole lot of negative magic and adrenaline in the way," her mom said.

"I sort of froze. Like my brain was screaming at me to move but my muscles hadn't caught up yet. I was scared because it was aimed at me, I guess. Not on purpose. But it was there, coming at me."

Katie Faith gave her a one-armed hug. "I know exactly what you mean and I had you at my side when Darrell came at me. You were alone and surprised. I'm glad Mac was there to snatch you up out of danger, but it just goes back to the fact that the wolves have created this mess and we keep getting sucked in to clean it up."

"*You're* the wolves now," Aimee told her.

"Yeah, marrying Jace makes me Patron too. And they *are* my wolves. I'm their witch. That was part of the oath I took and made to them. But I'm still a witch and this is bigger than any one pack. This is a threat to the magic that keeps us safe."

"We'll definitely talk about it on Saturday at the Consort," her dad said, features grim.

"Is there any way we can get your mom and dad off to Asheville early?" Things were getting so heated that Aimee was even more concerned about Katie Faith's dad's health.

"I've been trying all week long," Aimee's mom replied. She and Nadine Grady had been best friends since they were just kids and were as close as sisters. If her mom couldn't talk Nadine into not attending, Katie Faith probably had even less of a chance.

Katie Faith sighed. "I even resorted to full-on guilt tripping. Bringing up Daddy's health, saying she should get him away from all the drama. But he won't hear of it and she's backing him up. He says he's plenty strong and this is important. I can't argue with that even when it makes me crazy with worry. She's still worked up over the scene at the Founder's Day dance and she's going to see it through."

The big town party had dissolved into an actual brawl when Scarlett Pembry had been so awful to and about Katie Faith and Jace's family. Nadine had gone all in on the female Patron of the Pembry wolves, erupting in a spill of violence and magic Aimee had never seen from Katie Faith's mom before.

Nadine Grady was well and truly pissed off and in defense mode. Her family was being threatened and nothing got a woman like her worked up more than something like that. You didn't hurt her kids or her husband and get away with it.

"I surely don't know what's gotten into that woman," her dad said of Scarlett. "She's always been unpleasant and unpredictable, but this stuff about Jace and his father's erasure is beyond bizarre. I know she was petty after Darrell left Katie Faith for Sharon, but what she did at the market and then at the dance, well, that's worrisome."

Katie Faith said, "Part of this is what Mac said. Wolves get all riled up and they often work it out by beating each other up." The eye roll told Aimee just what her friend thought of that. "Pembry is at loose ends. No one is really in charge. That's what Jace says anyway and I agree. He and Mac met for a beer earlier this week. They're going to try to see if they can get somewhere."

"I don't know why he doesn't just take over! Take the job from his dad and get things back on an even keel," Aimee told them. He certainly was big and scary enough. Now that she'd stopped being scared all she could seem to think about was how grrr-arrrrgh-scary he'd been as he'd been tossing werewolves all over the parking lot at the grocery store.

"He can't," Katie Faith began to explain. "Well, he can but it would be really bad. Wolves are all about hierarchy and rules. If they don't have it they sort of lose their way. Like bratty kids I guess. Anyway, Jace says Mac has to build his base first, go through all sorts of stages with the pack and then take over. Otherwise it causes more trouble and then Mac would leave himself open to challenges and dissension from pack members."

"You're all very complicated."

"Witches are complicated too," Katie Faith said with a snort. "I think Mac is exactly what the Pembry wolves need. But Dwayne always played favorites, even at the expense of the pack. Darrell, that dingus, is the golden boy. Wolf. Whatever. Which has to make it pretty hard for Mac for that reason."

"Then why call him back from London? That seems sort of mean." Aimee felt badly for Mac. She had siblings but she'd never felt like her parents favored any one of them over the others. Though certainly she knew there were times they liked one of their kids more than the others.

"Dwayne might like one son over the other, but he can't ignore the truth. They called Mac back to take over. Pembry was the strongest pack for the last several years. That's not so true now. It definitely won't be true in six months. I guess we'll see if Mac's strong enough to steer them through this storm," her dad said.

"I need another piece of corn bread to digest all this stuff," Aimee said as she buttered the slice her mom put on her plate. "Everyone thinks life in a small town is so sweet and normal. Ha! *This* is what happens in small towns."

"At least our drama comes with bake sales and corn bread, though. Don't forget the tight butts in Wrangler jeans too."

"You're a sage sometimes, Katie Faith."

"Right? I was just telling Jace that a few days ago. He thinks I don't know he rolled his eyes when he turned around."

Chapter Four

Mac headed straight to his parents' house where, given the number of cars out front and in the driveway, everyone else had headed as well.

Everett and his uncle Bern caught up with him outside. "Just wait a second," Bern warned. "You can't go in there half-cocked or you've lost before you even start. Darrell is in there no doubt laying out the story however it suits Ronnie and his buddies best. How *you* handle that is important. You need to be thinking more and feeling less just now."

With a growl of annoyance, Mac paused to calm down before he ended up challenging his father.

Before he was ready.

It wasn't a game but if he didn't play it like one, he'd be signing the future of the pack over to the hands of a fool who'd make mistakes that would take years to correct.

Chaos at the top meant chaos through the ranks and it was the height of irresponsibility to charge at it like a bull. He was a werewolf and he needed to act like it.

So, he remembered what was true, not necessarily what was fair. And then he got himself under control and stood taller.

Bern had been watching closely, but once Mac gave a nod of thanks, they all headed to the door his mother had just opened.

Her energy spilled out enough that he felt it from feet away. She was upset and spoiling for a fight. Not necessarily an unusual state for his mom. She was, and had always been, what his father affectionately called *spirited*. It was just part of his mom.

But since he'd been home, he'd wondered daily just exactly what was going on with her to send her off into such a lather. This was more than worked up. Or high-strung or whatever.

He worried about her and wished she'd open up to him a little. She was his mother, *spirited* or not, and he loved her. Something was wrong and he wanted to help.

She'd avoided talking about it though, the times he'd tried. So he'd keep at it until she let him in or he figured it out. He didn't get his stubborn streak from his father.

She hugged him once he got to her. "Your brother already told us what happened. The Dooleys started the fight," his mother said before her gaze flicked to her brother-in-law. "Bern, didn't expect you tonight."

"I'm unexpected that way, Scarlett." His uncle grinned, but showed more teeth than he normally did. They'd never been the best of friends. His mother was guilty of a lot of things, but she was always totally on her husband's side and saw Bern as a threat.

Inside, in the dining room, Darrell was telling their father some fanciful tale about a truckload of Dooleys beating the hell out of poor little Ronnie down at the market.

His father was outraged, predictably. When he noted Mac standing there, he waved a hand. "Did you hear that bullshit? Carl's just going to let Jace Dooley's wolves do whatever they want now? Must be nice to be related to the cops and have the laws enforced whenever Carl decides to."

Starting a feud with Carl Benton was a *terrible* idea and he needed to quash that before it got any worse. "Carl does his job and he does it well, so let's not jump down his throat. I was just at the market. That's not what happened." Mac remained standing, speaking directly to his father while ignoring his brother.

"Ronnie already told me the story," Darrell said.

"Well, if he told you that story you just gave Dad, he's lying. Like I said, *I was there*. I broke the fight up. It was one-on-one. Two wolves barely old enough to shave. Ronnie was only around to stir shit once the danger of getting a beat down passed. No truckload of wolves. Just Pembrys embarrassing us yet again by acting like assholes in public."

"Why is it so hard for you to side with your own?" Darrell muscled to his feet to get in Mac's face. But Mac held his ground easily, mainly ignoring his brother as he continued to speak to his father.

"Ronnie's making things worse. Every time there's some kind of problem around here, he's part of it. Darrell is helping by repeating all these tall tales when not a one is true. It's stirring everyone up. This isn't junior high."

"He's asking you a question, son. One I ask myself too," his father said.

That hurt. A lot.

He shoved it away. Mac narrowed his gaze at his dad and let his wolf show. "You're seriously asking me why I won't lie to you? Why, after seeing something

with my own eyes and knowing this lie Darrell is telling is not just untrue, but potentially harmful, I won't
what? What is it you'd like me to do? If you're telling
me lying is actually the best thing for this pack because
the truth is too painful, it's my turn to call bullshit.
Real leadership is hard. A lot harder than just being
told whatever makes me feel warm and fuzziest while
the whole world goes to hell all around me. That what
Darrell brings to the table?"

"You watch your mouth," Darrell snarled and this
time, Mac did pay attention. He cuffed his brother so
hard he fell back over the couch and hit the wall behind.

"Shut up and let the adults talk, boy," Everett told
him.

"Macrae! What are you doing?" his mother demanded.

Without turning his attention away from his brother,
he answered, "What y'all should have done years ago.
You're letting your son swing his pecker all over town,
stirring up trouble and for what? You bored, Darrell?
I've got some real work for you if you need a job."

"Everyone needs to settle down," Dwayne said as
he watched Darrell make his way to his feet. As Mac
figured, their father didn't move to help. He pitied his
brother, who'd take this new future with Mac at the head
of the pack far harder than their father cared to admit.

They'd made his brother into the petulant monster he
was. Just like they'd made Mac the wolf to finally deal
with the mess they had created in town. Both brothers
had been formed and placed into a role. At least Mac
wasn't a shit-headed loser and tool like Darrell was.

"What do you suggest we do then?" his father asked,

not even addressing the lies Darrell had been telling them about Ronnie and the fight at the market.

"First thing is, we deal with Ronnie. Because if he's flapping his gums all over town with this bullshit lie, he's going to end up starting a riot. I warned him off at the grocery store so he's violating that order by lying about what happened just to make trouble." Mac turned to his uncle. "Can you get him over here?"

"Why you askin' him?" Darrell demanded. "You're just trying to railroad Ronnie."

Because it wasn't his business, nor was he anyone Mac sought advice from, he ignored his brother.

Mac's uncle spoke to Darrell, uncle to nephew. "He'd have to be important for us to want to railroad him, boy. He was told in public to rein his behavior in and he didn't. Ronnie doubled down, setting himself to even more destruction and lies. If we don't make an example out of him, everyone else is going to think it's okay to do whatever they want, whenever they want. Or worse, that there's a set of rules for Darrell's friends and one for the remaining pack. And one more fight could very well spark an open war with Dooley or the witches."

One they weren't in a position to win. One that had the potential to ruin the community for good. They needed to stop that from happening. Even if his father was too blinded by his affection for Darrell to actually do anything about it one way or the other.

Werewolves weren't human. They didn't run their lives in the same way. Violence was part and parcel of their existence and their governance. But the wolves in the pack respected a well-played hunt. They needed to see Mac's takeover as necessary and deserved. More than a fist, but a beating heart. A brain. All used in service of the many.

The army had made him harder. Faster. He'd been without a pack of wolves so he'd become close with the guys in his company. They'd been his pack in a very real way. Mac had learned to be smarter. To never stop training and learning.

Once he'd been battle hardened, he'd gone to London to work on his brain some more. He'd come back what they'd sent him away to become. But no one was going to pull his strings.

The wolves in the Pembry pack would support the strongest wolf. Either way. But if any of them had doubts, or felt he didn't do things the right way, the most clever way, things wouldn't stabilize for very long.

That was tradition. That was what kept them together even during the toughest times. He'd take over and he'd do it in a way that left absolutely no doubt he was in charge. He'd deliver the firm hand and the generous spirit the wolves needed to replace the chaos they had now.

"I'll go get him." Everett nodded once and headed out, saying he'd be back shortly. Huston—who'd been pretending to casually lean against the doorway—stepped into his place at Mac's side.

"Seems *you've* got yourself a plan, Mac. Care to share that with your Patron?" his father asked, leading the way to the kitchen just beyond.

"Let's cut the crap. You knew what was going to happen when you called me back here from London. This pack is in a mess and you need me to clean it up. And that's fine. I'm committed to doing that. But most of this tension is avoidable." He remained silent for long moments after, just to let the words his father needed to hear sink in.

"Ronnie has no control and he's been allowed to act a fool because he's buddies with your kid. That's lazy and we can't tolerate it another day."

"He's not your concern. He's my friend and our cousin and he's protected," Darrell said as he stomped into the room.

"We don't work that way. We're *all* protected until we step out of line. Ronnie has. He's not the only one, but he's certainly at the top. With some others." Mac gave his brother a look.

"If you think you can get away with hitting me, you're wrong."

Mac turned on Darrell, getting right into his face, nose to nose. *Definitely* violating his personal space. "That so? What do you have to say about it? You want some more? Come on then because God knows you need to be knocked down a few more times."

"You two stop it this instant," their mother snapped, trying to get between them.

But that wasn't what werewolf parents did. They were supposed to let their children learn to defend themselves and also to learn they'd get their asses kicked if they stepped out of line.

So, Mac gave no quarter, not moving and leaving it to Darrell to step away. "Stop protecting him. That's the problem here," Mac told her.

"Everyone calm down," their father said. "You two should be working together instead of against each other. And never letting a Dooley get between you. We're better than them. Act like it."

Without moving, still staring his brother down, Mac

said, "I'm totally calm. What I'm not, is tolerating any of this bullshit. Not from Ronnie and certainly not from Darrell." His brother dropped his gaze, which hadn't ever gotten higher than Mac's chin anyway.

"You can't let those Dooleys think they're as good as us. They need to remember their place. Even if they managed to sucker Katie Faith over to their side," his mother said, touching Mac's arm, trying to draw him away from Darrell.

The powerful witch and new Patron of the Dooley wolves was nothing even resembling a sucker, but Mac let that part pass because his mother was clearly going through something.

But.

"I'm not playing along with this foolishness. We gonna act like we're the Rockefellers or something? Huh? Momma, this is crazy. We don't have to be at odds with them all the time. We're all family and friends. We've all been family and friends for generations. There're plenty of mixed households here in Diablo Lake. That's a strength, not a weakness. We're not the enemy and neither are they."

His parents had lived here in isolation for so long they had no real idea of what it was like out there to be different. How much discipline it took to keep control even when things got sketchy.

That was thinking so outdated it was dangerous to continue to allow it without challenge.

"I said, enough!" His father's thundered command rang through the air, still strong enough to snatch the next reply from Mac's lips. "I don't like it that Ronnie thinks he can make up stories like this. It's dangerous.

Mac, I'll let you decide his sentence but I'll ask you to remember he's family and not an alpha."

"We just got finished saying that we're *all* family, Dad." Mac would back off for the time being. Mac wanted to choose the time and place. Wanted to have a little more backup in place. More wolves openly his. And he wanted his father to declare him Prime before he had to do it on his own.

Everett called out that he'd arrived back with Ronnie in tow.

"I'll handle it," Darrell said as he attempted to push past Mac, who stopped him cold.

"You've done enough. I've got this. So I don't have to do this to *you*, how about you knock it off too?" he said quietly. "I don't want to be at war with you any more than I want a war with Dooleys."

Darrell would have said more, but their mother pulled him back, allowing Mac to leave and handle the discipline of the wayward wolf.

Chapter Five

Generations before, when Diablo Lake had become their home, the witches began calling themselves as a group a Consort. Miz Rose, one of the Consort's elders, always joked that it was because one of their forebears hated the term *coven*.

Aimee didn't much care why they'd chosen it originally, she just knew she loved the term. Loved the intimacy of it. And that's exactly what it was to share magic with a group of witches. Intimate and special.

As she walked around town, she'd catch wisps of magic she knew belonged to this or that person. Sometimes those two signatures would meld into something else entirely when they practiced together.

It was special and something she never felt less than grateful to have as a gift. It made her part of something larger than herself and gave her a sense of forward motion. Like she was doing the things she was meant to do.

She'd stopped by Katie Faith's to pick her up on the way over to Collings Garden—what Miz Rose called the space on her property where the Consort routinely met.

Collings Garden was the heart of their community. It was where Aimee had learned to first practice her empathic magic while using filters to keep herself protected. She'd worked in the garden, teasing and coaxing the earth's energy into shaping itself however Aimee intended. To nurture the other plants, to use some of them in her tinctures and salves used to heal and help.

She learned that while the size of her magic was limitless, the use of it, the ability to hold it was what she needed to master. What she still worked on every day.

And she'd learned it there at Miz Rose's knee.

They parked in the half-circle drive and headed over the crunch of the gravel path until they reached the pavers that led the way through the massive yard the house sat in the center of.

There was a glass building, not really a greenhouse—Miz Rose called it the solarium—in the north corner of a thriving riot of a garden. Each time the witches met there they added their magic to the earth, nurturing it.

Over the years it had only gotten more and more lush to the point the air was positively teeming with magic.

And in turn, every time Aimee left that space, she felt alive. Centered and full of energy. A nice symbiotic relationship witches had kept alive in Diablo Lake from the very beginning.

They nurtured the magic the land at their feet blessed them with. The magic they used daily in and around town. Back and forth. Give and take. Balance.

Inside the solarium, most of the others already gathered. Katie Faith's dad had baked up a huge batch of his world famous blueberry-pecan muffins so pretty much everyone had one, along with tea or coffee.

Folks gave Katie Faith a wide berth until she'd had a cup of coffee or two. Her dad put an extra muffin on her plate and kissed the top of her head so she lost a little of her surly morning attitude.

Leaving her friend to that, Aimee rolled her eyes and found her parents. "Hey, you two." She hugged them both before grabbing a chair next to them.

"How's it going?"

"Got a call last night from Mac Pembry telling me he'd handled the problem with that fight at the grocery store," her dad said.

"Good. For God's sake, all these grown adults acting like toddlers. It's ridiculous. Did you get a similar call from Jace?"

Katie Faith grunted as she joined them. "Yes, he did. I was there when he did it. He does not like to have to admit when he's wrong. Damn. I really felt bad for the dumb kid who got into that fight. Kid, listen to me. Jeez. He's in his twenties. Jace sent Damon out to deal with him. And the wolf's dad probably also kicked his ass. Thank goodness JJ and Patty were out at their lake place so they don't have to see this."

Jace had taken over the Dooley pack only very recently from his grandfather so he'd had to instill his own brand of discipline and order too.

It was nice to have that in with the wolves, but it also made it more complicated when it came to them acting like jerks. She knew and really liked wolves in both packs. And her best friend was the pack witch now, essentially, for Dooley. But it wouldn't be fair to pretend Dooley wolves weren't also part of the bigger problem in town, just as the Pembrys were.

"I'd like to think it was just a blip, but the energy in town gets worse by the day. Have you been to the library lately?" Like the grocery store, there were times Aimee went in to pick up books and the tension inside was too much to bear for longer than just a few minutes.

Aimee's mom nodded. "Yes. Which makes it worse because the library is ours."

Witches, her mother meant. It was true the witches, much like the shifters, tended toward specific kinds of work in town. Witches ended up in jobs where they could use their particular gifts. Empaths like Aimee were social workers, doctors and nurses, teachers and counselors. Because of the rivalry between shifters, the police chief was nearly always a witch, though only about a third of the police and firefighters were.

To have a kerfuffle in the library, like the ones they'd been hearing about at the high school, meant the ability of witches to keep a balance was fraying.

More bad news.

Miz Rose came in then, so business could officially get started. They piddled around with some basics first while everyone continued to eat. Dealt with budgetary issues. Some community-service projects, but it wasn't very long before they got down to the meat of what was really wrong.

"Aimee, tell them what you told me about Jeremy's plants," Miz Rose said.

"I went over to check on Jeremy's sister, Myra. She's getting much better by the way and thanked everyone for the casseroles and soups you've been taking by. Before I left, Jeremy took me outside to show me he's got some sick plants. A few with frostbite," Aimee told them.

The people around the table nodded once she cleared that up. Myra Ruiz was a third-grade teacher who'd been hit particularly hard by pneumonia and had to spend a few weeks in bed recovering.

"The spots were small, but unmistakable."

In a climate like theirs, growing tomatoes outside anywhere else during the winter would be impossible. In Diablo Lake it was a common occurrence. So sick plants meant the magic that kept the heart of town beating, the protections and blessings the ground gave back to her inhabitants, was weakening. The time for hoping things would get better on their own, or due to action by the wolf packs was past.

And that meant they needed to address it once and for all.

"I still think you should speak on behalf of the witches here in town Monday night at the city council meeting. Address the mayor and the rest of the council members," Katie Faith told Miz Rose.

Miz Rose chuckled with a wave of her hand. "This problem calls for a new voice. Mine's an old one. My power will always be part of Diablo Lake, but it's time to hand over the reins to the next generation. You and yours."

"I think Katie Faith should do it," someone said.

Katie Faith shook her head. "I'm married to a Dooley. I'm the Patron now. I will always be a witch, but you know the Pembrys won't hear a word I say because of that. Let Aimee speak."

"What?" Aimee wrinkled her nose, curiosity warring with reluctance. "Why me?"

"Because your magic is inviting. Soothing when you want it to be." Her mother looked her over carefully. "Nadine and Scarlett have blood between them. Avery too. Katie Faith is seen as part of the Dooley wolves so she's going to be suspect."

"She *is* very suspect, I agree. Plus, Scarlett seems

to have some sort of strange obsession with her, which makes me nervous," Aimee added.

Nadine said, "Me too. Honestly that woman gets worse by the day. I tried to talk to Dwayne about it but he dodged me. Said she was all upset and would cool down soon enough. Told me to be nice. You know how I feel about that."

Katie Faith spun on her mother. "What? You went to them after promising me you wouldn't?"

"I promised you I wouldn't go after *Scarlett*. Dwayne was walking on a public sidewalk and I spoke to *him*. I didn't promise not to." Nadine's chin stuck out just like Katie Faith's did when she was stubborn.

"And," Miz Rose continued, her voice raised just enough to make Katie Faith and her mother stop arguing, "Aimee, your dad is the police chief. He'll be speaking anyway in an official capacity. You can talk about things he can't. Your mother, well, she threatens too many people." Miz Rose winked at TeeFaye.

"Fine." Aimee held up a hand, not wanting this argument to get any worse. "I'll be the spokesperson." She usually hated being the spokesperson, but she was good at it, she could admit. Had been on the debate team back in high school and even considered a run for mayor a time or two. Especially when the town had elected a doofus like Dwayne and needed a change.

Miz Rose's expression said she'd never harbored a doubt. "Good. Now everyone eat up and we can talk a bit more about how we're going to do this."

Chapter Six

Her mom gave her a tight hug before they got out of the car. They'd just parked across the square from city hall. The curbs up and down the street had plenty of parked cars.

"Looks like a crowd tonight."

Aimee reapplied her lipstick and gave herself one last look before she sighed and looked to her mom. "No need to emphasize that."

"Why not? You're going to do great. You're good at public speaking. People like you." Her mom paused. "I'm proud of you, sugar bear."

"Yeah?" Aimee squeezed her mom's hand.

"Even if you did cut off all that pretty hair and then dyed it blue like I don't know what."

Aimee laughed. "No one gives a compliment like you, Trula Faye." Trula Faye was better known as Tee-Faye and she had a great sense of humor and was fierce as hell when she wanted to be. Which was pretty often.

She'd been lucky to have grown up with such a great example of what it meant to be the best person you can be. Aimee had been raised to understand her gender and her magic were gifts rather than the curses others might try to make them out to be.

Her mom tugged the ends of her hair and gave her a quick kiss on the cheek. "It's cute hair. Suits you. I just wish you'd tell me what it is that prompted it."

As if she'd tell her mother she'd been having sex with a married guy for three years. It was bad enough that *she* knew it; there was no way she'd dump that on her mom. Shame still soured her stomach from time to time. She had this empathic magic and it never told her he'd been lying or had ill intentions!

"I wanted a change." After a week, she'd begun to get used to the way the cold felt at the back of her neck. And it gave her an excuse to wear scarves to work so that was a plus.

She was careful not to avert her eyes from her mom as she spoke. TeeFaye knew when people lied to her.

"You just know that *I know* you're avoiding the subject. Don't think I didn't notice how you sidestepped my asking you to tell me what happened. And don't insult my intelligence by saying you wanted a change. Well, sure you did. We all do when something big happens and we need to cut our hair or buy a ridiculously expensive purse you have to work overtime for the next month to afford. Are you okay?" This time she was all concerned mother.

Aimee swallowed back a knot of emotion. "Yeah. I am. I don't want to talk about it right now. Not with you. I don't... It's embarrassing."

Another thing about TeeFaye was that she was a big personality. A lot like Katie Faith, when Aimee thought about it. No question as to why she loved her best friend so much.

TeeFaye would have slashed some tires or set some

clothes on fire in a driveway. She'd have been at Katie Faith's side punching buttholes.

Aimee though, she just wanted to get the hell away from that horrible, ugly moment when Bob had told her the truth and made her part of his grotesque pantomime.

Her mother brushed her hair out of her face. "You have nothing to be embarrassed for. Not if I know you as well as I think I do. And if you do, well then you'll be embarrassed, you'll earn your forgiveness and we'll all move on. Because nothing will change who you are to me."

"I needed to hear that. Thank you." She took a deep breath. "Right now I have to go in there tonight and be an adult. Take on the weight of responsibility as the voice of the witches in this town. When I tell you what happened, it's going to wreck my calm, and I really need that tonight."

Not because she was weak. But damn if she'd let any of them see her stumble even for a moment.

Her mom's face tightened and then she sighed. "All right. All right. Come on then. I'm even more proud of you now." Her mom got out of the car before she could say anything else.

And right out front was a whole gaggle of Pembrys and Dooleys, already getting loud, all that shifter magic biting at her skin, and instead of the usual pine-tree-bark-warm-in-the-sun scent, it was acrid.

With a growl of annoyance, Aimee stomped over, pausing at Katie Faith's side. "What the heck is going on?"

"JJ and Dwayne started arguing about something. I don't know what. Jace, along with Mac, broke them up. Patty and I got pushed to the side. Scarlett's over there somewhere, thank God. They're having some sort of heated argument done in fake pleasant tones."

"Jeez Louise. Do they ever stop to remember the rest of us in this town might want to go about our day-to-day lives without all this stuff? It's like a terrible soap opera."

"They're better than the *Housewives* though. At least you'll be sure to get lunch before punches get thrown around Diablo Lake."

Aimee and Katie Faith laughed for a moment until they turned back to the situation near the front doors.

Jace stood with his grandfather at his back as they had an exaggeratedly calm discussion with Mac and Dwayne.

"We gonna have this meeting or what?" someone called out from the crowd. "I have to get dinner on the table and some laundry needs folding."

"This is wolf business, you aren't needed here," Scarlett said as she bustled forward to get in the face of the woman who'd spoken, which pushed Aimee's buttons in a big way.

"Excuse me?" Aimee demanded. "This *should* be wolf business, yes, but you've all made it town business. You can't just hold the town hostage because y'all can't run your own families. Last I checked, this wasn't a pack meeting, it was a city council meeting. Remember there are many in this town who aren't Pembrys or Dooleys and who like to, you know, have moments in their lives when it's not all about y'all."

"Oh, look at you, badass," Katie Faith whispered to her.

"Whatever. I am so over all this nonsense. It's getting so you can't do anything in this town without some sort of shifter bullcrap ruining it. No offense to those who married into the pack." She winked at Katie Faith.

Scarlett put her hand in Aimee's face and said to Katie Faith, "You better tell your little doggie to heel."

Magic surged up from the soles of her feet until the air crackled between her and Scarlett. Enough that the older woman stepped back just a smidge.

"I know you did not just put your hand in my face and risk me ripping it off your arm," Aimee told her.

Several more witches bunched up at her back, lending support.

"You think you can threaten me? This is my town! You're just a nobody." Scarlett's face sheened with sweat as guilt and nervousness seemed to come off her in waves.

Aimee lassoed up her power and flexed it just a bit. Wanting Scarlett to feel the wall of magic heat she could—and would—use to defend herself. "That's not a threat, old woman. That's a promise. I'm done with you trying to intimidate us all. I'm not defenseless. If you need a lesson, just let me know."

"Jesus." Dwayne hustled over. "Ladies, let's take a breath here."

"I've taken plenty of breaths, Dwayne. But your wife is out of line—as usual—and we're all pretty done with it. And you too," Aimee said. "She needs to get her hands out of people's faces and keep her attitude to herself or risk the consequences."

"What consequences?" Scarlett sneered but before she could say anything else, Billy, one of Darrell's brothers, pulled her aside, putting his arms around her and talking to her quietly.

"You can't talk like that and not expect a reaction," Dwayne said using his reasonable voice.

"Go suck an egg, Dwayne." Aimee only barely resisted giving him the finger.

A few people gasped, some laughed. But Dwayne just stared at her for long seconds. "There's no call for that talk."

For real?

"You know what, you self-righteous hypocrite? There's all the call in the world for it. You're not doing your job. Control your wolves. Control your wife. Control your kids! Don't you stand there and *scold* me for finally saying what the rest of us have been dying to say for years now. She comes at us with threats and anger and thinks we'll just let it roll off? Fuck you."

Under her breath, Katie Faith snickered but didn't interrupt because Aimee was on a tear.

Dwayne's face paled just a little at the curse.

Aimee continued while she had the chance. "The fact is, this town is home to more than you and your kids running up and down the avenue causing a mess. Your constant fighting is affecting everyone here. You never even consider that, which makes you a terrible mayor as well as a terrible Patron."

Dwayne sneered. "You don't know a damned thing about it. You just plant some flowers and take meals to the elderly and leave the governing to those who know what to do."

Did he just tell her the equivalent of get back in the kitchen?

"I will when I see someone who does know. You act like we *owe* you the mayor's office or something. We've been waiting on you to govern and we're all still here.

Waiting. And what do you give us? Lectures about how
we should stick to planting flowers and let you do the
decision-making? Oh, 'cause it's hard and that's all we
can manage?"

"Girl's got a point, Dwayne," Avery called out. "Take
your lesson like a big boy."

"This is wolf business. She's got no point because
it's not about her. You neither." Dwayne pointed Avery's way.

"Like a broken record." Aimee waved a hand at them.
"Every damned day *we* get pulled into it. And every
damned day one of you tells the rest of us it's not our
business when you go out of your way to make it our
business. I don't want it to be in my face. I don't want
to have tomato plants getting frostbite because this tension is eating away at the magic in the earth here. But
it's happening. And you're making excuses and doing
nothing. Months and months this has been going on.
Your wife is all over town stirring the pot, getting in
faces, starting fights. Darrell and his friends are acting
like drunk frat boys."

"You think it's so easy, why don't you do it then?"
His voice was sullen and defensive. Not a good look.

"Run your pack, you mean?" Of course that wasn't
what he meant at all, but she didn't care.

Thing was, Dwayne Pembry wasn't a totally bad person. Back when she'd been younger, he'd been a decent
enough mayor. Until Darrell dumped Katie Faith and
his pettiness had led to him getting booted from office
the first time. Just then she sensed his fractured feelings of responsibility for everyone. But he wasn't strong
enough, or whatever, to follow through by ensuring his

wolves did the same. He had a problem at home, so to speak, and it was screwing things up everywhere else.

He needed to be confronted with this so he could accept it. Own it and then make his changes. He'd been on the verge of losing control of his pack and the town for years and had survived more than one battle.

He couldn't win the way he was going now. Worse, Dwayne seemed all too willing to let everyone suffer rather than make the changes he'd need to. Why, she had a feeling was more complicated than his own desire for power. But at that point, a mess was a mess and it needed cleaning up.

"You goddamned witches!" Scarlett yelled out and that time everyone gasped, turning to face her and that angry expression she wore.

Scarlett had a lot of energy. She was a polarizing force in town and had been, from what Aimee understood, her whole life. Plenty of folks had stories about some terrible thing she'd done or said over the years.

But this was just so totally out of proportion, even for her. The guilt and anguish spicing her anger was what caught Aimee's attention, reminding her that people had lives no one else could see from the outside.

A wild light in Scarlett's eyes only made things more tense as she kept hollering. "This is all your fault. Everything was fine until Katie Faith Grady came back to town and now look! Dooleys reaching above themselves all because of a witch. A witch flapping her gums at the mayor as if she has a right."

Aimee held on to her temper by her fingernails. "I *totally* have a right. It's in the Constitution and everything. I don't know what your problem is, Mrs. Pembry. Whatever it is, you're clearly in pain and I'm sorry to see it. But you can't act this way. I'm not going to allow it."

She was angry, yes, but she didn't want to hate anyone. She felt bad for Scarlett. She didn't have to like the other woman to know some kind of something was going on with her. But it wasn't going to stop Aimee from saying what needed saying. For the good of everyone.

So she took a deep breath and continued. "I'm also over and done listening to you take your bad mood out on Katie Faith. In the market. In the town square. At the Founder's Day dance. As far as I can tell, *you're* the one who's been the problem in the months since Katie Faith has returned. Diablo Lake is her home. It's mine too. It belongs to everyone here. If you don't like witches, that's your right, I suppose. But we aren't your hired help and we're done with you acting like we are. This town and the way things are run should be about *all* its citizens."

"Who knew you had all that in you, girl?" Jace said loud enough for people to hear.

Katie Faith raised her hand. "I did."

The squabbling at the edges grew louder until finally, Mac whistled loudly to get everyone's attention. "I'm going to suggest that given tempers right now we adjourn until Wednesday. That gives us all two days to cool off and we can get back to it," he called out.

Aimee looked to Miz Rose, who nodded her agreement. It would be better done when things were less tense.

Hopefully.

One thing was clear though, things could only get worse if they kept on the way they were. JJ looked pale and drawn, Jace worried about his grandfather as well as the general pulse of the town and his wolves. Darrell had shown up to shove at Mac, who manhandled his brother away, back down the steps and off to the side in a heated conversation.

Good luck to him trying to talk sense into that dumbass.

"Let's get out of here. I'll give you a ride home," she told her parents.

"We're headed over to Nadine and Avery's so we'll go with them." Her mother hugged her. "I want you to tell me, but I'm guessing you aren't ready after that scene."

Her mom got her. How lucky she was.

"Yeah. I'll talk to you soon. It's not like you're going to let me *not* tell you now."

"Glad we're clear." Her mom gave her one last hug, followed by her father and they all headed out.

"You should come over," Katie Faith told her.

"Your house is going to be full of wolves all worked up about stuff. You have to be their mommy."

Even though her friend rolled her eyes, there was truth in what Aimee had said and she couldn't deny it.

"You kicked butt tonight."

"I will always get your back. Especially when that crazy bitch makes yet another pass at you. Did you piss in her Wheaties or what?"

Katie Faith's sadness rolled from her in a soft wave. "I don't know what her thing is. It's not like *I* left her son at the altar, hello. Also, have you noticed the way Mac keeps looking over at you?"

"Mac Pembry? Nah, he's just trying to get a lay of

the land. Jace does the same thing." And wishing otherwise was dumb.

"Liar, liar, pants on fire." Katie Faith snorted. "Sure, he does that too. Wolves do that. But he's been looking at your boobies and that isn't necessary to get a lay of the land. He's totally cute."

"He's a werewolf. A Pembry. Jesus on a skateboard, Katie Faith, Scarlett is his mother. I said good day."

"He's so cute, though. And I can highly recommend werewolves as romantic partners. If you know what I mean and I know you do."

Aimee laughed. Not that she hadn't thought about Mac's romantic partner potential several times since he'd come back to town. Especially since that day he'd hauled her up and away from the fight the week before. *So strong. Damn. He smelled good too.* Threw out testosterone like crazy, which left her a little loopy and slightly defensive every time.

"It's not like you'd be smooching *her*." Katie Faith broke into her thoughts.

"You just got married. A body'd think you had better things to do than trying to arrange my dating life. Go home, weirdo. I love you and I'll talk to you tomorrow."

"Don't hide your light under a bushel, Aimee," Katie Faith said.

"Laws," Aimee muttered as she turned to head away from the scene. She'd been all worked up and ready to speak her mind and the whole night had gone sideways in the worst fashion possible.

Darrell stepped into her path with an ugly look on his face and in the background she heard Katie Faith swear.

"You got a big mouth on you." Darrell's body language was aggressive. He invaded her personal space on purpose. Tried to crowd her.

Wanted to cow her. *Oh. Hell. No.*

"Blue ribbon for your clarity." Aimee fake smiled at him as she attempted to dodge around his bulk. But he adjusted so she couldn't.

"One witch tossing your worthless ass out into the street not enough for you?" Katie Faith's voice bristled with antagonism as she stormed up to Aimee's side. "Fuck off, Darrell. Why aren't you home harassing your wife instead of out here trying to scare people?"

"Says the dumb bitches attacking old ladies like my mom."

Aimee stepped in between them. Jace kept a very close eye on his wife as it was. If he got it into his head that Katie Faith was upset or felt threatened things could get bloody.

In fact, she noted Jace stalking their way already and there was probably little chance of avoiding an incident.

But before she could say anything, Mac shouldered up, putting an arm around his brother and bringing him to heel.

Loathing crawled over Darrell's features for a brief moment and Aimee took note of the discord between them.

Mac said, "Darrell, you left our discussion early. I still have some things to say. You and I need to let these fine ladies get about their evening. So much excitement already I'm sure everyone would regret it if anything bad happened." There was a lot of emphasis there on getting Darrel to knock it off. A lot of power in the words and plenty of compulsion too.

"Did you hear what she just said to me?" Darrell bellowed like a man-baby.

Aimee rolled her eyes. "Just in case you didn't, we told him to fuck off. And you can too if you think we're going to take abuse from any more Pembrys tonight. Or, quite frankly, any other time."

Mac shook his head. "No, ma'am, I'd never think such a thing."

"What the hell is going on over here?" Jace growled on approach.

Mac turned his focus on Jace as he held Darrell in place. Like he was showing another pack that he was handling the situation.

"Just getting on our way and letting Katie Faith and Aimee do the same," he told Jace in a serious tone. "Y'all have a safe drive home." Nodding, he pressganged his brother away.

"Close one," Katie Faith muttered.

Jace eyed them carefully. "What went on?"

Aimee flapped a hand quickly. "Darrell was a dingus. But that's not news. You two get on home. That's where I'm headed too." Where it would be quiet and no wolves would be anywhere. And she could change into pants without a zipper and rid herself of her bra.

Like the Lord intended.

"You want to stay at our place a while?" Jace asked.

"Thanks for the offer. But I'm good. I'm not worried about anything that shithead can do to me. I think Mac is going to slap him upside his head though." She hoped it would be more than once.

"He'd better or he'll have an even bigger problem on his hands."

Katie Faith gave her a quick hug before she and Jace headed off toward home.

Once she got across the street and headed to her car, she heard Mac call her name so she stopped with a sigh loud enough so he'd better understand how close she was to going off.

"What?" she demanded. "Haven't you and your family done enough tonight?"

He put his hands up in defense and even in the light of the street lamps he was beautiful. "I haven't done anything."

Aimee harrumphed. "Again, I ask, what?"

"Just making sure you were okay."

"Keep your jacked-up family away from me and mine and I'll be perfect. If you can stop a war from erupting because your brother and father have such small dicks, that'd be icing," she told him as she got into her car.

Chapter Seven

Mac stood there in the street, watching her drive away.

That was unique, he had to grudgingly admit. He rarely had to chase them. Or. Never. But he never wanted to catch anyone for longer than a day or two. Until her.

Right then he had to fight back a flood of possessiveness as her taillights faded.

But the problem here—one of them anyway—was his damned brother constantly causing trouble. Darrell had attempted to scare Katie Faith and Aimee. Part of Mac wanted to rip his brother's arms off and beat him with the stumps. A big part. Okay, all.

His family should have nothing to do with him and Aimee and whatever he'd manage to get her involved in. Starting with his pants. But they were his family after all, and that meant of course they'd be a problem.

He turned on his heel and stalked back to his truck. He'd have to deal with his family soon enough. Especially because Darrell waited for him with his cousin.

"I'm really close to leaving you bloody right now, Darrell. So I'm telling you to keep your trap shut and open your ears."

"I don't have to listen to you," Darrell spat out.

Mac popped him a quick one in the nose. Enough to make him bleed and make the point about how easy it would be to do it again.

Darrell howled and started for Mac, who popped him again twice more before he pivoted, sending Darrell to the ground as he lost the target he'd been lunging at.

As he lay on the pavement, holding his nose—already healing, the fucking baby—he complained long enough for Mac to telegraph that he was going to be punched again, and then Darrell shut up quick, not wanting any more pain.

Mac left his brother on the ground as he knelt next to him. "You're making my job a lot harder than it has to be. And that makes me really cranky. If I *ever* catch you trying to scare witches or anyone smaller or less powerful than you again, especially in the name of this pack, I will personally make sure you're stripped of membership and shunned. You will not start a war, Darrell. Hear me? And you will not terrorize women like a goddamn bully. You disgust me. Now get the hell home and if I see you again before I tell you I'm ready, you'll be spitting out teeth."

He turned, giving Darrell his back, letting his brother know he had no fear of him at all. To Huston he said, "Make sure he gets his ass home. He makes any stops before that, I want to know."

His cousin nodded before moving off to follow Darrell.

Rage roared through his veins. Aside from the pact that the wolves were supposed to abide by—namely never using their power unfairly—his brother had no call to try to harm or intimidate *Aimee*. She was strong.

Hell, when she told him off… Well, each time she did, because she seemed to do it a lot, he got off on it.

But teeth and fur, claws and ferocious beast strength could break her. Catch her by surprise or off balance and if she wasn't ready, she could get caught in the crossfire. Which was unacceptable.

He'd keep a very close eye on his brother. Yes, there was no way around a challenge. Pembrys were going to self-destruct unless they got some real leadership. So his dad had to step up or get out of the way immediately. His hope of a peaceful transition like the Dooleys had just gone through was waning.

He got into his truck, scrubbing his hands over his face before sighing. He needed to talk to Aimee, make sure she truly was all right and also speak with her about the situation in town. Try to defuse things. And maybe ask her out. *Yeah.*

It'd be part of him truly moving back to Diablo Lake. Plus she smelled really good. And he wanted to lick the magic off her skin.

First the job. Make nice with the witches to defuse this a little. Then the romance.

Half an hour later, she opened her door to find Mac standing on her porch.

"I thought this was done for the day." She crossed her arms over her now braless chest.

"You're nice to other people." He said this like it was new to her.

She cocked her head, eyeing him warily. "*I'm a very nice person.* But that doesn't mean I'm a doormat. And it doesn't mean I don't push back when someone shoves me. Nice doesn't mean weak."

He smiled and it sent a slow shiver of delight over her skin. He had a really great mouth.

Even from where he stood she caught the scent of wood smoke on his clothes, pine and cold, clean air. What must he have been like in London? Far away from this place with these stars, did he have that same sort of capable masculinity emanating from him?

"I bet no matter how hard any of those other guys tried, everyone's gaze flicked your way when you entered a room."

She hadn't meant to say that out loud. Everything moved in horrified slow motion as the words left her lips for him to hear. And then his smile slipped, changed and then it was something else entirely.

Something sort of dirty and naughty and she liked it.

Aimee swallowed hard, her pulse thundering.

"Everything about you is unexpected," he told her, sounding like he didn't know if he was mad or not.

Katie Faith was the unexpected one. Aimee was solid. Predictable even. She frowned at him. "I just meant in London or in the army. I've met army guys before."

One of his brows slid up slightly. "I'm an alpha wolf." He shrugged. "It tends to catch attention."

Lord, yes it did.

That and his butt.

"Did you know I can taste your heartbeat?" he murmured, leaning in close. "I can scent your blush as it heats your skin and the way your body chemistry changed. It's delicious."

Holy shit. He'd essentially just told her he knew he got her wet.

And she'd be lying to insist anything else. What she

felt right there as he stared, looked at her like she was something he planned to lick from head to toe, was the most intense thing she'd ever experienced.

Made her feel like an amateur because this was big-league attraction.

She put a hand to her throat but didn't deny. Didn't argue.

The chemistry swirling between them was a thick current, catching her, holding her. Not that she would have attempted to break free.

She cleared her throat and found some words. "I knew. In general, I mean. Katie Faith is married to a werewolf. She dated Darrell for years before that so I'm not ignorant of your heightened senses."

"Why do you sound so mad then? When your scent is just for me?"

"I don't know. I don't like not knowing, which makes me mad too. You're very sexy, did you know that?" He made her blurty. Which agitated her even more.

"Are you going to invite me in, or are we going to keep having this weirdly entertaining conversation out here?" he asked. "I promise not to bite. Not unless you like that sort of thing."

Exasperated and totally tingly at the image *that* conjured up, she stood to the side and motioned him into her kitchen. "I just made hot tea. You want some?"

He stood there and breathed in deep, his eyes closed, body tensed as every bit of him seemed intent on sniffing or smelling or whatever he was up to.

She knew he was big. She'd been next to him and up against him now twice, but in her house he seemed massive. The intensity of his concentration only seemed to make him larger, more compelling.

Just standing there he took up most of the oxygen and it was hard not to sway just a little, caught in his power as he so intensely cataloged whatever smell he was smelling.

Then, without anything else being said about it, he snapped out of it. "Sure. Got any cookies?" He plopped down at her table and began to poke around in the bread box. "What are these? Can I have one?"

A lot more like a bear than a werewolf just then. But she kept that to herself.

"Those are pecan sweet rolls. Merilee made them for the Counter. You can have one, but the other is mine and you should know up front I am mean when anyone steals my food."

"Cross my heart I will not steal your last sweet roll." He made an X on his chest. "I'll even bring you some extras if that means you'll be nice to me."

She poured his tea into a mug and indicated the sugar and milk if he wanted some. "I'm sorry I was short with you. Again. The first time at the market it was because I was still freaked out and mad about nearly being knocked over by two giant wolves. No one likes feeling that vulnerable. And tonight because something was said about someone I love like family and your damned mother has done a lot of damage with her mouth. I know she's your momma and so of course you love her." Aimee rolled her eyes. "But together with your brother, she's bound and determined to cause some sort of fight everywhere Katie Faith goes in her own hometown. What sort of person does that? But you didn't say it and I shouldn't have included you in with them. Though I do expect you to rein them in."

He could make Pembry a better pack. If they allowed

him to. But she had her doubts about that. His parents were so focused on Darrell taking over as Patron, even though they'd called Mac home and knew he was going to take over. They seemed to wallow in some fantasy that both things—Darrell in charge and Mac taking over—were possible at the same time. Or maybe they just wanted him to do all their dirty work to get rid of Darrell so they could still be on Darrell's side in a way. Which made Aimee angry. What parent did that? They'd set up some sort of situation where no matter what Mac did he'd be the villain in some sense. So they didn't have to come out and say to Darrell's face that he wasn't the wolf for the job? Ugh.

He watched her as he ate his sweet roll and drank his tea. His energy was intense, yes, but it was easy being with him. She didn't feel like she had to fix him or shield him or even be mad at him. That was a nice thing.

He said, "I accept your apology. And I want you to accept mine because I know this mess hurts Katie Faith and her family and I hate that Avery's health is in jeopardy and this nonsense makes it worse. You shouldn't have to be afraid to be out and about or have someone try to ruin your day. I get why you were upset. Both times. *I'm trying.* Please understand that. I'm trying to make the changes we need at a speed they'll actually work in."

His tone and the sigh at the end tugged at her. He was torn. That much was clear. And he'd probably already figured out that his parents were using him as the cudgel they didn't have the spine to be themselves.

She found herself really wanting him to share. "Before you say anything else, I think you should know I'm a little empathic. I can't read your mind or anything like that. But we all give off emotions, even when we try to lock them down. I try to be up front with people. I never want them to think I pry."

A new blush heated her chest and cheeks.

"Really? That's sort of cool. Well, wait. Is it cool? Come to think of it, that might be annoying or scary given how people can be sometimes." His reaction let her admit she would have been really sad if he'd reacted negatively.

Instead he seemed interested rather than repulsed. Which made her like him even more.

"It's a gift and like all gifts, they come with blessings and flaws. I can shut it out in crowds but I'd hate to live in a big city. It helps me do my job better. I'm still learning how to use it." It hadn't saved her from her foolish mistake with Bob, but stone-cold liars were often really good at it. "Miz Rose says she still learns new things about her power. So if she can, I guess I'm glad to do it as well."

"Huh. Okay, I get that. So. I'm sexy?" One corner of his mouth hitched up and punched her in the gut. So much desire filled her that all her renewed guilt over the whole situation with Bob melted away.

"You seem to bring out the blurt in me. You know you are so stop pretending to be modest. What's your mom's problem?"

He leaned back after wiping his mouth. "Wow, you're all over the road there, Aimee. How about we get back to how sexy I am? And then we can promise to never include details about my mom when we're talking about sex or who is sexy."

Lord. He was trouble. Except this trouble was well over six feet tall and had shoulders wide and strong, and he looked like Paul Bunyan only… Well, no, not Paul Bunyan, but like the paper-towel guy. Yeah, that one.

She was a rule follower usually. But he made her want to break them all. Or at least the good ones that might end up with kissing him. Or fucking. Whatever. Wow.

At least his wolf sense couldn't smell this conversation she was having in her head.

"My mother is fiercely protective of the Pembry wolves."

He had to go and ruin that lovely little fantasy she was having about him with that? "Is that an actual answer to my question, because if so, that's dumb. You think she's the only one who feels protective? And yet none of us are poking old men trying to recover from a near-death health crisis over it but her."

"Are you always like this?"

"Right, you mean? I am. Way more than people give me credit for," she muttered. "Or do you mean annoyed that as dumb as your family is, *you* look good enough to take a bite out of?"

"I don't have the slightest idea how to deal with you."

She laughed then. "I'm not a puzzle to be solved. Anyway, you need to be kept on your toes."

"Are you the woman to do that?"

This was bad. She should avoid this moment. Laugh it off, shoo him away and masturbate instead.

"I don't know."

He cocked his head. "Do you want to be?"

"Yes. Parts of me right now are all shouting yes. My brain says no. I shouldn't. But you have such a pretty face, it's hard not to get all caught up in it."

"What if I said I wanted you to get all caught up in it? Like if it was between your thighs?"

Delicious shivers of delight wracked her as they both crossed that line.

There was no misunderstanding he was referring to oral sex. Not any more room for misunderstanding how much she wanted that to be happening either.

She blew out a breath. "So. You know this could end in total disaster, right?"

"I'm not sure I can think right now. All my blood has rushed from my brain to my cock. But whatever to all that. I want you. You want me. Fuck everyone else."

"I can't imagine anyone in your family would be okay with this."

"None of them are going to kiss you. And not all my family are bad."

"You're going to kiss me?"

"I sort of feel like if I don't I'd be missing out on something really good. And you want me to. So I'm happy to oblige."

"That's good because my appetites are insatiable."

He laughed, leaning over to drop a kiss, a brush of lips and the warmth of his breath against her mouth.

"That one was an introductory kiss. Free of charge."

"It was okay."

Her mouth tingled so there was that.

His smile told her he wasn't insulted. "Don't put that review up online, okay? I have a reputation to uphold."

"I'm thinking you'll have to give me a few options so I can judge appropriately. You don't have a Consumer Reports page so I need to do my research. I'm very responsible."

"This is hands down the strangest conversation I've ever had with a woman."

"I doubt that. I know who your mother is." She gave him a look.

"I thought we decided we weren't going to talk about my mother right now?"

"Well, you said that because you want to kiss me instead of talk about how out of bounds she's acting."

"Just so you know, I'd pretty much always rather kiss you than talk about my mother."

He was so funny. How had she never known this? *Damn it.* Funny men were a weakness and this one also had wide shoulders, soulful eyes and an ass you could bounce a quarter off.

"I understand that, Mac. I surely do. And yet, the topic is pretty important."

He leaned across to kiss her again, this time there was no sweet brush of lips. This time he eased right in, his tongue sliding over her bottom lip and right into her mouth like he was meant to be there.

Oh, his taste. Dear heavens above. It rushed through her system like little tiny sparklers of pleasure.

He slid a hand—a big, strong hand—around the back of her neck, holding her close as he deepened the kiss.

She grasped the front of his shirt, more to keep from melting into a puddle of goo than anything else. Her heart pounded as he nipped her bottom lip hard enough to elicit her gasp of pleasure/pain.

If this man did anything else as well as he kissed, she was really going to enjoy getting to know him.

Then again, he was a Pembry and his mom was a total kook and his brother was a psycho.

And yet, she had no intention of breaking the kiss.

* * *

Mac had never tasted anything like Aimee Benton. And now that he had, he found he had no interest in any other flavors.

Ever since the night when he'd broken up that fight and pulled her from the fray, he'd been unable to stop thinking of her.

She tasted like fine, smoky scotch. Her energy, her magic was golden and full of light and sensuality.

It didn't matter that they were improbable.

What mattered was the way she felt as she surrendered to the kiss. The fire in her spirit. The fantastic rack didn't hurt either.

Aimee was someone he could see as an equal to his own power. A witch who, though generally genial, had a very tough spine.

He wanted more.

He was pretty much as hard as he'd ever been and there was probably no chance he'd get inside her that night. Two days ago he'd have said never. After that kiss though, he knew it was inevitable.

Mainly because once he'd set his mind to something, he rarely failed. And also because he knew how much she wanted that too. Something else he liked about her was that if she wasn't interested in anything else with him, she'd tell him straight up.

Admittedly, he kept kissing her to keep her from overthinking and to make his case that he would be worth the time and effort.

That and he liked kissing her, so why stop?

He sipped at her. Savored each moment as he took her bottom lip between his teeth, tugging gently.

Her moan in response seemed to physically grasp

his cock and squeeze and he had to swallow back his own entreaty.

The back of her neck was so fucking soft and smooth he wanted to rub his face along it, preferably as he took her from behind.

She wriggled to get closer, which only made him madder to have her.

"Let me take you to dinner," he said as he cruised kisses across her jawline to her ear. Unfortunately he had to go back home to deal with that scene at city hall. He'd only come over to apologize and it had been longer than he'd planned on.

Not that he regretted their kiss. Or whatever else they'd just started. But duty called and it sucked so he figured he'd better lock her in at least for the next step.

"Right now?" The disappointment in her voice made him smile as he sat back.

"Tomorrow night. I need to go home right now and deal with the scene at city hall earlier. Believe me when I tell you I'd rather be here than there."

Understanding lit her eyes and she nodded. "Bummer. But I get it. Uh, dinner in public though? Like Pembry wolves would see us?"

"You ashamed to be seen with me?"

She made a face and snorted. "Yeah, I make out with guys all the time but they have to be really special to be seen in public with."

"You know what I mean," he said.

"No. I think you need to know what *I* mean because I'm not interested in you if you can't admit there's a problem at your end, not mine. Like I'm going to complain if people in this town see us eating together? That's the least of all the problems you need to handle. We both know what's happening right now in town."

"Okay, okay. Fair enough. Yes, in public, and who knows what my family will think. I already told you we aren't all like my mom and brother. My uncle and cousins like you."

"Jeez, don't get a complex or anything."

He would have been annoyed but the grin she wore let him know she was just teasing. He liked her.

"So. Dinner tomorrow. I'll pick you up here? Say, seven?"

"All right. That works."

She got up to walk him to the door where he lost himself in her for a few more kisses and rushed out before he decided not to go at all.

He skipped heading to his parents' house, stopping off at his uncle's first. He'd called and left messages with his father and Darrell, and wasn't surprised to see none of them had responded.

"Where have you been?" Huston asked.

"Told you I had to handle something. I went to talk to Aimee Benton. Apologize for what happened earlier."

"Really now?" His cousin gave him a look. "Must be why you smell like a witch."

"I was in her house. Of course I smell like her." They'd all see him out with her the following night anyway. That and he had no desire to hide it. He liked the idea of people knowing he had plans for the delectable Ms. Benton.

If people watched them—and they would, because everyone in town was nosy as fuck—they'd also see a wolf with a witch. They'd see the normal stuff like dating and a budding romance. Normalcy was what Diablo Lake could use a heaping helping of.

Well, normal for Diablo Lake.

"Is that your story?" his aunt asked with a smirk.

"I truly did go to her house to apologize, yes, ma'am." Mac avoided direct eye contact.

She snorted. "You're over there all up in her because she's adorable."

Aimee *was* pretty damned adorable, as it happened. But that was something he'd discuss at another time.

Right then he had to handle Pembry business. "What's going on with Darrell and my father? Have they been over? They're ducking my calls."

His uncle's expression told Mac what he thought of that. "I saw him corralling your mother into the car. Lights are on at the house so I imagine they're home. God knows where your brother is, but he's not making trouble at the moment so I'll take that as a win," his uncle said.

"Before he left he wouldn't tell me what JJ said to him or how the fight started. Do you know?" Mac asked as he plopped down on the couch.

"If I were to take a guess, I'd wager it had something to do with Josiah Dooley, but I don't know for sure. You know your dad doesn't say much to me unless he has to these days."

"The witches are pissed. He's stirring up a hornet's nest and I don't know why. But I do know there's nowhere to go but more tension unless we can work this out."

His family was tearing apart and it weighed heavily on him. The knowledge of what was to come if things kept heading in the same direction.

He hated it. Resented it. And it didn't matter. Because he had to clean it up.

"Anyone want to tell me why my mother is losing her shit so much worse than usual? This seems like a lot more than her normal high-strung behavior."

His aunt and uncle averted their gazes and he barely withheld an impatient sigh.

Barely.

Secrets never stayed secret. Not forever. And this whole thing was headed for a spectacular crash.

"Scarlett keeps her own counsel, Mac. If she has things to hide, she's not sharing them with any of us here," Huston said.

Mac hadn't gone to a goddamn war zone to come home to shovel secrets for anyone.

He stood and headed toward the door. "This festering stuff has poisoned our pack. I got dragged back here across the world to clean up a damned mess and it makes it a lot harder when no one wants to speak honestly."

Though he tried not to slam out of the house, he knew he failed as he stomped down the steps leading to the yard beyond.

"You know the law," Huston told him as he caught up.

"I'm sick and tired of trying to handle this bullshit with one arm tied behind my back."

"Dude. I get it. Okay? We're not the enemy."

"What the actual fuck? Why is everyone getting in my way instead of helping?"

Huston shook his head. "Let's go for a run. You're all kinds of messed up right now. Get yourself under control. Especially if you're going to go rubbing up over Aimee on the regular."

Mac growled but stalked to the woods just beyond. He'd cut short some pretty spectacular rubbing all over one another to return home to this?

Huston was correct though. It would indeed be on the regular. Now that he'd tasted her, he planned to taste her a lot more.

A run would help him get himself reined in. He needed to burn this all off before it singed him.

He did one of the few things that always felt exactly right. Mac slipped his human skin and let his wolf come and take over. He tore into the trees, his cousin already ahead of him on the trail.

Chapter Eight

"Okay so I didn't tell you this last night, because it happened late and I figured you and your husband would be doing filthy things to one another." Aimee grinned as she waggled her brows at her best friend. She'd come into the Counter, the soda fountain Katie Faith's family owned and ran, to dish a little on the way to her next home visit. "I have a date. Tonight. With Mac Pembry."

Katie Faith's eyes got wide as she said, "Get out! I want to know every single detail right this very moment."

"He showed up at my door after that whole thing outside city hall. To apologize, though I *was* mean to him at first."

"You were not. You snapped at him I bet. But you're not mean." Katie Faith said it with so much conviction it made her smile.

"Well, he said how I was nice to other people and it made me mad. So I told him I was nice to people but that I wasn't a doormat. And then he came in and we made out for like twenty minutes. Oh my God."

"You're very nice!" Katie Faith sniffed her annoyance before her tone went a little lower. "Is he a good kisser? Duh. I bet he is. You wouldn't tolerate a bad kisser. Plus, look at him. He just looks like he'd lay one on you that had you making very bad choices."

"Right? He's *such* a good kisser and he takes charge." She fanned her face with her hand a moment at the memory. "He held me by the back of my neck and got all growly. It was...dominant. Not underrated."

Katie Faith's knowing look made Aimee want to giggle with glee. So she did. "Like Christmas and my birthday all at once."

Katie Faith gave her a thumbs-up. "I always thought bossy guys were idiots like Darrell. Bluster and pecker measuring to deal with their various complexes and stuff. But Jace, well, he's as bossy and dominant as they come and it's not to deal with any complex. He's the real thing. Which means he's also protective and loyal and courageous. And for me? He's a big giant softhearted dude and that's pretty freaking cool."

It was, as a matter of fact.

"So he asked me to dinner tonight. He's picking me up at seven," Aimee continued.

"Wow. I'm so giddy. I have a werewolf and now you will too."

Aimee snickered. "Hit the brakes there. It's a date, not marriage."

"But now that you've made out with him you're going to go back for more. And if he can't keep you that's on him." Katie Faith nodded as she finished.

"I'm not sure, but I think you just said I was easy," Aimee teased.

"Only when you want to be. Which is the best kind, in my opinion," Katie Faith said.

"Okay, that I can get on board with." There was no reason to be ashamed of liking sex. She had this attraction

with a really smoking-hot guy. If they got horizontal—
or vertical, he seemed the stand-up-sex type—she had
no reason to pretend she didn't want it.

"But this is going to be in public. Which seems, uh,
a bold choice. What do you think?" Her judgment felt
strange. She wasn't used to questioning it, but that was
before she'd found out about Bob.

"I think he's a werewolf and you're a powerful witch
and he's going to want to show you off. I like Mac. I always have. I'm not a fan of some of his family, but he's
always been good to me. Where are you going? Do you
know?" Katie Faith handed a Vanilla Coke her way.

"I don't. But it's Diablo Lake. There are two places
that seem likely so the pub or Salt & Pepper. Why?
Are you going to show up with Jace and be all, oh, my,
what a surprise?"

"Of course I am. I think it could actually be a good
thing for us all to be seen together being cordial. The
town could use some stability. Also I'm nosy and I want
to be there to see how hard he puts on the woo. It'll keep
Jace on his toes too." Katie Faith snickered.

Aimee snorted. "It's a good thing that boy has super-
powers. You're a trial. Anyway. I can call you when I
find out. But if I tell you to go, you best take your pretty
butt away. I can't get at all his good parts if you get him
all worked up in the bad way."

But Katie Faith was right about it being a positive
thing if they were all seen with each other.

"*And* you need to tell Jace before you arrive. I don't
want you springing this on him in the middle of my
date." You had to set limits with Katie Faith or she got
a little wild sometimes.

But there was no doubt her life would be so much worse without Katie Faith in it.

"I need to get to work." Aimee finished up her soda and dropped money on the counter. Katie Faith just glared at her, but she knew not to argue. Aimee was going to pay and that's all there was to it. "Talk to you later." She blew Katie Faith a kiss as she left.

He brushed his palms down the front of his thighs before he got out of his car. Mac loved this neighborhood. The houses were small with prodigious, heady-scented gardens. He paused before knocking on her door, breathing deep. Pine and roses. The wall of trees just beyond her back door lent the pine, and the trellis and porch columns were covered in fragrant climbing roses in full bloom.

A witch lived there, that much was for sure. But there was more. It was *her*. It was the magic, that unique scent and energy that only Aimee had.

He knocked and hadn't succeeded in wiping the smile off his face before she answered.

She smiled back immediately. "Right on time."

He got the feeling she was a punctual person. He bet she'd never been tardy for class.

Then he noticed what she was wearing. A bright blue shirt. Snug enough to highlight her curves. Her skirt similarly hugged her long legs leading down to boots that managed to be sexy and practical at the same time.

"Wow." He studied her face. Her eyes had been made up to emphasize the color. *The lipstick.* "I like red lipstick." He grinned and her smile got bigger.

There she stood looking like delicious temptation. Bold and totally in charge.

"I find it incredibly sexy that you're so confident," he murmured as he bent to brush his lips against hers.

"Now it's my turn to say wow." Her voice trembled slightly, inciting his wolf. "You look great."

He'd gone for a button-down shirt and jeans, so he was glad she approved. Also because he'd spent an inordinate amount of time deciding what to wear. And changing twice.

"You want to come in or are we pressed for time?" Her mouth tipped up at the corner. "This is kiss-proof lipstick. We could test it. It comes with a money-back guarantee so you'd be doing it for science."

"Why, Miss Benton, you're quite the temptress this evening." He followed her into her front room where she closed the door and turned to face him.

"I'm glad it's working."

He backed her against the door, his body just shy of hers. "It works, all right."

Hands on her hips, he bent his knees and kissed her long and slow, tasting her carefully.

"Yeah, so I think this lipstick is a keeper," she managed to say after he broke away. She had no idea if it had smeared on her or not, but it wasn't on his mouth and if it attracted kisses like the one he just laid on her, it was definitely a keeper.

He grinned and then his stomach growled really loudly.

"Okay I get it. You're hungry. And Katie Faith has called me already three times to see where you're taking me and telling me how hungry she is too. I should have said, *oh, by the way, there's probably no way to avoid Katie Faith and Jace showing up wherever we're going tonight*. She's nosy and bossy and my best friend.

Plus she thinks it'll be good for the town if we're all seen together not fighting in the middle of the street. My only excuse is the kiss you laid on me made me loopy. Er. Loopier than usual."

"So this is a double date?"

"No. Well. I told her no. You've met Katie Faith so it's a roll of the dice really. I let her know I'd call when I was ready to have her show up. I don't think we need them at our table for dinner. Maybe for pie after? I mean, Jace isn't a bad guy. Maybe you know that. You probably do because you were in school and you're both alpha wolves and I'm babbling now."

He kissed her again because it pleased him to do it and she tasted so good. "Babbling is okay. We can have dinner with them at the pub. That's where I figured we could go. They can leave after pie though. How's that plan instead?"

She laughed. "That sounds like a very good plan."

Chapter Nine

Mac couldn't deny his pride at the way people reacted as they entered the Red Roof Inn together.

The hostess, one of his cousins, took them to a table he'd thankfully remembered to reserve in advance. The place was already humming with conversation. Music played over the sound system and it smelled like pizza dough and beer.

Not bad at all. "Oh, we'll have two more people with us," he told his cousin as he held Aimee's chair out and then helped her sit.

"I've never had a positive chair-holding-out experience. It's always sort of random and out of sync and then I have to surreptitiously redo the whole sitting and chair-moving process. But you did really well. Thumbs-up," she told him as he joined her.

"You're very strange and it totally turns me on."

"That's an unexpected and yet awesome compliment. Thank you."

He tipped his chin at the sight of Jace shouldering his way through the crowd, protecting Katie Faith from getting jostled. Mac approved of how he was with his wife.

He knew Josiah's reputation. It would have been hard to grow up in the shadow of that. He also knew a little something about growing up in someone's shadow and having to prove yourself.

What Jace appeared to have with Katie Faith told Mac he was already a better man than his father ever had been.

Aimee's face lit up when she caught sight of her friends. She waved at them as they made their way over and sat.

"I ordered a pitcher at the bar on the way in," Katie Faith told them.

"Because you're one of heaven's own angels, that's why," Aimee said. "We just sat down two minutes ago so we haven't ordered yet."

"Kismet. Now food. Oh my God, I need food." Katie Faith looked to Mac. "Hi. Why do you eat so late?"

"Why do you eat so early?" he asked back.

"I'm hungry early. Normal people are, you know."

"When she gets hungry, or you wake her up early, she's really awful. Like a rabid raccoon. She'll be better once she eats and gets some liquor in her," Aimee explained to Mac.

"Fair enough." He and Jace then tipped chins and clasped forearms and the tension eased.

The crowd, who'd been watching carefully, also relaxed. It was always sort of amazing how seemingly small things like being together in public made a difference with folks.

"Who's getting what?" Katie Faith asked. Jace got up and returned with a bowl of bar snacks and the pitcher.

"These should help everyone's evening." Jace set the bowl near his wife who gave him a grateful smile.

"That's her way of saying we all need to order things she wants to eat a bite or two of. I figure you're a werewolf and can defend yourself and your food if need be, though. You have to be firm with her." Aimee winked at Katie Faith.

It wasn't that Katie Faith wasn't bossy. She totally was, but Aimee moved with it. Pushing back here and there but the two of them weaved together the order in a flow of insults, bizarre inside jokes and laughing.

"Are they always like this?" he asked Jace.

"Yes. Accept that now. They have a penchant for trouble too. Best to just nod and go with it. You can't outlast them. Katie Faith's like a kitten. Don't tell her I said that." Jace smiled slightly as he looked over to his wife briefly. "Now here's the part where I say Aimee is like my little sister and I'd be vexed if she got hurt or misused."

There wasn't any pretense that this was a first date in any human sense of the term. They both knew what it was to find a female who'd piqued the interest of man and wolf. He enjoyed women, yes he did. He hadn't been a monk; no he'd had plenty of wonderful, pleasurable moments with them over his life.

But he'd never mistaken any of those for anything but temporary relationships. Fucking was one thing. But Aimee represented *more*. He'd have to get to know her better, but she made all the chaos seem to part and quiet a little. And that wasn't anything to sneeze at.

She came with an extended family who all wanted to protect her and he liked that even as it ruffled his feathers. Which was one of many reasons why it was clear he was interested in something serious. "Understood," he said with a nod, meaning more than one thing.

For the time being he'd allow this protection because she was close with her friend and her friend's husband.

But maybe one of these days *he'd* want to protect her. Maybe she'd be someone he considered his.

"Do people always stare at you when you're out or is this a new thing?" she asked him as the food arrived.

"I'm a good-looking man." Mac shrugged and she laughed. He liked it. Craved it even. Amusing her. Having her be interested in what he had to say. He hadn't realized just how funny she was at first, but by that point he got it. Another super sexy quality she possessed.

"You're a *very* good-looking man. I can't lie." She put hot sauce on her pizza, which made him suspicious. But there was that compliment so he went with that.

"Oh, *very* even? Well, thank you, ma'am." He liked flirting with her. There'd been a lot less lightheartedness in his life before she came along. "It could be they think it's strange to put hot sauce on pizza."

"You're supposed to be worldly, Macrae. Take a walk on the wild side. A little hot sauce makes most everything better." She took a bite, humming in delight.

"Worldly?"

"Essentially anyone who gets to live somewhere else is worldly. Plus it was across an actual ocean so bonus points."

She made the weirdest sort of sense. It fascinated him.

The wolf thought so too. Wanted to puzzle her out, to play and pounce each time she delighted him.

Aimee leaned in, placing a hand on his forearm, leaving little zings of electricity in her wake.

His magic surged in response, but when her gaze locked on his, it settled, caressing hers, like a whole body embrace. All the tumult left him in a warm flow.

He mouthed, "Wow," and she smiled. A small, private smile.

And though it had felt as if an hour passed while they just stared at one another, it had just been a few breaths.

The rest of the world settled back in around them as the sound began to register again.

"They're probably looking because he and I are sitting at the same table and not fighting," Jace said.

"That and the whole date-with-a-witch thing. You know," Katie Faith said, "general Diablo Lake nosiness."

"Don't forget his handsomeness," Aimee added, her attention shifting to include the others at the table.

"I would never," Katie Faith told her with faux solemnity. "It's probably why Eileen is staring at him like she wants him for dinner."

He looked around and caught sight of Eileen Drewry at the bar, sending him what his aunt liked to call a come-hither look.

No, thank you. He turned away quickly, before she got any ideas.

"Well, he's not on her menu tonight so she needs to keep looking," Aimee said quietly to Katie Faith.

"He's a prime slice of man meat, Aimee. Going to be hard to expect everyone not to look. And try to touch. I'm just saying."

"Okay, ladies, let's not scare Mac just yet," Jace said, doing his best to hide a laugh.

"Is this like hazing?" he asked Jace, not at all offended to see Aimee showing her teeth to another woman trying to get his attention.

"I'll let you know when and if it ever ends for me."

He lifted his glass, saluting Jace with it. They'd need

to talk about the mess between their two packs but not right at that moment.

That night was about being a guy out on a date with a beautiful woman he'd had a soft spot for for years.

"So, you should come in." Aimee tipped her head toward the house.

"Yeah?" He went ahead and followed her into the house.

"I try not to say things I don't mean. Unless it's about presents my grandma gives me. Then I say they're great!" She flashed him a smile.

"Well, that's the rule. I have a great-aunt like that. Knitted the most god-awful sweaters for me every year on my birthday."

She grinned. "Which one? I know several of them." She led him into the living room.

"Opal Chambliss. She still makes me things. Scarves now, though. I can deal with that." He grinned.

He really shouldn't be so adorable. It was bad for her constitution. Somehow. Whatever. It was his fault she was all goofy and addled by his testosterone and magic.

"I'm not trying to make you goofy and addled," he said around a poor attempt not to smile as he flopped onto her couch.

She'd said that out loud.

Jeez-a-lou.

"Well, stop it." She waved a hand his way.

"But I don't want to stop it if it makes you addled. That means I'm hitting some sweet spots." He inched closer.

"I think you're going to be a lot of trouble. You are, aren't you?"

He nodded. "Yes. I think so. But I'll make it worth your while."

"You're really good at this stuff. It's like my knees are magnets, repelling the other."

He guffawed, which only made her want him more. So she got her skirt up enough to climb into his lap, facing him.

"I don't know where you get the stuff you say," he told her as he kissed over her jaw to her ear.

"I'm talented. Obviously." She'd tried to sound flirty, but the thing he was doing to her ear with his tongue resulted in her sounding like she'd climbed three flights of stairs.

"I can't argue with that. You're very talented. I'd give you a gold star and a blue ribbon."

"I look forward to finding all sorts of things to grade you on. Notably things that include you and me being naked. Or on the way to it." She paused as he nibbled the hollow of her throat.

"All through school I thought you were the quirky, perky girl who said *please* and *thank you* and followed the rules."

She laughed. "Yeah? Well, I was. And I always thought you were the unobtainable older boy who'd do all sorts of exciting things with me. At the time I originally thought that, of course I didn't really know the whole depth and breadth of just what two people could get up to. But even then I thought you were lickable. Just not for a girl like me."

He flipped her onto her back on the couch, settling between her thighs, her skirt really hiked up by that point.

"You're a buffet of wonderfully fun bad choices, aren't you?" she asked as he kissed her.

"Let's find out," he replied, his hands sliding up her rib cage. "I prefer to think of it as an array of sensual choices." One flick of his fingers and a button at the top of her blouse slipped free.

His gaze held hers a long moment—she knew he waited for her to object or change the trajectory of their evening.

Her shiver of delight was a low, slow, heated wave. Damn if consent wasn't sexy as hell.

She stretched up just a bit to bridge the gap between them and nipped his bottom lip.

He let out a trickle of a growl. Not the scary kind.

The heat where his lips slid over the skin of her neck just below her ear made her gasp. Scalding. Branding. Leaving an impression of his lips that'd last far longer than just that night.

He did his magic and two more buttons on her blouse sprang free to expose the bra beneath.

She was so glad she'd chosen that particular bra earlier. It was one of her favorites in a blue similar to the blouse. Her boobs perched up, quivering on the very edge of overflowing the cups because of how she'd arched.

He bent, brushing his mouth over the curves of her cleavage, breathing her in. *Wow. Oh wow.* He did something to her that was exhilaratingly terrifying. The intensity of what they made together was fantastic. And yet it was so unusual she was wary.

"No offense or anything, but this couch is small and I'm getting a cramp in my thigh from trying not to lean all my weight on you," he said with an adorably frustrated frown.

"Is that your way of saying you want to see my bedroom?"

He paused and then snorted a laugh as he stood.

She just took a look at what she'd been blessed with and sighed happily before she rolled to her feet.

"I'm going to lock my doors. People will barge in if I don't," she told him as she locked the front and pulled the shade on the window down. "I'd turn off my porch light, but Mrs. Burrows has that little dog of hers and he goes absolutely crazy when all the cats come around in the dark. They really do it to mess with him, sweet little thing."

He grunted and she grabbed his hand on the way past. She threw the back-door lock as they headed through the kitchen to get to her bedroom.

"What's that sound for?" she asked.

"Dogs."

She tried not to laugh and succeeded. Mostly. "I forgot you guys had a thing about dogs as pets. But you're wolves. Werewolves! Totally different from Pookie. That's the dog's name. He's not exceptionally bright, but he is generally happy and only barks in the dark. Maybe he's afraid of the dark. Huh."

He just stared at her so she pantomimed locking her lips and throwing away the key.

He rolled his eyes but hummed his pleasure when she turned on the lamp in her room.

"I like it in here. That's a big-ass bed."

"It's a pain in the butt, that's what it is. But I love it anyway. My great-grandpa made it for my great-grandma. It was a wedding present."

She ran a hand over the wood frame, smooth from generations of people touching the footboard as they passed. The carvings were simple, but beautiful. Big-headed roses in full bloom connected by swirling leaves.

It was a custom size, so she'd had to get a mattress custom made to fit. But it was a place she spent a lot of time in. Big enough to lounge, work on embroidery, read, watch movies, all that stuff.

She was a homebody and her bed was a place she loved to be.

And right at that moment, she really loved that she was about to be in it with Mac.

"Woo-hoo!" She pointed at him. "I think you have way too much clothes on. Or too many clothes. Yeah, that one. I bet you've got something pretty awesome underneath your pants and stuff."

"Or you could help. Many hands make light work and all that."

She thought about it a moment and then stepped to him, unbuttoning his shirt and shoving it from his arms.

"Wow. You're...wow." Beyond words, she flapped a hand his way. "What the hell do you do to look like this? Do you work out eight hours a day? You ate pizza! I saw you eat four slices and you had a hoagie and pie with three scoops of ice cream. Your stomach is ridiculous. I have major reservations about getting naked now that I've seen this. And a nipple ring? Did you have that in the army? Did it hurt? How does it stay in when you change? It's so sexy I'm going to... Well, I'm going to pass out."

Then again, she could just stand there a while and drink him in. Good gracious, what a specimen.

He shook his head, coming toward her faster than she realized he could move. The heat of his body against hers, even through her clothes, made her dizzy.

This close all her senses seemed saturated with him

and that was before her shirt was off, his mouth in the wake of the fabric.

"I find it astounding you'd think so when it's you who looks this fantastic without a shirt. Yes, it hurt. The magic of the change means it's there when I take my human form again. No, I didn't have it in the army."

He answered all those questions as he got rid of the bra and she shimmied out of her skirt while he got his pants, underwear and socks off.

"Now. Yeah. Now I think we've got so much to discuss." He backed her to the bed and she ended up flopping onto the mattress with him leaning above her, blocking out all light with those wide, muscled shoulders.

"I can conjure up a dozen things to do with my mouth that don't involve talking."

He slid his body against hers as he climbed up the bed, pulling her to his side before wrapping his arms around her. "See, thing is, I've been thinking about a lot of those very same things ever since that night we bumped into one another at the bar at the Red Roof Inn."

She couldn't help the warmth on her face as she blushed, so charmed and flattered. He made her feel fucking beautiful.

"I've never in my life been more glad I have an IUD. Because I can have you in me naked. Gloriously, wonderfully naked."

The werewolves-not-being-susceptible-to-STDs-thing was awesome, as far as Aimee was concerned.

"You just say whatever comes into your mind, don't you?" He tested the weight of her breasts in his hands a moment.

"No. I do have manners, you know. But I'm not playing around when it comes to wanting to come and come hard. I'll do the same for you, but I like sex and I really want to have it with you and I'm glad I don't have to deal with having to use a condom."

"You have wonderful manners. With most people anyway." He licked over her left nipple, which made the wisecrack she'd been about to make die on a moan of delight.

"You're just used to everyone saying what you want to hear. And frankly, look at you. I'd do it too. Luckily, you appear to be susceptible to my particular charms." She managed this around a tongue that was pleasure thick, resulting in slow, nearly slurred speech.

"If only people told me what I wanted to hear," he muttered. "Luckily, between you and me, we're all good to get to the coming hard part."

"You're a great date. I'm just saying."

Anything else she may have said she forgot when he used his teeth on the other nipple. Tugging until she nearly begged.

Need licked at her skin, drove her as she dragged the edge of her nails down his back and sides. His snarled groan set her afire.

It was so totally hot shit holy wow she just threw herself into it, soaking it up.

She tasted like magic. Sweet and spicy. It clung to his tongue and lips, that thing that made her who and what she was.

He rubbed his face all over her delightful breasts, noting each gasp and moan. Learning what she liked best so he could give it to her again and again.

She was so much more than he'd imagined, and he'd

imagined a lot. Strong and bold, she arched, urging him on. Demanding what she wanted.

When she wrapped her thighs around his waist, the heated slick of her pussy stroked against his cock and left behind a wave of dizzied pleasure.

He wanted her. All of her. And when she wrapped a hand around the base of his cock and squeezed, he wanted her even more.

"Wait," he wheezed.

"I don't want to. Now." She squeezed again and then slid her fist up and down to make her point.

"I never rush a job, Aimee," he told her as he kissed down her belly, thinking a little more clearly when she let go of his dick.

He took his time at the sensitive skin at her hips and then across her lower belly until he finally reached just exactly where he needed to be.

"Remember what I told you yesterday about being between your thighs?" he murmured.

"I've been playing it over and over in my head ever since you said it."

It wasn't practiced dirty talk, it was just how she was. Blunt, but not cruel. Maybe it was that so much of his life was taken up by artifice and constant tension because of lies and secrets, but it soothed him to know she said what she thought the way she did. "Damn, what you do to me."

So soft. He kissed and nibbled at the insides of her thighs until he spread her open and took a long lick, humming.

The sound she made seemed to echo through him, jangling to his bones. He'd wanted to be there for hours, but that gasped groan shredded his control.

And that was before she reached down, ran her fingers through his hair and then yanked him closer.

His cock seemed to ache in time with the pounding of his heart as he ate at her, licking and sucking.

"Yesyesyes," she chanted, urging him on until he decided to take her over into climax. "Holy cheese puffs!"

He was still laughing when he kissed his way back up to her mouth, taking it in a long slow kiss.

"You're laughing at me?" she asked when he'd broken away to catch his breath.

"Hell yes. Holy cheese puffs," he repeated, laughing anew.

"I have a problem with cursing so I'm trying to use alternatives."

"You did tell me to fuck off just last night."

She snickered. "Well. I did just tell you I have a problem. Thank you kindly for that amazing orgasm."

"There's more where that came from. Why don't you climb aboard?" He tipped his chin at her just to see if she'd get pissed or dig it.

One brow raised, she swung one of her legs over his lap and straddled his waist.

He loved the way she looked above him, tousled and sex flushed. Her eyes had gone half-lidded, her lips kiss swollen, parted slightly.

"You're so fucking beautiful," he told her.

Her mouth curved up. "Thank you."

"Now get yourself all around my cock."

Her slumberous eyes widened a moment as she sucked in a breath. Oh yeah, she liked that.

Good. He did too.

He watched the flexing and tightening of her thigh muscles as she teased herself all around his cock.

So wet and so hot, he had to clench his jaw to keep his control.

Finally she grabbed him and angled herself down, took every bit of him in one quick, mind-bending movement.

All he could feel was her. The way her inner walls hugged him. White hot and slick. He dug his fingers into her hips and began to move her body as he thrust up, taking over.

Aimee bent to lick over his nipple before tugging on it gently. He grunted and she tugged a little harder.

He stuttered a curse at how good that felt and tried to keep his pace even. He wanted to draw this out. Take it slow.

But she took his restraint and control as a challenge, and squeezed her inner muscles around him until he wheezed. Though he'd been keeping the pace and movement, she added a little swivel each time as he got all the way inside.

His vision narrowed with each thrust as she dug her nails into his sides.

Knowing he would eventually fall victim (or victor) to the lure of her charms, he walked his fingers down her belly to her clit.

As he watched her face, he slowly circled the pad of his middle finger around and around.

She moaned and got even hotter around him. "Again," he urged.

A nod as her gaze locked with his. She added a move that had her grinding herself against his fingers, which nearly pulled him into orgasm right that moment. As it was, he barely held out until her head fell back and she came all around him.

On and on until he couldn't take another moment without climax as he held her tight for long moments until at long last, they settled back side by side in her humongous bed, sweating and panting.

The best date he'd ever had.

Chapter Ten

"I'm not sure I'm ever going to be satisfied in any other bed." Mac stretched out his arms, grabbing her quick and hauling her close. He felt so warm and lazy there with her. Perfectly satisfied.

"I'm pretty awesome," she said.

"You are. I also meant the general size of the mattress."

"That's awesome too. But it can't make you a cup of coffee or get you off. Which is a drawback I've come to find."

"You've got me around. I can do both. I'm not as good at coffee as I am orgasms though."

Her theatrical, put-upon sigh made him roll his eyes.

"When I was a kid I remember being so mad that being a witch wasn't like Samantha in *Bewitched*. Like why can't I just blink up a four-course meal? Oh, I get to be great with roses? Big deal! I want to crinkle my nose and make some damned French fries." She tucked some hair behind her ear. "I can't believe I need another haircut. I love it short, but it grows so fast I need to have the back of it shaved. I probably should go for one of those long bobs. They call them 'lobs' but I'd rather call it a blob."

"Sometimes I have no idea where conversations with you go. I mean, don't get me wrong, it's usually worth the journey. But yeah, you're like *D&D* sometimes. Lots of wandering around."

She pinched him and then made an annoyed sound. "You have no body fat. I find this suspicious. Did you truck with dark arts to get that belly? Remember I asked you earlier and you didn't answer. Probably dark arts." She shook her head with a sigh.

"No dark arts. Sorry to burst your bubble. I'm a werewolf. We have really fast metabolisms. I exercise every day, but mainly because of the werewolf thing. Plenty of room to run here. Not so much in London. As for your hair? I've got some basic skill in using clippers. When you're in the middle of a desert you need to keep your hair as short as possible. We learned to barter and to give haircuts."

"I've often thought how sad it was that you can't actually bite someone and make them into a werewolf. I'd surely love that metabolism."

"I bet you have." That and all sorts of off-the-wall stuff he was sure.

"Like, that's not something lots of people wonder? I mean, it's not like I made that up. It's in books and stuff."

"Fiction books."

"Well, werewolves actually do exist. So."

He failed at holding back a snicker. "Just not ones that come from genetics instead of bites. Like how it actually works…" He caught himself and snorted. "I'm catching it from you. I'm going to start meandering through every conversation now, right?"

She laughed so hard it gave her the hiccups but it felt

damned good there in her gigantic bed, the scent of sex and magic in the air.

"Tell me stuff. What was London like?" she managed once she'd returned to bed after a foray into the kitchen for snacks and some sugar to cure the hiccups—though he wasn't sure he was ready for a sugared-up Aimee.

"I think you and London would be a great fit. It's a mix of young and old. Great pubs. It's familiar enough but still different. Really fantastic mass transit. Shiny red busses and lacquered black cabs. Excellent fish and chips. Lousy coffee but I haven't had a good cup of hot tea since I left."

"Funny, I was away from Diablo Lake for two years as I finished up all the coursework and practicum stuff I needed to work in the program I do. I came back on weekends and all that jazz, but I never actually felt *home* anywhere else. That doesn't mean I don't want to travel though. I'm saving to take a trip two years from now."

"I was gone for seven years. Because of the military I got to travel more than I would have otherwise. The world is so big and yet really small all at once. But you're right. Diablo Lake is home. For better and for worse, I guess. Where do you want to go on the trip you're planning?"

"I'm working on two different itineraries. One to Japan and one to Italy. I'm not sure which one I'll do yet. The research is fun."

"I've never been to Japan, but it's on my list. I've been to Rome. Busy. Talk about old! Every block you walk down there's so much history woven into everything. The traffic in Rome is one of the few things I can honestly say made me truly fear for my life. But they have excellent coffee."

"I approve of your love and appreciation of coffee. Why'd you come back?"

He sucked in a breath and then got himself comfortable, getting the pillows behind him propped just right.

"I only had a year left to go in my program so I'd have come home soon enough anyway."

She hesitated a while before speaking again. "Because of all this stuff going on between Dooley and Pembry?"

"Among other things, yes. You're correct that there's a problem and that wolves aren't handling it so it's involving the whole town. I'm trying here."

She rested her head on his shoulder. "It must be hard. I'm sorry."

It seemed at that moment that a warm wave of comfort flowed through him. Her magic, he realized and then wasn't quite sure how to feel about it.

"What do you mean? What must be hard?"

Aimee scoffed. "Don't sound so nervous. I'm not going to fistfight you right here in my bed. I wouldn't want to embarrass you with my physical prowess and make you sad that you're not as badass as me. Since I had you inside me just a few minutes ago, I figure I may as well get to know you better."

He failed at withholding a wince. "I apologize. Suspicion is my nature. Not fair, but there you go."

She nodded, taking his meaning and accepting his apology. "I mean leaving a situation you were in to come here when everything is in flux and your brother is getting all this attention and he's not half the wolf you are."

He frowned because that was pretty accurate. And then he let out a breath. "It's complicated."

Aimee continued, "I know I'm blunt. Not as bad as some can be. But I say what I mean and if you ask my opinion, I'm going to tell you. Everyone wants something from you here. They want you to make decisions. Want to you to fix things and lead. They want your power or your influence. I want stuff from you, but not your power. And I don't need you to fix me or make my choices. I just like the man. Wolf. Wolf man."

With one arm, he squeezed her to his side briefly. He didn't want her to feel as if he suspected her of any of that. But it was true otherwise. It was hard to know who to trust.

Aimee though? He could breathe around her. Even though their situation was complicated he knew what they shared was something he could find solace in rather than have to avoid.

"I was raised to lead, to make decisions and take care of problems. It comes with the gig. Not everyone in my family is the same as Darrell."

She waved a hand lazily. "I grew up here and I count just as many Pembrys as Dooleys as friends. But that doesn't make it any easier on your heart to have to go against your brother, I'd wager. Even when he's as big a tool as Darrell."

"He's spoiled. I have hope he'll grow up. Someday."

She harrumphed at that. Yeah, he wasn't sure that would ever happen either.

"Tell me about your job," he said to change the subject.

She told him about all the people she visited. How she connected them with the services they needed. He heard the affection in her tone when she discussed her clients, even the prickly ones. Was glad witches and shifters had someone like her looking out for them when they needed it the most and he said so.

"It's my gift. My magic is nurturing magic. Healing. I can do other things, but that's what I feel I was called to do. I'm lucky because we have a secure funding source, something social services, especially rural ones, always have to worry about. I get to help people. I learn their stories. Each one of them has so much to offer. My schedule is pretty much my own. I drive a lot, but I use the time for audiobooks and podcasts. Best of all? I get to provide services to the folks here in Diablo Lake. Sometimes I'm the nearest some people will come to a doctor unless things are really dire."

He really liked this woman with her weird sense of humor and giving heart.

"That's pretty awesome. I've been meaning to talk with Miz Rose about the possibility of a doctor in town."

"Really? That's a fantastic idea. I brought this up a few times to the city council but some people always got in my way."

"My father is old-school. He got rich holding on to every nickel and he sometimes forgets the penny smart, pound foolish saying. I'm the CFO of the pack, essentially. The money we'd save in the long run, especially given the benefit to our pack members, if we had a doctor in town once again would be significant. I guess I can talk to you instead of Miz Rose. Since she scares me and you just make my dick hard. Though, if I'm totally honest, I can admit there are times I'm scared of you too."

"Are you trying to butter me up?" she teased.

"Why? Do you like that sort of thing?"

"You're getting the hang of this, Prime." She nipped the meat of his pecs.

"I'm not officially Prime."

"You don't need a declaration to be what you so clearly are. What kind of name is Macrae anyway? You have a brother named Darrell, your dad is Dwayne, how did they come by Macrae?"

"My great-great-grandmother's maiden name was Macrae."

"I like it better than Darrell. Then again, that might be because Darrell is a turd and has ruined the name for me forever. What's the story with your brothers anyway?"

"In what way? Because that question could mean a dozen things when it comes to my family."

"Well, Billy is okay. He's not a total idiot and he's not throwing fists at the market, a bit too passive but we can't all be super wolf. Darrell is mainly who I mean. Samuel, well, he's a work in progress, but I have hope he can turn himself around if your family supports him when he needs it."

Samuel was the baby of the four boys. As for his problem? He wouldn't say it out loud and embarrass his mother, but everyone who came after Darrell got less attention. Samuel got scraps. He and Billy at least had something before Darrell had been born. And then his aunt and uncle had pretty much stepped in with Mac to be his support system. Samuel always pushed everyone away and it was sad.

"Sammy's thinking of going into the military, though I'm trying to talk him out of it. There's a fucking war going on and he's just casting around looking for ways to avoid jail time. Maybe he would benefit. I know I did. But he's got poor discipline and poor control and I just don't think he can handle it."

"What about a community-service-project-type thing? Would it be all right if I looked around to see what might be available for him?"

"You'd do that for Samuel?"

She snorted. "Of course I would. It's not only a nice thing to do, it's part of my job. It'd be nice to have some of the younger shifters working toward being more stable." She yawned. "You sleeping over? Keep in mind that you can say no and I won't be insulted in the least."

Normally he'd be out the door. He never wanted to give any impression of being more involved than he truly was. Sleeping with someone was incredibly intimate. It left you vulnerable to someone else in a way few things did.

"I think I'm going to have to get used to this, uh, more plainspoken way of communication."

"Don't mock. I could be one of those coy, simpering women who pins all her hopes and dreams on her man. I don't need to be propped up and my sense of worth isn't based on anyone else. But I like to sleep after sex and I have to be up early and the city council meeting is tomorrow night. You can use the shower in the guest bathroom in the morning. I think there are extra toothbrushes and stuff."

"I'd like it if you simpered, I think. I mean, if we were alone and you were naked."

"How totally unusual for a man to say," she mumbled as she burrowed under her blankets.

He didn't want to move. Her warm, curvy, naked weight rested against his side. The room smelled of magic and sex. The bed was more than roomy enough even if he'd wanted to move away from her.

But.

"I have a meeting first thing in the morning. I need to go home because that's where my suits are and I have to drive down to Knoxville." Normally, he'd have been glad of that excuse, true as it was. But he did find some disappointment in his gut that he had to go.

"All right. I suppose I'll see you tomorrow night at the council meeting."

He cursed under his breath and she snickered.

"Let's hope things are calmer this time around." He rolled from the bed with a sad sigh and she sat up, the blanket falling down to her waist, exposing her tits and making him nearly trip over the pile of his clothes.

"This is Diablo Lake. It's going to be chaos in some way. Let's just hope it's the kind without bloodshed."

"After the meeting, you and me? Drinks? I'd invite you to my house but I don't really have one. I mean, I do. I'm living with Huston, but you know what I mean."

"I do. But I have no roommates so you can come here. Bring a suit if you want to sleep over after you satisfy my carnal urges."

He snorted as he got his clothes back to rights.

"I'll see you tomorrow." He leaned across to where she perched, kissing her quick and pulling away before he got caught up in her again and never left.

"Bye. Thanks for the orgasms. Lock the door behind you." She snuggled down into her bed once more and that image of her stuck in his head until he fell asleep in his own, much smaller bed, less than an hour later.

Chapter Eleven

The next evening, still a little delightfully sore in all the right places, Aimee blew out a breath before she opened the door. An early dinner with Miz Rose, Katie Faith and the moms was usually a fun event. Especially once the moms started in on the white wine.

Tonight was different though. They had a lot to discuss and most of it didn't have fun involved at all.

Still, the scent of White Shoulders greeted her as she was pulled into a hug from Miz Rose. "Come on through, sweetheart. Everyone's in the kitchen."

The crew in the kitchen was made up of blood relations or those as good as, like Katie Faith and Nadine. Aimee's mom waved and then gave her a quick hug.

There was a large spread so she filled her plate and settled at the big table as everyone ate for a few minutes.

"Have any of you heard anything official from the wolves?" Miz Rose asked as she joined them all.

Katie Faith said, "The Dooley wolves are duly chastened and apologize profusely for what happened night before last. I've also encouraged them to hasten toward a resolution with the Pembrys."

"I can't get the mayor to return a call and he wasn't

in his office today. Apparently he's pretending to be sick instead of a coward," Miz Rose told them with a sniff.

Man, if Miz Rose came at her with that attitude she'd be hiding under a table. Maybe that was where Dwayne was just then.

"I know Mac is trying to deal with it," she told them before thinking about how it would make people react.

Everyone turned to look at her and that was when she realized her oops.

"What?" Aimee asked, though she knew exactly what.

"How is it you know what Mac Pembry is or isn't doing?" her mother asked with a raised brow.

Aimee's cheeks heated with her blush. "Oh. Well. We're, uh, dating." If she counted the makeout session as the first date and the night before as the second, it was fair to say they were dating instead of fucking. An important distinction when one was talking to one's momma.

"When did this happen?"

"Really recently. Anyway, so he and I had dinner with Katie Faith and Jace last night. I believe he's genuine about wanting to make things better. I just don't know if his father will get out of his own way to let that happen. They keep pushing Darrell and if you ask me none of them want him as Patron except his buddies. Makes me question Dwayne's leadership so much more the longer this goes on." She shrugged. "But I'm not a wolf. In any case, all this silly ducking of phone calls and the like is weak." She realized she had to decide whether or not to go to Mac with that.

She cared about it differently because he was more to her than a hot dude she boned. There was a vulnerability about him when it came to his father. A weight he shouldered without complaint, but one she saw nonetheless.

It made her protective of him.

"Is this a serious thing?" her mother asked, totally off the official subject and straight into Aimee's business.

Aimee sighed, staring back her mom's way. "It's very new."

"I didn't ask you if it was new or not." Steel edged her mom's tone.

Southern mommas did not mess around when they asked you a question. TeeFaye was no different.

"It's not casual. That much I know."

"You and me need to take some time later, all right? We didn't finish our conversation the other night." Her mother's narrowed gaze told Aimee she hadn't forgotten that promise to tell her about the situation with Bob.

Great.

She nodded.

"So we go in tonight and demand to be heard," Miz Rose said to everyone, getting them back on track.

Aimee said, "We've made it clear multiple times that the worsening situation between the wolves is negatively affecting the town and the people who live here and are protected by her magic. Katie Faith, what was that business between JJ and Dwayne?"

Katie Faith rolled her eyes as she shook her head. "He's pokered up but I'm guessing it's about Jace's dad. He's gone off on a hunting trip. His own version of ducking calls."

"So this is old business. *Personal* business and it's getting in the way of the rest of us." Nadine's mouth flattened into a line that spelled trouble.

Aimee added, "But it's *not* pack business. I mean, it is because it involves the wolves, but it's about people. It usually is. So we have a better chance of solving things that way. We just need to know what each one of them needs and find a way to get them close enough to that to solve this."

"Which is sort of your jam, right?" Katie Faith asked. "You're the empathic nurturer."

"I'm not a contract negotiator, for heaven's sake!" But she was good at figuring out what people needed and then finding ways to deliver.

Katie Faith's mom interrupted, "Dwayne won't listen to reason. He won't listen at all. How can we fix it around him? I like Mac, I always have and I'm not the only person in town glad to see him back. But he's not even Prime."

Which meant he'd have to challenge his father or his brother, maybe even both. Dwayne must have known that when he called Mac home. If not, he certainly had to know it by now. And what the hell kind of father did that to his son? He'd stacked the deck against Mac in so many ways and yet in the end, Mac would have to overcome all that and take over to drag the Pembrys out of this trouble.

It made her sick and suddenly she loathed Dwayne more than she ever had. Worse, she had lost all trust and confidence that he could run the town to the benefit of all the citizens.

"Dwayne needs to go. He's a lousy mayor and he's holding the rest of us hostage."

The room went silent as they all looked to Aimee, smiling.

"I agree. And I've taken the liberty of going over the town bylaws. We can challenge him and call for an election to be held within thirty days." Miz Rose pushed a sheet of paper her way. "The relevant information is there."

"Me? What?"

Miz Rose gave her a look. "You're going to run for mayor and beat the snot out of Dwayne Pembry, silly."

"I'll run your campaign!" Katie Faith told her. Even as Aimee shook her head Katie Faith continued speaking. "Before you start to argue, just stop. You *can* do this. Didn't we just say this was your jam?"

"In fact, I think you'd be amazing at it." Aimee's mom reached over to squeeze her hand. "You've always been a leader. Quiet determination, but the most determined person I've ever known. We need to heal after we get this town back on track. You were born for this."

"I'd be lying if I denied I hadn't thought about it. But the fact is, I have a full-time job already. How can I fit it all in? I don't want to ask the people here in Diablo Lake to get rid of one do-nothing and go replacing him with someone just as bad."

Miz Rose waved that away. "I'm old enough to remember other mayors. Dwayne has everything funneled through him because he's got control issues. But you wouldn't have to run it that way. The job isn't meant to be a full-time position. Most everyone else has worked a day job while holding the mayor's office too."

Aimee chewed her lip a moment. "If I delegated to representatives of the different packs and the cats, as well as the witches in the Consort, we could have a much better, more representative form of government. And then the load is redistributed to a larger group, which is more democratic and less overall work. I hope."

Her mother grinned. "You *have* been thinking about this."

"Told you. It makes me really mad, you know? Mad

that Dwayne acts like he's *owed* that job. And one he pretty much sucks at. The roads aren't being repaired. The signal as you enter town has been broken for months now. Witches already healed the tree that'd been dying in the town-square park, but we had to do it on our own, without permission because he farted around so long playing games. The school needs the funding for another teacher and he won't even have a damned committee meeting scheduled to deal with it." Aimee curled her lip a moment.

"There's so much antagonism and drama that we can't even have a city council meeting anymore without having to reschedule for another day. And he's doing *nothing* to fix any of this. It's like he's frozen in headlights or something. Whatever it is, I'm just totally sick of it. I don't want to be mayor forever. But I think we need a break from Dwayne. To cleanse the town's palate before a new leader takes over."

"This is the part where I play devil's advocate even though I think you'll be a great mayor, okay?" Katie Faith asked. At Aimee's nod, she continued, "He's going to see this as an attack against Pembry."

"Maybe." Aimee shook her head with a snort. "Most likely he will even though it isn't. I can't control his feelings. Not that I won't be careful. I'm not stupid. My aim is to approach this in a way that's best for everyone when I can."

"How's Mac going to feel about this?" Katie Faith went on.

She kept her wince back, but the pressure of her mother's deepening attention landed on her. "I hope he won't take it as an insult because that's not what it is. But I can't control his feelings either."

She really liked him. A lot. And she didn't want to

hurt him. She could only hope he'd see what she was doing for what it was. Regardless, she was going forward because she truly felt it was what was best for everyone.

"He should understand politics. Jace did and he's all superbossy wolf with most everything else. I bet Mac will think it's hot that you're doing this. Gonna get his werewolf DNA all riled up."

"I think not having this discussion right now would be best for me," she told her best friend.

It then dawned on Katie Faith that Aimee's momma was sitting right there and perhaps werewolf hotness wasn't a topic for that time.

She mouthed, "Oops."

"Moving on. So, we'll challenge Dwayne tonight and I'm the one who'll run for the mayor's office. Is everyone sure about this? We haven't polled the entire Consort about this."

"We already discussed this before the last city council meeting. The Consort is in agreement through representatives who all spoke for the witches in this town. You're well liked. Trusted. Better than that, you're respected." Miz Rose smiled. "You've taken care of a lot of people in Diablo Lake or their kin so they know you, or feel like they do. Your mother is right, you'd be amazing at being mayor."

Aimee rapped her knuckles on the tabletop. "All right then. Let's go make trouble for the man."

"Hold up, sweetheart," her mom called out, linking arms with her. "I'll ride in with you. Makes no sense for me to drive as well. Your dad will meet us there and I can come home with him after."

"And so I can tell you my story," she said as they got into the car.

"Well, naturally."

Despite being embarrassed, she found herself feeling unburdened as she related the situation with Bob to her mother. It also helped that her attention had to be on the road and then finding a good parking space as she told it.

Once she'd parked and turned the car off, she turned, allowing herself to face her mom. "He made me the other woman. I'm just so disgusted with myself. Humiliated that I made such a mistake."

There was no harsh judgment on her mother's face. Not for Aimee anyway. The fierce lines on her features were in defense of her child, not against her behavior. "You didn't do anything bad here so stop being disgusted with anyone but him. He's in the wrong. He lied to everyone here and now he's trying to push it off on you." She made a disgusted sound.

"I'm a witch! I *should have known* he was hiding something. I can tell with everyone else. Maybe I didn't want to see it. I dated him for a few years on and off. I never thought he was the one or anything. We had fun. It wasn't serious. He had kids and a wife that whole time and it never even occurred to me." Aimee banded her arms over her stomach. Not being able to rely on her magical gifts had really left her off balance.

"Some people are good liars. They're good liars because they're deluding themselves too. That's why you missed it. Also, darling, who on earth does that? He had his own apartment for his dalliances. He lied to everyone including you."

"He never seemed like a sociopath! He opened my door. His job is helping disabled poor people. He really did seem to care about that."

"Hitler loved dogs." Her mother rolled her eyes. "So

he's not entirely evil. Big whoop. He had no reason to tell you at this point except to make himself feel better. It's like he walked back over to you, punched you in the gut and then walked away again."

Aimee nodded emphatically. "I wasn't sad when we broke it off. And I didn't miss him. But this left me feeling so used. He made me into something I wouldn't have chosen to be. And he did it without my consent."

Her mom pulled Aimee into a fierce hug. "I want to head down there and beat the pee-whining shit out of that man. This is *not* on you." She gave Aimee's shoulders a little shake as she pulled away, just to underline that point. "You were raised better. You're not who he tried to make you into."

She hadn't realized just how much she'd needed to hear a pep talk like that until her mom gave it to her.

"Thanks, Mom."

"I love you. Now. The next thing we have to discuss is Mac. You'll bring him to dinner this Sunday."

Not a suggestion or a request.

She could have argued that it was too soon to have him over to her parents'. But that would have been a lie. Her mother knew it and she knew it. So she accepted that, like a lot of other ways, Diablo Lake courting was often different than it was elsewhere.

"If he's still talking to me after I announce in front of God and everyone that I'm out to steal his daddy's job."

Her mom snorted and then opened her door. "If the boy's that weak, leave him be. But I doubt he is or you'd have been bored. Come on then, Ms. Mayor. Let's get moving."

Chapter Twelve

Aimee was glad they arrived early because not ten minutes after they got seated, the room had swollen with people until it was near to bursting. It looked like half the town turned out.

Miz Rose had a seat on the City Council and looked over to them with a nod from her place at the big table on a dais at the front of the room.

"Is it weird I'm excited? Like we're on a caper," Katie Faith said quietly.

"Yes, it's weird. But you're weird. I'm sorry to have to inform you of this. I know it might come as a shock."

Katie Faith socked her in the thigh so hard she knew she'd have a knot there later.

"You're going to give me the church giggles and then Jace is going to frown at me."

"How can you tell the difference? He frowns all the time." Aimee looked over at her friend's husband as he came in, his grandmother on his arm. "Anyway, if you're giggling and trying not to, you'll be too busy to get up to any real trouble."

"You have a low opinion of me," Katie Faith sniffed around a snicker.

"Hush. I've got to look leader…uh…leaderish. Or whatever. You know, in charge and stuff."

"Leadertastic?"

"Leadermaster."

"Leadermistress?"

"No. That's dumb."

Katie Faith's suppressed laughter had given in to shaking as she tried to hold it back. Of course this silliness made Aimee less nervous and a lot more amused.

Nadine, sitting on the other side of her daughter, handed Katie Faith a hard candy of some sort along with a look that told her to get herself together.

"Eat your butterscotch and hush," Aimee murmured and grunted as her friend's elbow dug into her ribs.

Mac walked through the double doors and she had to pause to appreciate all the man brought to the table. His gaze had that implacable thing the wolves tended to give off when they were on duty. Tough. On full alert and ready for anything that might come.

He wore a suit. But he wore it like a warrior. *Damn.*

His gaze flicked over the people in the room until he found her. A smile marked his fantastic—and talented—mouth.

She waved. If any other females saw that connection, good. Mac was a virile male in his prime and he looked so gorgeous it made her warm all over.

He leaned over to speak to Huston, who also turned to face her with a grin. Huston was another one of the Pembrys she'd always liked.

She waved at him too, though less cheekily.

Mac and Huston began to weave their way through the crowd as Dwayne came in with Darrell at his side. The energy changed then as Mac's attention hardened. He changed course, moving to his father instead.

"I feel bad that I'm not going to tell him before we

do this. I don't want him to feel ambushed," she said to her mom.

"This is his world, sugar bear. He's going to understand and know you need to do what you're supposed to. If he's right for you, he'll not only understand it, but he'll respect it. If he doesn't? Well, then he's a fool just like his daddy. Better to know that up front before you invest one day more of yourself in him."

"You're good at this stuff." She rested her head on her mom's shoulder for a moment.

"You're not hard to love. You make good choices." She glared at Aimee. "Don't even try to take ownership of that matter we discussed in the car."

Busted.

Dwayne sat and rapped a gavel. "Before we get started tonight I'm going to warn everyone here to be civil or you'll be ejected. I will not allow any more disruptions."

But he'd been the one to start the last fight!

At first, the room went dead silent as pretty much everyone thought that very thing. Then Aimee stood, strode to the microphone and spoke.

"I'd like to be placed on the agenda."

"We're busy." He had the audacity to sneer her way. The witches began to whisper, their energy sharp and angry.

"According to town bylaws, any citizen can approach the council at the beginning of the session and request to be added to the agenda." Aimee wasn't going to let him rile her up and lose focus.

"That may well be. But as we couldn't get our business done two days ago, we have a very full schedule."

"I'm looking at the official agenda." Aimee held up

the piece of paper Miz Rose had given her earlier. "You even have citizen commentary as an item. It's already there."

He tried to argue with her. She watched him look for ways to maneuver around her.

"As we don't need the mayor's approval to add an item to the city council agenda, I've added you." Miz Rose had her own gavel but the way she rapped it sent out a peal of sound along with magic that seemed to put a period on that subject.

Before an argument could break out over it, Aimee turned and went back to her seat.

And as she sat and listened to a report about pot-holes and another about repairs needing to be made to the bridge leading back out to the main road from town, she was convinced she was doing what was necessary.

When Miz Rose called her name, she stood and headed to the microphone again. Mac watched her and she smiled his way, hoping like hell that he wasn't going to be angry or upset over what she was about to do.

"State your name, Family and whether you're a resident of Diablo Lake," the council secretary told her.

"I'm Aimee Benton, a witch, born of witches and a lifelong resident of Diablo Lake. Under article four of the Diablo Lake charter and section three of the council rules, I call for a mayoral election to be held within thirty days."

Mac had been watching the curve of her backside, thinking about the state of her underthings when she up and challenged his father for the mayor's office.

He'd been sitting in a knot of wolves and it said a lot about the state of pack unity and the health of the town in general that there was only a very small outcry—his mother, brother and a few of his dad's cronies and confidantes. The rest of Pembry either smiled or remained silent.

"Did she warn you about this?" Huston asked in an undertone.

"Nope."

"Huh."

"Yeah." Mac wasn't sure how to feel about that. He didn't feel used. But he wondered why she hadn't mentioned it the night before.

One thing he knew for sure was that his father had asked for exactly this. How he reacted would seal his fate.

Darrell stood, growling, and before Mac blinked, Jace was up at Aimee's side. Which agitated Mac's wolf because *he* was the one who should be defending her.

She turned to Jace, speaking quietly. Mac had to force himself to remain seated as the exchange happened and then decided fuck that. His wolf wasn't much for staying still at that moment. So he quickly moved to Darrell, shoving him back into his chair.

"You, shut it and get yourself under control. Now," he ordered his brother.

"I don't take orders from you." Darrell's dumb mouth made the words and Mac wanted to punch him so much he allowed himself to fist his hands a few times.

Mac got his face close enough to Darrell that his brother actually flinched. "You *will* or I swear by all that is holy I will beat your ass right here in front of every living soul in this town. You know I can. You might even know I want to. So go ahead on."

Darrell broke eye contact. Once that was resolved,

Mac returned to his seat to watch this battle of wills between his father and Aimee.

"Miss Benton, you have no authority to do any such thing," Dwayne said in such a condescending manner Mac knew immediately how that would go over.

And his sexy little witch didn't disappoint when she simply stared at his father and said, "I'm sure you wish it was so. Me? I'm just disappointed the mayor doesn't know the rules of the town he's taken an oath to run. Read the relevant sections I noted. I'll wait."

"You complain about how things are going and then you add fuel to the fire. That's not very responsible of you, young lady."

She smiled brightly for a moment, totally surprising and then confusing his father. As she'd intended.

Her voice was calm and soothing while still commanding attention as she continued, "Two nights ago after you were in yet another manner of altercation in a public space, you challenged me to do a better job. So here I am. I'm announcing my candidacy for mayor. I'm of age. I belong to a Family and I'm a resident. The declaration needs to be made at a city council meeting or in paper. My printer is broken so this'll do nicely." It was prim and stern and nurturing all at once. Like getting a lecture and a hug at the same time.

Applause broke out and then his father, red faced and flustered, repeatedly rapped his gavel on the table and shouted for order.

Everyone quieted down, but the energy remained joyous and in support of the woman at the microphone.

If she'd been angry or very emotional, his father would have mocked or discounted her. But she came at him head-on, like a warrior would. The wolves understood that and from the solemn respect coming from the cats, they did too.

And she did it not in a brutal, aggressive way, but a sure, confident assumption of power. There was no way his dad was going to talk himself out of this.

She was fucking magnificent.

Mac had never in all his life been more attracted to someone. She was every bit an alpha. She just fooled people on account of being so weird and adorable they underestimated her.

And when she came she smelled like pomegranates and snowfall. That sense memory sliced into his head and he had to close his eyes a moment to get himself under control.

Until his brother spoke again. "We can't let that bitch get away with this," Darrell snarled and not for the first time Mac wondered what the hell his brother's problem really was. He had a wife who loved him. A couple of kids who were healthy. A job he was proficient at.

But he'd always had a sense of entitlement and it had led him to a myriad of bad choices and personality defects. Mac loved his brother, but laws he wanted to smack the shit out of him at least twenty times a day.

Mac grabbed the back of his brother's neck and held him in place while he bent to speak into his ear. "You will shut your mouth and get it together. You're the reason we're in this mess so do me a favor and let the big people do their work and you get your butt back to the kids' table."

Darrell tried to struggle, but Mac's hold was too strong and soon enough he stilled.

"I'm going to kick your ass for this," he whispered to Mac.

"You're a fool if you imagine that could ever happen. We're at a public meeting and you are going to stop acting like a moron so I don't have to beat you in front of everyone. Mom's already on the edge. Don't make it worse."

Sharon, Darrell's wife, took his hand and squeezed. She didn't say anything, but his brother did blow out a breath and ease back enough so Mac let him go.

"You're out of your depth, missy," he heard his father say to Aimee as he tuned back in.

"Whatever you say. I do hope we can keep this race civil and remember this is all for Diablo Lake, not ego or entitlement." Her tone was so prim Mac was absolutely certain he was going to hell for how turned-on it made him.

His dad burst out, "I say this is a fantasy. You can't upend this town for some sort of frilly hobby."

All the women in the room turned their attention on their mayor—and not in a friendly way. Mac managed not to cringe but only out of self-preservation.

Aimee's bright smile didn't fool Mac one bit. Her eyes told a different story. "Don't make this so easy, Mr. Pembry. Save it for the debate."

With that, Aimee turned on her heel and nodded at her people, who up and followed her out. The Dooleys took their direction from their new Patrons and left as well.

Miz Rose stood and turned Dwayne's way. "I know your mother, Dwayne Pembry, and she'd be so ashamed of you right now. As ashamed as I am."

She gave a look of utter disdain and stalked out, head held high, pocketbook on her arm like the good Southern woman she'd been raised to be.

Once she'd gone and all that was left were Pembrys, his father raised his arms and slammed his fists down onto the table so hard one of the legs broke and things flew to the ground.

Mac watched, disgusted by the display.

No one had perfect control. He sure didn't. But you didn't throw a tantrum in public. Ever. His father was the Patron, it was his job—his role—to keep his wolves calm.

His mother screaming, his brother acting like an idiot and his father breaking things didn't make for calm. It only riled up an already tenuous situation.

Someone had to be in charge or things could easily slide into something far more dangerous.

Mac stood and addressed his wolves, letting his beast show in his gaze and through his voice. "All y'all go home now. Nothing left to see or do here. Everyone keep themselves under control. The last thing we need is anyone making this worse. You hear?"

Darrell started to argue, but Huston shoved at him and told him to shut up.

"We just gonna take this?" someone shouted. One of Darrell's buddies.

"Take what? She's running for office, not slitting our throats while we're sleeping. This reaction you're having? It's not normal. You get me? We look weak when we get upset over something so simple and everyday."

"What do you know about it? You ran off," Darrell snarled.

"I know I served my country and then went and got myself more education to help run this pack. I know I came back here to a fucking mess where full-grown wolves actually cower at the idea of a little wisp of a witch running for mayor. If she wins, so what? We're still Pembrys. And we still need to handle all the problems facing this pack. Including this stunning lack of discipline."

"You're just saying that because you're fucking her."

Darrell had made more than one mistake. First, saying such a thing was a problem for him. Then of course, he'd said it while within arm's reach of a faster, stronger wolf.

Mac looked down at his brother, tossing him a handkerchief. "Clean up your face. Next time you speak like that about her I'm going to make it so you can't use your mouth to speak, or eat, or breathe again. You got me?"

His mother tried to push him back but he stared down at her. "Back off."

"What did you just say to me?" Her eyes, damn, there was something going on inside his mother and he had no idea how to fix it. Or if he could.

"*I said, back off.* He needs to be disciplined. I'm handling that and I don't want any interference." If she wasn't going to do it, if his father wasn't, Mac would and no one was going to get in his way.

He used all the power in his tone. Pitching it like an alpha would. Like a Prime.

His mother stepped back, all her angry energy seemed to drain away. And then she lowered her gaze.

In front of a whole room of Pembry wolves.

A wave of power rolled through him as their allegiance began to settle with him. Noted the look on his father's face—satisfaction, pride and grief.

It was the point where he became Prime in a way no one could deny any longer.

Werewolf packs were incredibly hierarchical and

class-based. At the very top was the Patron. The boss in charge of everyone. Sometimes it was a couple like it was currently with Jace and Katie Faith as Patrons of the Dooley wolves and as his parents were for the Pembrys.

The wolf who'd take over from the Patron at some point was the Prime. Jace had been named Prime of Dooley when he'd been a young man and had been trained by his grandfather to take over.

But for Pembry, there'd been no Prime announced. Even though it had been patently obvious for a long time that Darrell didn't have the power to hold the pack. He'd never be Prime and he'd never be Patron.

And right then, as Mac looked at his father, they both knew Mac could take over at that exact moment without much effort.

His dad had acted, or refused to act in such a way that while Dwayne could have declared Mac Prime, he hadn't. Being named Prime by the current Patron would have signaled to the rest of the wolves in the Pembry pack that a peaceful transition of power was coming. It would have calmed them significantly.

Instead, he and his mother had hidden their heads in the sand so they didn't have to disappoint Darrell.

Sadly, because his parents hadn't done their jobs, Mac would. And in the end it would hurt Darrell even more. And in that moment Mac hated them for doing this to him.

Nothing to be done about it, especially right then. So, Mac turned his attention back to Darrell. "The mayoral campaign will *not* get personal. Between you and me though? I'm very personal now. You will go out of your way to be mighty careful how you speak about Aimee. I won't tolerate any of your bullshit."

"I see you over there lining up behind *my* son, Bern. You couldn't take over so now you want to latch yourself onto my boy to ride him into the Patron's seat? That how it goes?" Dwayne said, trying to get the focus off Darrell.

Before his uncle could speak, Mac got between them, addressing his dad. "No. You put us all here. So I'm telling you we're not doing this because someone has to be in charge. Anything that's not useful, swallow it."

"Are you sleeping with that girl?" his father asked, sidestepping the fact that his son had just ordered him to keep quiet in front of the whole pack. "Just how divided is your loyalty?"

Mac didn't flinch, but only because he had such good self-control.

"Seriously? Can you really ask me that?" Mac had been leaning against the edge of a table, but to underline his point, he stood to his full height, letting his power emanate from him. More power began to flow to him as the wolves of their pack turned his way and metaphorically and physically submitted with a lowering of shields they held between man and wolf and bowed their heads.

It hung in the air between him and his dad, the weight of power and allegiance in the room shifting to Mac.

There was a razor-thin edge at that moment as father and son continued to look at one another. He didn't want to have to challenge his father. Especially not before the election. All the chaos and upheaval they had at the moment was bad enough.

Now that he'd assumed his position as Prime—taken it as his wolves had freely given their loyalty and power to him—he had a little more room to maneuver and get things into place.

It was inescapable that he'd have to challenge his father and he wanted it to be on his terms. Mac wanted to choose the time. Mac wanted to occupy the Prime spot at least a few days, learn to use all that power he now had access to.

He needed to stalk his prey a while longer so when he took his father on, there'd be absolutely no chance he'd lose and give his wolves over to more of the same from his father until everything frayed to dust.

Mac showed his dad all those things as he gazed over at him. "Get your priorities straight. You've got a race to run. That is if you're sure you actually want to *be* mayor. Focus on how you're going to get yourself reelected in a town where a lot of folks *don't* think you're doing a good job. As for my personal relationship with Aimee, that's not going to be open to argument or personal commentary. I'm Prime of this pack and unless anyone has some evidence of actual wrongdoing on my part, I won't tolerate idle attacks on my loyalty."

His father held up a hand. "You're right. You're right. She's got some spunk, that Benton gal. Comes from an old family. But I'm going to win. Because I'm a Pembry and this seat is ours. Not no witch's. You get them in here and suddenly *our* needs are the ones getting ignored. Just you remember where and who you come from. Them witches are all up in Dooley business now that Katie Faith is with Jace."

"This isn't at all what I meant when I said run this town like we know you can." Mac turned to the wolves at his back. "Everyone, go home. We're going to be just fine. No matter who the mayor is. We all live here in

Diablo Lake. Together. And we have for generations. There's no need to get worked up over this."

Wolves filed out, some—many—of them stopping to touch Mac on their way past. He kept calm. Tapping into what they needed. Reassurance. Not an incitement to riot.

He also made sure his father noted it. Saw that Mac was already acting as Prime so he could go along with what Mac had just announced—act like it was his idea—or back off and shut up.

Chapter Thirteen

She wasn't surprised by the knock on her back door.
Or that all her chemicals did a dance when she caught
sight of his features under the porch light.

Damn, he was so big. So beautiful. She'd never wanted
someone so badly in all of her days.

The emotions she picked up confirmed that he was
angry and maybe a little hurt and suddenly she didn't
want him to feel that way with her. Not the hurt part.
The angry part they could work out.

"I know it was a surprise. I didn't not tell you on purpose. It just happened today. I mean, I'd have done it either way, mind you, but I would have told you up front."

"Can I come in?" He tipped his chin and she stepped
back, waving the way.

Once she closed the door and they stood in her kitchen,
the impact of his wolf and the magic he carried as a
shifter surrounded her.

"Wow. So. That happened, huh?" She pointed at him.

His serious look melted as he laughed, stepping close
to pull her into his arms. He buried his face in her hair,
breathing her in as their magic caressed and combined
in ways that made her entire body an erogenous zone.

"What you do to me, girl." He shook his head as he stepped back. "I became Prime tonight."

She hugged him tight, pleased for him. "That's amazing. Congratulations!"

The tension radiating from his muscles fell away and she snuggled in tighter, needing him to know she was there for him. *With him.*

If he wanted that after they put everything out on the table anyway. Because she really liked Mac and wanted to pursue something with him in the long-term sort of way. But it wouldn't work if they weren't honest.

"I'm not mad at you for challenging my dad for the mayor's office," he said after pressing a kiss to her lips.

"Oh. Well, good."

"Things are going to be really complicated. Especially between now and election day."

She took his hand, tugging him into the living room where she went back to her place, tucking her blanket in around her legs as she settled. "I just made a pot of hot chocolate. There's enough for two mugs if you want. If not, there's stuff in the fridge."

He glowered a moment, continuing to stand, staring down at her.

"What now? If you're breaking things off, fine, but let's skip the hot cocoa if it's all the same to you."

He snorted, shaking his head. "Hot chocolate sounds just fine. I'll get another mug and take off my shoes."

She watched him poke around through her cabinets until he found a mug and came back to join her. Not on the other end of the couch, but right up on her. In her space.

He got under her blanket, draping her legs across his lap, tucking it around her feet.

She wasn't a werewolf but she knew enough of them and her best friend was married to one so she understood what that was. He was marking her. Protecting her. Making her house a space that was his as well.

If he'd been a threat to her, the magic she'd poured into the land her house sat on, into the walls and floors, would have set off an alarm of sorts.

Instead, it settled around them both. Not something that had happened with anyone but her family and Katie Faith.

Her magic was so totally ride-or-die for this werewolf. Probably the rest of her too.

"I'm not breaking up with you. Is that what you want?" he asked after he filled his mug.

"Hell no. But I'm going to be totally honest with you, okay?"

He nodded. "I expect no less."

"I think this race is going to get mean. I think your father is going to say rude, spiteful things and I'm not going to tolerate any nonsense. Which means your family is going to be spending a lot of time being mad at me and me at them. You and I have nothing to do with that. It isn't about me and you. Or about witches versus Pembry wolves. It can't be. If we let it, everything between us will begin to go bad."

He took a deep breath. "I can respect that. I wouldn't expect you to not stand up to ugliness and I'm going to do the best I can to keep that out of this campaign. I just not even an hour ago warned all the Pembry wolves at the city council meeting, *including my father and Darrell*, that we'd keep this race civil. And I underlined that with my dad and Darrell when it came to you as my woman. Because you are." He nodded to underline that.

Mac leaned to put his cup down, taking hers as well. He enfolded her hands in his. "You know this is serious. I've known you since we were all kids. I'm Prime now and my wolf knows—like the man does—that you're what he wants. Every time I see you I want you. And now that I've had you? Now that you've had me," he added with a smirk. "I don't want to let go. I'm all in. But I'm being honest with you in return because when you're all in with me, it's forever. And as you may have noticed, I come with a lot of baggage."

Aimee sucked in a breath. He overwhelmed her sometimes. Which sort of freaked her out. But also, mainly, it felt right. Like he was the lock she was meant to fit.

She wasn't human. Never lived like one when it came to culture and social hierarchy. Her magic had already begun to root into his, which she told him.

"Notice I'm not arguing here. When you came into the house earlier I felt that you'd become Prime. I felt your wolves and their power coursing through yours. My magic knew yours immediately. Understood the ways it had changed."

He tipped her chin up with a fingertip and kissed her long and slow until her bones had melted and she sighed when he pulled back.

It should have felt like it was moving too fast. It should have been a moment of panic where she argued with herself about how this was not logical.

"I like that you respect me enough to tell me the truth."

She'd never been complimented like that, but, yeah, it worked.

"I've got *so much respect* coming your way. I bet you can't wait."

He shook his head, smiling. "I promise that anything you tell me in confidence will never be repeated. I want this—" he motioned between the two of them "—to be rock solid."

She held out a pinkie and he took it with his own. "Pinkie swear."

"Okay so now that we've lowered the cone of silence I need to say that your dad was a condescending asshole tonight."

He thought about how his dad hadn't acknowledged that Mac was Prime. Even as there'd been a flash of pride in Mac, their dad had given the bulk of his affection and attention to Darrell.

"Yeah. He was. On the other hand, you were fucking amazing. I was so proud of you standing up the way you did."

"It's not usually me that does the flashy up-front stuff. That's always been Miz Rose or Katie Faith. I was nervous, I can't lie. Luckily your dad was such a turd he ended up making me mad and I forgot about being anxious." She gave him a look. "I did see you haul Darrell back on his ass."

"I told you I underlined what I wasn't going to tolerate when it came to you and how they acted."

She blushed a little. "Yeah? And what does your momma think?"

"I don't know. She left before I could talk with her about it." They'd ushered her out before Mac had finished with his father.

"Well. Stay out of arm's reach. I know you probably learned that lesson even though Darrell didn't."

"Even when he played football he forgot that."

"Another reason why he'd be a terrible Patron. How'd he react to you being named Prime?"

"I just assumed the title. My dad didn't argue. I imagine by morning it'll be announced far and wide."

"Wait." She held up a palm. "What do you mean he *didn't argue*?"

"I mean, I don't know how to explain it. But as I was there tonight it just happened. I felt the moment when the wolves turned to *me* to make things right. And when I decided I was Prime, I just *was*."

"Wow. That's really cool. But how did he announce it? Or memorialize it? Or is this another way of doing it and I just didn't know until today?"

"I could have fought for it and assumed the title. But there's no one I'd fight. Darrell knows he can't beat me. He most assuredly does after tonight. And he had the chance to challenge me several times and he didn't. This was a bloodless coup."

Aimee frowned at him. "What aren't you saying?"

"Nothing, it's totally normal for a wolf to take a title by assuming it and the pack not challenging that."

She didn't believe him, but he could see she hadn't thought of a way to get around that yet.

"I'm proud of you."

He stole a kiss. "Thank you. Speaking of parent reactions. Your dad won't coldcock me for being with you?" he asked.

"I'll do you one better than that. My mother invited you for Sunday dinner. They eat at four thirty. Don't be late. If my dad has to wait to eat he gets so grumpy."

"Uh. Okay." He knew at that point he had no such welcome to offer her. Not from his parents anyway.

He figured his grandmother and aunt and uncle would take that place though, in welcoming her to the family.

His phone started buzzing and he groaned.

"Go on, Prime, answer that." She nudged him.

"I don't want to. I'm here in our bubble and I don't want to go."

"You're adorable when you pout. Damn it. How can nature be so unfair?"

He groaned but answered. "What?"

"Just wanted to check in to be sure you were okay," Huston said, not ruffled at all by Mac's gruffness.

"I'm here with Aimee just now."

"I put a guard on you. Don't argue. You're Prime and things are hinky. You won't even see them."

"Them? There's more than one?" Mac demanded.

"Not at a time. But there'll be a pool so someone can be on you twenty-four hours a day." They'd discussed some of this as necessary preparation to take over.

"Okay. Fine."

"Tell Aimee I said hey."

"I will. Don't leave a light on for me. I'll be staying here." He waggled his brows at Aimee, who snickered behind her hand.

"Call me when you wake up." Huston hung up the phone and Mac tossed his to the coffee table.

"I'm supposed to tell you hi from Huston."

"You're staying over, huh?" One corner of her mouth tipped up.

"I've got an overnight bag in my trunk. I was hoping we'd be in a make-up state of mind versus a break-up state of mind. I'm glad it's the former."

"Me too. But I'm not so dumb I don't know we won't

fight. A lot. You're very bossy and I don't like being bossed."

"Yes, you do."

She blushed again. "That's different!"

He pounced on her, getting tangled in her blanket, laughing and stealing kisses.

He rolled to his feet and picked her up, blanket and all, carrying her to the bedroom, where he deposited her onto the bed as if she weighed nothing.

That wasn't overrated.

She wanted him so much it caught her breath a moment as he whipped his shirt up and over his head.

"Like Christmas early."

He dived on her, his hands and mouth kissing and caressing even as he managed to get her totally naked without breaking a sweat. Within another few breaths he was naked as well.

"Damn, boy, you got some moves on you," she teased.

"I have to keep you interested, don't I?"

She embraced him, holding him with her legs around his waist too. Shuddering when he rolled his hips, brushing his cock against her clit.

"That's the fucking way," he snarled.

Like she'd argue with that?

But he backed off and it was her turn to snarl. "Why? What? Why are you stopping?"

"Because I'm not a seventeen-year-old boy. I have self-control and some finesse."

She rolled her eyes. "I don't want that right now. I want you in me."

"Oh." With a piratical grin, he thrust into her with

one hard movement, leaving them both gasping for breath.

He was big. Big enough that it stung a little. And big enough that the sting warmed into pleasure as he dragged free of her body and plunged back in.

She dug her nails into his shoulders, into all that muscle, the play and flex against her hands nearly as hot as the pressure he managed to work around her clit.

He really did have some major finesse.

She was so tight and hot inside sweat beaded on his brow nearly immediately. That soft, sweet heat gripped him, not wanting to let go and he nearly lost his mind with the pleasure of it.

She held on tight, urging him just how she liked him, which turned him on even more. She trusted him with herself, with her pleasure and the vulnerability of expressing it to someone else.

He licked down her neck, loving the little sounds she made, especially the squeaky one when he found that perfect spot just below her left ear.

He should have been mindless with it, with the need to have her; instead that depth of want made everything clear. He knew what he wanted without a single doubt.

"Make yourself come," he whispered against the sensitive skin of her temple.

There was no hesitation. She slid a hand between their bodies until her fingers found her clit. He stroked into her, grinding his body against those fingers each time.

Her breath got shaky and her inner muscles began to twitch and contract around him. Her already inferno-hot pussy superheated again as she came with a cry she muffled, her face pressed to his neck.

By that point he was lost to the need to come. His body took over, delighting in each touch and caress as she ran her hands over his back. The scent of her orgasm, of her magic meeting his hung in the air, heavy and sensual. Teasing his senses as he came so hard he forgot to breathe until he sucked in on a gasp.

Even after he rolled to the side, the muscles in his thighs and calves jumped as he lay there, fingers tangled with hers, panting like he'd run a mile.

"I like your house a lot better than Huston's," he muttered.

Laughing, she rolled into his side, resting her chin on his chest. "I should hope so."

"I'm not going to hide that you're my woman." In fact, he wanted everyone to know.

"That was very cavemannish. Cavemantastic. Whatever you wanna call it. I wasn't aware it was an option for you to hide that we were dating."

"We're not dating. Humans date. I dated humans. You're mine."

She pinched his side.

"Hey! I'm yours too."

"Oh. Okay. But you know, you might think in a month that I'm more trouble than I'm worth."

He sighed. "You're trouble all day and night. But you're most definitely worth it. And not just for the sex."

"Thanks. I guess. I definitely like you for the sex. I mean, the rest is pretty good too. Except for your parents, but I'm willing to try and look past that."

"That's a thing we'll have to keep working on."

"Or, you keep working on it. I have my own kooky

family to handle and no offense or anything, but yours seems like a lot of trouble. You're big and strong and so I'll leave it to you."

He grumbled, but held on to her anyway. The weight against his side, her thigh slung up over his, her arm draped across his belly, it all worked together to soothe and excite at the same time.

"So. You're running for mayor," he said.

"Yeah. I am. I can't make excuses for it. I wish I didn't have to, but I do."

"I think you'd be good at it. The empathy you carry is important. To everyone." It felt like a betrayal of his father to say it, but it was true.

"Empathy is within everyone. People just need to listen. I do think my gifts are a good fit for the job. He's going to be angry though. I don't necessarily like it when people are angry at me."

"My mom can be good practice."

She snickered. "I'll try not to insult her. In front of you I mean. She's your mom, I get that. You want to defend her and I get that too."

"She's wrong. Blaming Katie Faith for this is silly."

"She knows that. There's something else eating at your momma and it's not Katie Faith. Maybe she's worried about whatever confrontation you and your brother are going to have. He's not going to take this well. You being Prime, I mean."

He wished he knew what his mom was so worked up over too. It alarmed him to see her so close to the edge.

"She's always been bigger than life. But this is different, like you said."

Aimee sighed, heaving herself out of bed and to her

feet. Which was fine with him until she pulled a long-sleeved shirt on.

Catching sight of his features, she bopped him with a pillow before shimmying into a pair of panties. "It's cold. For those of us who aren't shifters, this is winter. I need pants and socks so stop pouting."

"I'm not pouting."

"Normally, if someone in town was feeling off, like your momma probably is, I'd talk to them. Check in on 'em from time to time. But she's... Well, I guess I haven't been as pushy as I normally am because of this mess between her and Katie Faith and I know she sees me as an extension of that."

"Are you...actually worried about my mother? After all she's said to you and Katie Faith?"

"Yes. Well. If there's something wrong, naturally I'd want her to get help. I'm not a monster."

He moved quick, grabbing her by the waist and hauling her back to bed, kissing her as she laughed.

"Let's do something else for a while. Pretend the rest of the town and its problems are far away for another orgasm or two. What do you say?"

She held his cheeks in her hands. "I say hell yeah."

Chapter Fourteen

Aimee knew it had snowed overnight before she even opened her eyes. Delight sent her to her knees to peer through the window to confirm that.

"It snowed!" she said as she shook Mac awake and went back to the view.

He looked really good in her bed, all sleep tousled and warm.

"Oops," she said, tipping her chin at him.

He looked down at his chest to see the love bite she'd left there. But instead of annoyance or embarrassment, he turned a look her way that made her nearly buckle.

"Never apologize for marking me. That it's still on my skin all these hours after you gave it to me is an interesting thing, isn't it?"

She turned from her perch at the window and didn't deny anything. "You guys don't mate though."

He rolled his eyes. "Sugar, we imprint. And I am most assuredly imprinted on you. That you could leave a mark that's lasted this long says you picked me right back."

Aimee crossed her arms over her chest. "Imprinting is like what then? I mean, I know Katie Faith and Jace are imprinted and bonded by marriage and pack magic and stuff." She put her hands over her mouth, eyes going wide with horror. "Please forget I said all that."

"Why? It's not a secret. I was at one of their wedding ceremonies and the other with the pack was similar to one we do in our pack." Mac stretched, reaching his arms above his head, arching. His muscles rippled— she really did think that would never get old—as he did and he groaned.

How on earth did she merit this delicious bit of maleness?

One of her favorite things about being in love with a werewolf was all the stretching they did. And groaning. And fucking. Damn he really loved sex. And thank the lord above because she did too. And sex with him was mind-boggling. He made her come so hard she frequently tingled a good ten minutes later. It was raw and vulnerable and sometimes she felt so exposed it was difficult not to panic a little.

But he didn't get panicked at all. He just seemed to always know exactly what he wanted. So. Totally. Sexy.

He didn't need to be taken care of. He respected her abilities to handle her business. And yes, he did get pushy sometimes, a thing werewolves did that she wasn't as enamored of as she was the rippling muscles.

Quick as lightning, he had her grabbed and hauled back into bed as she laughed, dizzy with love and snow on Christmas Eve.

Snow!

It was snowing at Christmas, which was her favorite. Aimee loved the smell of snow, so crisp and sweet. Loved the way it made everything sound and look different because it reflected the light the way it did.

"Dude, it snowed."

He grinned down at her. "We're already ping-ponging through topics? You only just poked me awake a few minutes ago."

"I know. It's the snow though. I love snow. I really do."

Mac leaned down to brush a kiss over her mouth. "I'm pretty sure you're like this every day. We'll play today."

And in the midst of her fantasy about having in-front-of-the-fireplace sex, she realized something else. It was Christmas Eve and she'd totally forgotten that when she'd invited Mac to dinner at her parents' house.

"I just remembered what day it was. You don't have to come to dinner at my parents' place. I know you probably have family stuff." And her father was a huge fan of holiday decoration so there'd be that to contend with.

"I know it's Christmas Eve. I don't have any other plans but to have dinner with your family tonight. Tomorrow I'll go on over to have breakfast at my grandma's house. Lots of little ones this year so we'll do the present opening over there and all that business. I'd planned on inviting you but you said you were busy with work and then your family thing."

Every year she and her family and extended family spent all of Christmas morning making things for all manner of care packages. They baked casseroles in the big industrial kitchen at Salt & Pepper to be stored in the freezer and given out as needed over the next two or three months for the senior-meals program.

Preserves, pickles and relishes, along with beans and rice would be divvied up into the baskets of non-perishables Aimee often took out as she visited folks in and around Diablo Lake.

All the people currently sewing, knitting and crocheting warm clothes would bring all those items then as well. At the high school, there was a closet where Aimee would leave many of these care packages so kids could nip in, take what they needed and not have to have a big deal made out of it.

The packs, the cats and the Consort kept it stocked over the course of the year and had done so for as long as she could remember.

At the same time, they made sheets and sheets and sheets of cookies they'd then take to neighbors and friends before their big holiday dinner, this year at her mom and dad's house.

Aimee had grown up with this as her holiday tradition for as long as she could remember. It made her as happy as the snow did.

"I don't give presents on Christmas Eve. So I'll bring your presents over tomorrow night. You bring your leftovers, I'll bring mine. We'll feast." He kissed the tip of her nose.

"All right. My dad's been smoking turkey and pork for the last week. Gonna be a very good time for sandwiches."

"Now. We were talking about imprinting just a few minutes ago before you changed the subject three or four more times. I shouldn't make light of the whole we-imprint-not-mate thing. The fact is, once that initial bond is made, that imprint where my wolf decides he likes you best of all and wants to keep you forever, it is sort of like mating. Whatever you want to call it, you're it for me."

"Oh." She blinked up at him. "Even though I'm the enemy?"

Ignoring that, he continued, "I know you wanted to keep things quiet with our relationship. But I'm thinking we're pretty much done with that. Half the town knows and everyone else suspects."

"You can't just announce that you want me forever and then change the subject."

He kissed her again. "I can't? And isn't it really part of the same subject anyway? Our relationship and being more public with it."

"Well." She frowned. "I like our little privacy bubble."

He snorted. "It's only a matter of time. Plus I want to assure your parents tonight that I'm not trying to hide you."

As reasons went, that was a pretty good one, she had to admit. "You don't even want to know if I'm imprinted on you?" she teased.

"I know you have. I can smell the way your chemistry changes when you see me, or even think about me. You got it bad for me."

She giggled. "You really need to build your self-esteem."

He nipped the skin at the hollow of her throat.

"You promised me bacon this morning," she said, nudging him. "I'm hungry."

"I'll make the bacon if you do coffee. And pancakes."

Aimee pulled a bright red hat on after she'd zipped her coat up. Flurries had come and gone as she'd bundled up while he smirked.

Naturally he could smirk because he was a volcano and wasn't that affected by the cold. It also made him look insolent in a nighttime-soap-opera way.

"You need gloves at least don't you?" she asked him as they headed to the back door.

"When I said we'd play today, I meant we'd play. My wolf loves the snow."

Excitement filled her belly as she leaned in to hug him as she danced a little. "Really? Yay! I've been wanting to ask you if I could, uh, meet your wolf."

She pulled her mittens on and then he led her out back. "Just a block over is a strand of trees and the edge of the meadow. Plenty of open space but it's private enough."

With that, in the shadow of her garage, he got naked.

"Can I watch?"

He stole a kiss. "Yes."

Aimee stepped back, clasping her hands in front of herself, full of glee.

He ran a hand through his hair, let his head drop back and with a shudder, it was as if the air around him opened and a wolf changed places with the man.

A wolf nearly as tall as her shoulder. Broad, rippled with muscle and a furnace-like blast of power, he shook himself, lowering his muzzle just a little.

As if she'd be scared?

"You're gorgeous."

And he was. Caramel with hints of gold.

"I know you can sort of understand me but not perfectly so I can deny this later. But. I want to squeeze you while giggling and telling you how fluffy you are. I also want to boop your nose. I won't do either of those things."

She really wanted to boop his nose though.

He approached slowly, placing himself against her so she had the opportunity to touch him as they headed the short distance to the little meadow he'd indicated. If anyone noticed them out, the witch and the werewolf, it wasn't unusual enough to even bat an eye over.

"Thank you," she told him as he leaned against her, giving her a brace to get over a rickety little set of steps across the creek.

Beyond, the field was full of untouched snow. It filled her with joy. So much joy she bounced around and flopped on her back, making a snow angel as Mac watched with what she thought might have been a smile.

Probably a smirk.

She rolled to her feet, careful as she could be to save the imprint she'd just made on the ground.

A few feet away, Mac waited, expectant. He dipped his nose, like, "get on with it already." So she scooped up some snow and packed it just right before hurling it at his backside.

He yipped at her, easily dodging the next volley.

For some time they played out in the snow, running, dodging snowballs as she laughed and his wolf was dazzled by her.

Dazzled and firmly imprinted and in full-protection mode. It was cold for human skins to be out for long. She was vulnerable.

His wolf bounded over, happily accepting the hug she gave him, her arms around his neck, face buried in his fur. She spoke in her words. He knew she complimented him.

Using his head to push against her, he managed to breathe her in as much as he could as they moved back to the den she shared with him. No other smells wor-

ried him as they got back and he was ready to give way
to his human skin again.

His witch dropped to her knees and hugged him once
more.

Safe. Knowing he could trust her with his most
vulnerable and exposed moment, the wolf let go and
the man resurfaced once more. And once he had arms
again, he closed them about her, holding her close.

"Your wolf is so handsome. And fast. I bet you let
me hit you with all those snowballs, didn't you?" she
asked as she handed his clothes over.

He had let her land a few hits. It wouldn't have been
as fun for either of them if he'd been able to dodge her
every single time.

"My wolf has scented your magic and I need to let
you know he's got no plans to ever let you go." That'd
been the absolute truth of it. The wolf saw her unique
nature, her beauty and power, as well as her fragility
and liked it best.

She tiptoed up and kissed him once he pulled his
sweatshirt back on. "Thank you. My magic really digs
your wolf and I'm honored that you trusted me enough
to share your change with me."

She understood. Understood what it had meant to
him to spend the day playing in the snow with her. She
didn't want him to pretend to be human. In fact she embraced what he was. Including his wolf.

He hugged her as the snow began to fall again all
around them. She giggled and he wondered if he'd ever
met someone who loved playing in the snow more.

"We've got a few hours before we need to head over
to dinner. Let's go inside and get you warm," he said,
tugging her toward the back door.

"You're supposed to like frolicking outside!" she accused. "You're a werewolf."

"We frolicked for quite a long time. Now the man wants to snuggle in front of a fire with his gorgeous woman before we have to get ready to go."

Her nose was red, as were her cheeks, and just looking at her filled him with so much happiness he wasn't quite sure how to process it all.

He'd muddle through, obviously, because he knew a good thing when he saw it.

"I'll even make you hot chocolate. Come on. You know you want to." He sent her a grin.

She rolled her eyes, but grabbed his hand and let him pull her toward the back door.

"You're like a baby seal," he told her as he helped her out of her boots.

"A baby seal? Is that the best you got?" she said, hanging up her coat.

"You have those big eyes and you have so much fun out there in the snow. It was the most frolicsome creature I could think of on the spot."

"Huh. Otters frolic."

"In the snow?"

"Sure! Why not?"

"I can't believe I'm having this conversation."

"I know."

"You sound so pleased with yourself."

"I'm an experience, Mac. We already talked about this."

He turned on the fireplace and they settled on the couch, watching the weather in the warm cocoon of the living room.

"Was that a test? Today I mean."

"Test?" he asked as he brushed a kiss against her temple.

"Like to see if your wolf was going to be cool with me?"

He laughed, taking her hand and kissing the knuckles. "My wolf is always pressing at my skin. He wants to protect you. Wants to look at you and be around you as much as he can. That he spent a few hours playing with you while you laughed and spit out magic like pixie dust was the best day ever."

She grinned. "Really? I had a wonderful time. I don't think I've ever had so much fun on a snow day. I'm glad it was with you."

"I did warn you," Aimee murmured as they pulled up in front of her parents' house. The big yard was decked out, every inch, in holiday splendor that glittered, sparkled, shone and blinked.

"Well, you said he likes to decorate. This is…" Mac shook his head.

"Wait'll you get inside." Aimee snickered as she got out and pulled some packages from the backseat while he gathered the food she'd brought with them.

Carl Benton came out to the porch and at the sight of his daughter, he lit up as bright as the front yard.

Mac realized he'd never noticed the brightening of anyone's magic the way he had just now. Like his connection with Aimee had turned up his radar by quite a bit.

Maybe it was just her and anyone connected to her. But it was beautiful to see the wash of blues, silvers and purples in Aimee's magic complement her father's similar tones, his a little darker and with more reds and greens.

"Come on inside. It's cold out here." He grabbed his daughter up into a hug and took some of the food from Mac, shaking his hand briefly before leading the way into the house.

Nadine was in the big kitchen with TeeFaye and Katie Faith. Merilee stood at the oven, peering inside a moment before she added two minutes to the timer.

So much noise and light and love. The house positively swelled with the connection these people shared.

This was a *pack* in a very real sense. The wolf within approved.

It was also a riot of every Christmas color imaginable. He counted three different holiday trees on his way through the house. Aimee hadn't been exaggerating when she'd told him her dad went *a little overboard* at Christmas.

TeeFaye grinned at the sight of Aimee. "Come give me a hug, darlin'. You been outside playing in that snow all day?" she asked Mac as she hugged her daughter.

"We did, yes, ma'am. Thank you so much for having me here tonight. I'm honored." He indicated the box he'd just placed on the counter. "I, uh… I brought some jerky and some smoked trout." He'd hunted the venison and caught the fish himself, did the smoking and drying himself.

For werewolves, presenting food or clothing to the family of their chosen partner was a point of honor. He was telling her parents that he'd always be sure Aimee was fed and protected. As Prime, he was saying she was an extended member of the pack as well as his family.

Aimee turned to him, surprised. "Thank you. You

didn't say you'd done this." She took his hand, squeezing it.

Katie Faith said, "He's not saying this, but a present like that, of food for his chosen partner's family, is a big deal."

"It's not like I never knew a werewolf before," Tee-Faye said. "Thank you for the food. Smoked trout is a particular favorite of mine. I hope you won't mind if I serve some with dinner tonight."

Mac nodded, pleased they'd appreciated his offering. Definitely pleased by the look in Aimee's eyes as he'd done it.

Jace strolled around the corner with Katie Faith's dad, who looked better than he had since Mac had returned to Diablo Lake.

"Go on into the living room, now. Everyone will be under my feet. There's snacks out but don't ruin your appetite," TeeFaye cautioned as she shooed them out with a wave of her hand.

Aimee stayed in the kitchen, sending him a good luck as he followed Jace, Carl and Avery out of the room.

Mac shook Avery's hand after telling the other man he was glad his health was recovering so well. He and Jace nodded before clasping forearms.

Then Mac noticed another tiny tree on the sideboard at the end of the room and one in the corner of the living room.

"I like a lot of trees at Christmas. But TeeFaye and I, well we've come to an agreement over the years that I can have no more than five trees in the house," Carl said, noticing Mac's glances at the decoration. "Stingy if you ask me."

"I kind of expect there to be a Santa for kids to take pictures with in here," Jace murmured as they loaded up on snacks. Warm spiced nuts and deviled eggs so good Mac had to force himself away from the platter after grabbing three.

Mac snorted, but kept it quiet enough he hoped no one else heard.

"Did you notice there were two fully decorated trees out front, one to either side of the porch railings? And there are more in the backyard. Thank God the dancing Santa blew up in a tragic accident," TeeFaye said as she came in with everyone else. "Tries to play like I'm so mean when it looks like an elf exploded in my house." Laughing, she dropped a kiss on Carl's forehead and plopped down next to him.

Aimee sat next to Mac, leaning in so they had more contact. Soon enough, her presence soothed his anxiety.

They all talked about this or that relative getting married or divorced. Who was graduating from high school and college, who just got a job with the county. Aimee's brother was due to have been with them that night but he'd gotten stuck in New York City on the wrong end of the same storm that had dropped all the snow on the ground in Diablo Lake.

"Have you never dated a witch before?" she asked quietly as they sat side by side at the big table in the dining room, surrounded by the chatter of this family he'd discovered he really liked.

"What makes you say that?" He helped himself to more turkey and Carl beamed at him.

"Because you seem a little stunned by us. Or maybe it's just me and my weirdo family." Aimee laughed. "Dad gave you that smile when you got more turkey because he did most of the cooking, including the turkey and ham. Mom did the sides and Merilee did the bread. I mean, in case you were wondering. And you were, but I didn't pick that up because I barged into your head."

He took her hand and kissed her knuckles. "I know you would never do that. I noticed your magic tonight in a way I haven't before. I think part of it is our strengthened connection and another part is that I haven't seen you this relaxed in an intimate setting with your friends and family."

He understood then. Her magic was very much part of her upbringing and identity. This was part of her tradition and culture and he got a deeper perspective on her and what drove her after seeing her this way.

Mac needed to talk to his aunt and uncle about Aimee. He wanted her to feel accepted the way her family was trying with him. He knew his father would never allow that. Knew his father took Aimee's challenge personally.

"Stop worrying about that right now and have another roll," Aimee told him as if he'd said that aloud, before she went back to her plate.

She knew him too. Not just that he tossed out emotion that she could read because of her gift, but because she listened hard. Wanted to understand him too.

"What brings you here tonight instead of doing something with the pack?" Mac asked Jace as they stood out on the front porch and watched Aimee and Katie Faith play in the snow.

Aimee's magic would catch the moonlight at times, glimmering in a way that was only hers as she held a hand out, palm up, and made bubbles that rose lazily on the breeze until they froze and then burst in a pretty shower of ice dust.

His wolf wanted to bound over and chase once more.

"We're doing Christmas with them in the morning at their work-party thing. Katie Faith says mainly I'll just be moving things and hauling stuff and it's all for the town so…" Jace shrugged. "Plenty of Dooley wolves need help from time to time so I figure we can make it part of our community work. Plus it makes my wife happy." Jace turned to face Mac a moment. "I'm doing you a favor by telling you your wolf is far happier and more at ease when your woman is satisfied."

Aimee's delighted laughter drew his attention away from Jace. They were so pretty together, the two friends bundled up against the weather, bits of snow clinging to their coats and scarves from the snowball fight they'd just won against Mac and Jace.

She and Katie Faith had their own magic in their friendship. The affection and humor between them sat on a foundation of trust and loyalty.

"I hope we can keep the election stuff outside this." Jace waved a hand around. "This is part of Katie Faith's family and Aimee is important to her. Plus, you're not a total dumbass like some others I could name, but won't because I'm trying to be a gentleman."

Mac guffawed a moment. "Right. Well. Aimee's a family-oriented person. That's important if she's going to be Patron with me someday." Some people might think she was too irreverent to be serious about running a pack.

But Aimee's strength was deep, solid and steadfast. Not always something people understood as alpha behavior at first glance. She was a calming, soothing influence even as she knew how to enjoy the little things that made life better.

Not the showy fire Katie Faith's power seemed to possess, but potent. Deep and wide. Full ⸍f compassion and humor. She complemented him so perfectly. Challenging him to see things from different perspectives, to be as steadfast as she. As loyal. Pembry wolves would know she was soft, but not weak. They'd trust her judgment and that she'd always call him out when he wasn't in the right. And they'd know she would also do the same with them. And they'd love her for it.

His beautiful, silly witch. Who'd challenged the Patron of Mac's pack. The Patron who also happened to be his dad.

Jace spoke again, breaking into Mac's thoughts. "Totally between you and me, okay? I know what this feels like, at least in part. If you want to talk as friends, I'm good with that."

"I always figured you hated Pembry."

"After what happened to my dad, you mean?" Jace sucked in the night air, scenting for danger, making sure his mate was content and safe. Mac had done the same. "It was Dooley who disciplined him. But no one other than him was responsible for whatever happened to him. I'm smart enough to know, in any case, that a pack is more than just one or two wolves. We can manage to steer our way through this crisis, Mac. But I don't know if your dad feels the same. No. I don't trust him to do what's best for the town right now. And I don't trust him to do what's best for wolves. I think the way he enables your brother to be a petty little asshole is lazy and dangerous."

Mac scanned the yard and the area just beyond. "How many guards do you have out there?" he asked.

"Two. It's overkill but Damon insisted. You?"

"I was told it would be one, but I realize it's two. Huston and Everett." There weren't any others around who'd be able to hear their conversation, which made it easier to be frank.

"You have my word that you can speak freely," Jace told him.

Though he knew what had to be done, though he'd been planning an overthrow of his own father, he still hesitated to say the words out loud to anyone outside his inner circle.

He needed to reach out to not only stop a war but also line up allies for the time to come.

"He's been in power so long he's forgotten how to be patient and put his ego aside while he leads. He's losing support. He's not providing the strength and stability the pack needs. You're right that he isn't putting the town first."

The knowledge that he was going to have to challenge his father had been with him for most of his life. It had always been a one-day sort of thing.

Sometimes the handover of power from one Patron to the next was a bloody affair. Contentious. Between rivals. Mainly though, it was relatively peaceful with an adult wolf taking over from a parent or other relative in charge. Like Jace had done with his grandfather the month before. There'd been a bloodletting, but it had been a ritual, for show more than to break or humiliate the loser.

"I expect, were I in your place, that you're shoring

up your support before you make your final move?"
Jace asked, his gaze still on his wife.

"I am. We're not so different, Pembry and Dooley.
Once the transition has taken place, I hope we can work
together to steer the wolves and this town out of this
mess."

"You have the support of the Dooley pack when
you're ready. I know Huston and Everett are good at
protecting you, but we've got your back if you need us."
Jace turned to Mac and they clasped forearms.

Behind them, Carl leaned out the door and called out
that it was time for dessert.

Aimee dashed across the lawn and leaped into Mac's
arms, hugging him tight. "Let's go get some pie. And
stop thinking about your dad."

He let her go and tried his best to forget about his
dad and to get back in the moment with her. He'd just
made an important alliance and had more strength at
his back. He was all about her for the rest of the night.

They hustled into the house after taking care to
knock the snow off their boots and coats for the promise of coffee and three different kinds of pie.

Chapter Fifteen

Just a few days after Christmas, out on client visits in and around town, Aimee knew the old wolf heard her approach the front door. Hell, he'd probably heard it when her car turned off the main road.

Shifters didn't like being snuck up on, or being made to feel as if someone was trying to sneak. He was old, but he wasn't useless. And she knew that was one of his hot buttons. So she let her heels make plenty of sound as she climbed the porch steps.

She rapped on the wood of his screen door and called out, "Hey there, Mr. Pembry! It's Aimee Benton. I was out this way and thought I'd stop in to see if you wanted any of this extra salve I've got."

If she'd said he needed it, he'd have rejected the help. Even though he did need it because his arthritis gave him a fair bit of pain he didn't want to admit having.

But if she said she had extra and made it seem like he was doing her a favor, chances are he'd take the help and use the salve. He might even let her inside, where she could see how much more of her help he'd take.

Jeph Pembry was at the end of a very long life. At a hundred and twenty-two, he liked to spend a lot of his time as a wolf, napping near the big wood-burning stove in the center of the room. He was a well-respected elder in the Pembry pack and Mac's great uncle.

He was also stubborn, as alpha wolves tended to be. The older he got, the more ornery he got. Mainly, he let Aimee have her way. Ate the food she brought over. Took her advice. Drank the tea and tinctures she made. But he didn't always get there without a lot of guile and charm on Aimee's part. Just enough more than his stubbornness.

Beneath his gruff attitude, Aimee was pretty sure he liked her and had fun sparring with her.

"Come on in, then. I 'spose I can use some of that gunk you make."

He opened his screen door for her. His color was good. Hair, as always in the same marine, high and tight, he'd had as long as she'd remembered. White as snow now, as was his wolf, she'd heard. He was neat and exuded a little pain at the edges, but otherwise, he was having a good day and wanted the company.

"I sure could use a cup of coffee." She held up a thermos. "Want some? I made a big pot this morning before I left for work."

He nodded, pulling down cups she poured the coffee into and then pushed his way. "I was just over at the Counter with Katie Faith. Merilee does the baking for them now. She sent home some cherry Danish. Want to share with me?"

He had a weakness for sweets so she wasn't surprised when he hummed his pleasure as he took the first bite.

"I've got some other stuff that I'm not going to be able to eat before it goes bad," she said, keeping her tone light. "You can't have the meat loaf because my momma made that for me." She grinned. "But there's some venison stew and I didn't have the heart to tell Ada Healy I don't much like venison. Want to take it off my hands?"

Ada was another kitchen witch like Aimee. She loved to cook and a few times a month she made batches of soups and stews, full of vegetables and whatever meat or game she had on hand and packaged it all up for Aimee to give to her clients when she went out visiting.

Jeph gave her the stinkeye long enough that she sighed. "What? I can take it by my parents' place later, I guess. My mom can put it in the freezer for another day."

"Ada's a fine cook. If you won't use it, put it in the ice box for me, please."

After she loaded the stew into his fridge, she tidied up his kitchen while leaving some of the apples she knew he liked in the bowl on the small table in the breakfast nook.

All the while, he told her about a rebuild he and his grandson were working on. She noted his hands seemed more gnarled than usual so she managed to talk herself into helping him rub the salve onto his joints.

"Don't worry, it doesn't smell like perfume," she told him as she began to gently knead his hands, rubbing the cream in. As she worked, she let her magic rise and wash through him, grabbing bits and pieces of stray anxiety, anger and pain as it did.

She hadn't done it without permission. A long time ago, she'd asked if he minded her using healing magic on him when she was there and he'd agreed. She'd never use her power against someone like that, even if it was to help.

"You smell like Mac," he said, a gleam in his eyes.

"Do I, now? Huh. I'm wearing essential oil today. Maybe that's it."

He cackled. "I been hearing talk all over town about you two. That boy is a whole lot like his grandma. My youngest sister. She don't like Scarlett much, which is why you don't see her around town as often these days. But she's got a spine of steel. And balls. Excuse my language. She's tough, I mean."

Aimee felt like balls were actually pretty weak. One kick or bump and the guy was out. Now, ovaries? *They* were tough.

"I know your sister." Rebecca Pembry was a total badass. Since Dwayne and Scarlett had taken over as Patrons from Rebecca, she'd headed up the Episcopal bake sales, the church parking lot swap and ran all the fund-raising like a well-oiled machine. Their booth at the Founder's Day celebration was always a place to stop for Rebecca's hummingbird cake and divinity.

"She's going to like that you're with Macrae. No offense, but your power added to this pack is a good thing Mac brings to the table. I'm going to call her when you go. Lord it over her that I knew for sure first." He gave her a quick look, like a little boy, and she was charmed even though she knew better.

"That'll be between Mac and his grandma," she said with a snicker.

"Up and challenging Dwayne for the mayor's office last week? Got the whole pack talking. Good on you, girl. You have some nerve. I like it. Dwayne needs to go. He has since the first time he got dumped out of office. I wasn't fooled by his claims to have changed. I'd prefer it be a wolf in the job though, no offense."

"That mean I have your vote?" she teased. "I understand why you'd prefer a wolf in office. But I guess that's why I'm running. Because the mayor's office should be about the whole town and not just one group of us in it. It doesn't *belong* to werewolves."

"Fair enough. If you're with Mac, maybe he could run instead."

She laughed. "Well, if he wants to run against me later, I guess he can."

He nodded once. Sharply. "You're a firecracker. Good. Macrae needs that. Took over as Prime without an announcement from his daddy, you know. Had to because Dwayne's too wishy-washy." He growled a little. "Man's useless. His father would be ashamed to see it if he were alive today. Darrell's just as bad."

She hated that Dwayne hadn't made a big deal of Mac being Prime. He deserved to have a dad who was proud of his accomplishments. Maybe in his own way, Dwayne was proud and he just didn't know how to show it and protect Darrell too.

Ugh. Whatever.

"I'm sorry your pack is having all this trouble. I'm not challenging Dwayne to make things harder for you all. I'm doing it to help the town. I care about Mac," she added quietly. "I won't ever hurt him like that. Not deliberately."

He nodded, relaxing as she moved to the other hand and began to massage the salve in. Her magic warmed her skin, warmed his as well, soaking in and hopefully drowning his pain.

The spell she used would most likely keep him pain-free for the next several days. Her magic flowed into him, filling the space where the pain always lived and hid, surrounding it so he couldn't feel it.

She spooled it slowly, like cotton candy, wrapping it around all the jagged parts inside him.

When she finished, he smiled softly at her. Just a brief moment.

Once she'd found her voice again—sometimes when she used her magic like that she had to take a few seconds to set herself to rights—she pointed at the tub of salve. "If you rub it in daily, in the morning when you wake and at night, that'll help too."

He thanked her in his gruff way and told her he might just be seeing her in two nights for the candidates' forum in town.

She told him to call if he needed her. But he was too proud for that, so she'd be back. And she'd bring some extra salve to the forum to tuck into his pocket as well. It was part of the play they acted out on a regular basis. Their version of affection. She gave him two honks of the horn as she started her car and he rewarded her with a sour expression before heading inside again.

Grinning, she pulled away from the house and went back to work.

Though the day was cold and had been snowing in fits and starts, Aimee had her hands in the dirt, where they liked to be, when Huston strolled up, Mac at his side. An unexpected sight this time of the day.

There was a mayoral candidates' forum later that night where the local paper and the rest of the council got to ask questions. Maybe that was it. Whatever brought them, it wasn't a chore to look at both men as they approached.

Her magic seemed to rush out, surround them both to see what their intentions were. She'd never really experienced that before so she went with it, letting the magic lead.

Satisfied, apparently, with the lack of dire intention on her visitors' part, her power trickled back into her gut.

"What brings you two out today?" She continued to clip her herbs, keeping them from the medicinal ones she had in a separate basket. She held up a bunch. "Dill? I seem to have way more of it than normal. I don't know why. More for pickles I guess."

"This is some kitchen garden," Huston said, reverence in his tone as he turned in a slow circle to take in the riot of life that filled her yard. "I don't think I've seen so many flowers in winter before."

"Thank you." Aimee didn't tell him the reason why it had been so damned fertile of late was connected to how often his cousin visited her bed. As her heart filled with the chemistry of a new romance, so had everything all around her come to life.

She knew they had something more than marigolds and dill to talk about, but she let it come. Enjoying the way her magic seemed to spring right to her will when she worked outside on a regular basis.

"I had breakfast with my grandmother today."

Ah.

She grinned up at Mac. "You can't blame that on me. Talk to your great-uncle Jeph. He smelled you on me when I went to see him day before yesterday."

"The minute you left he called Nan and got her all worked up. She's already planning on how many children we're having. Just so you know, she says four will do nicely." Mac knelt next to where she'd been working.

"You call her Nan? Like for Nana?"

"One of my older cousins started it and it stuck. If she tells you to call her Nan you're in. Rebecca is what company calls her."

Aimee looked up at the sound of Huston's snicker. He shrugged without arguing.

"You know that's a lot of pressure, right? When I meet her officially what if she tells me to call her Rebecca?"

Mac rolled his eyes.

Huston said, "She won't. She's an astute judge of character."

Aimee sure hoped so, because otherwise it would suck big-time.

"As for her request for babies, four seems like a lot of Pembrys. I don't know about that." Also, she wasn't having any babies anytime soon. Not even with this gorgeous wolf kneeling next to her smelling really tasty.

"We can practice a lot until we get there."

She rolled her eyes.

Finally, Mac said, "My grandmother gets headaches. Do you have anything for that?"

"A number of things." Pleased he'd come to her, she stood, brushing off her knees. "I'll make tea and you two can give me some details and we'll figure out the answer."

He held his hand out and she took it without a thought. When she touched him, her magic seemed to crackle around them both with something like static electricity.

His eyes widened a little and she winked. "Katie Faith told me that might happen. Apparently she and Jace have that too."

By the time she'd washed her hands and switched from her work shoes into her house slippers, Mac had already put the kettle on to boil, totally at home in her kitchen.

"I wasn't sure what sort of tea you'd want, but I got the water on."

She tiptoed up to kiss him quickly. "Thanks. I was thinking of some spice tea. It's really tasty but not too sweet. I made it myself."

"Of course you did."

She gave Mac the eye, but he just smiled back all solemn-like.

Aimee began to clean and prepare the marigold into a paste. "I hope you guys don't mind if I work while you talk. Since I've got the town hall tonight, I want to have all the things I need for my home visits tomorrow finished up."

Mac watched her, interested. "As long as our being here won't mess up your magic."

Aimee let her internal walls down as she began to slowly rock the pestle over the flowers. Magic flowed steadily into the mortar bowl, changing slightly when she added a few other things to get the consistency right. Her magic was part of the recipe, something uniquely hers, something she used to create the right remedy for the right person.

"It won't. I've been making tinctures, pastes and the like since I was a kid." She added a little comfrey, nudging it to be extra soothing. "Tell me about her headaches. She hasn't contacted me about them in the past so whatever you can tell me would help."

"She said sometimes the pain is so bad she has to lie down in the dark until it passes," Mac said at last, concern for his grandmother in his tone.

He went on a while, giving more specifics about

the sort of pain she had, Huston adding details here and there.

Aimee finished the paste and transferred it to three different jars, her lips moving as she added some basic protection magic to them.

"I suppose she won't consent to see a doctor? I can connect her with a medical practice that has shifters and witches on staff. She should get a workup. It sounds like migraines, and I'll go visit her to bring some tincture I have and ask her some more questions. But a neurologist can be sure there's nothing alarming going on."

Mac shook his head. "I tried already. She said her mom had the same kind of headaches. That it was a family thing. You can only press her so long before she throws you out of the house. Nan's got *opinions*."

Aimee snorted a laugh. "She gave birth to a lot of bossy wolves. I imagine she has to be tough to have survived this long dealing with your daddy."

Huston's startled guffaw made her smile.

"I'll talk to her when I take over the tincture myself. She's probably right. This is pretty common with female shifters as they near the century mark. Happens to the cats too. I'd feel better if she at least spoke with a doctor. I know you said she's got opinions. And good for her. But I deal with crotchety old shifters weekly. Believe it or not, I'm pretty good at getting my way."

Mac raised a brow. "You don't say."

She flicked her wet fingers his way, sticking out her tongue.

"She already went to the doctor," Huston said at last.

Mac turned, mouth dropping open to speak but his cousin held up a hand.

"She made me promise not to tell anyone. That was

the condition on which she'd allow me to take her to Knoxville. I talked to the doctor after she had an MRI. It's a form of migraine, like Aimee just said. But she doesn't like the pills they gave her so she doesn't take them."

Human medication didn't usually work on shifters. Their metabolisms ate through most before they could work. There were some pain relievers and the like, but many of them came with side effects because of their unique physiology.

"Some shifters react worse to the medication than the headaches. I expect that's what happened." She turned to look through the apothecary cabinet standing in her mudroom.

There she kept the various supplies she needed for the remedies she created for her clients. At her touch, the doors sprang open, though they wouldn't for anyone else. A pulse of magic tickled her fingertip as the locks recognized her.

"I can stop by her place on my way to the town hall tonight," she called out as she tucked two dark brown bottles with dropper lids into the pocket of the apron she wore.

Thinking again, she grabbed some of the cream she made for her dad's shoulder pain before drawing the doors closed and resetting the magical lock with a few words and movements of her hands.

"There something dangerous in there?" Huston asked her as she came back.

"Where?"

"You had the cabinet locked. Is it safe to have that cabinet in a room with all those windows? Someone could break in and steal whatever's inside."

"I told you to stop watching all that true-crime stuff on cable, didn't I?" Mac said.

"I lock my cabinet for several reasons." As she spoke, she washed her hands and set about organizing the basket of supplies she needed. Each client was getting a separate muslin bag with whatever she brought them. Sometimes it was medicinal, other times it was a book or a puzzle. Just something to brighten a day.

"My cabinet is where I keep my Work. Capital *W* magic work. It's irresponsible to not take care in how I use the power I'm gifted with. I know you think that room would be easy to break into." She smiled then, showing teeth. "It's not. The cabinet is a way to keep whatever batch of medicinals I make fresh. They're organized." Color coded and indexed by client, but she didn't need to tell them that. "It's handy to have it all in one spot and somewhere visible so I won't forget. Witches like organization, I don't know if you figured that out yet. I also lock it because it's my space. My magical energy is there and I don't want anyone else poking around without my permission."

Huston nodded. "Makes sense. I don't think you should go over there before the town hall. Just tell Mac and me what she needs to do and we'll relay that to her."

Aimee frowned. "Why? If she's planning our babies, she can't hate me. Or I guess that's how I'd imagine it going. But your family is…uh, you're all outliers. Yeah, that's the word. So what's the story?"

"There's a pack dinner before the candidates' forum," Mac told her. "She'll be there so one of us can pass it along."

Aw, he didn't want her to feel bad that she wasn't invited to the family dinner before the forum later that night. She smiled to let him know she was teasing. "No consorting with the enemy before the event?"

"It's not that. You know it isn't. Normally I'd say go over there and meet her. But tonight she's going and only because my dad called to invite her personally. Nan's not a fan of my mom." Mac winced.

As Aimee certainly couldn't argue with that perspective, not having much like for Scarlett either, she just said, "Okay."

She wrote up a card with directions for the tincture and tucked it along with the bottles into a bag, handing that over to Mac.

"It tastes gross. That's just truth. But it should help her. It won't help if she doesn't use it. I find a fancy way of making that point so I trust you'll do the same."

Huston stood. "I'm, uh, going to the car. I'll wait for you there," he told Mac. To Aimee, he said, "Thank you for helping Uncle Jeph and our nan."

"Wait a sec." Aimee handed him the cream she'd pulled from her cabinet. "You appear to be favoring your left side. Bruise? Soreness from working?"

He grinned. "My brother and I got into a fight after we went on a run last night. I've got a massive bruise on my right hip." Usually things like that healed very quickly for shifters. But at times when it was combat between two shifters, the wounds received would stick around longer than usual.

"This is good for bruises and muscle soreness. Just rub it on after you get out of the shower and any other time you might need it. It's arnica and a few other things. Nothing spooky." She winked.

"Thanks for this too." Huston held up the jar.

Mac waited until he'd gone before hugging her and laying a long slow kiss on her.

"Thank you. For everything. I'm sorry I can't be with you before the forum. Are you sure you're okay with me doing this dinner tonight?"

Since they'd been together, they'd been trying to keep everything low-key. They weren't hiding their relationship, but given the renewed tension since she'd challenged Dwayne for the mayor's office, they'd been quiet and private in what Aimee liked to think of as their love bubble. Which was so schmoopy she didn't call it that out loud.

"You have shit to do as Prime, Mac. I get it. I'm not insulted. I'm having dinner at Salt & Pepper in an hour anyway. I'll have a bite of cheeseburger in your honor." And count her lucky stars she didn't have to do it while at the same table as his mother and father.

"Now that my grandmother knows for sure that we're together, I expect everyone in town will soon enough."

"Yeah I figured as much." She shrugged, hoping like hell they were strong enough to make it through what was sure to be a tumultuous time over the next several weeks until election day.

"Truth be told, I'm glad of it. I don't like not showing you off."

She smiled up at him. "You're really going to get me sexed up later, just so you know."

"I'm always glad to hear that reaffirmed." He kissed her again. "Good luck tonight. I'll meet you here after?"

"We're going to the Counter after for milkshakes. Come by then. I mean, if you're not doing something with the pack. If you can't make that, I'll text you when I'm done and you can meet me."

He frowned and she laughed because he was so cute when he didn't get his way. "I know. It's hard when everything in the universe doesn't change itself to suit your preferences."

"It is! I'll just have to endure, I suppose."

She swatted him on his very adorable ass as he left, wishing her good luck one last time.

Chapter Sixteen

Mac's father pulled him aside just before they went into the city council chambers for the forum. "I heard some new rumors floating around town about Katie Faith."

Mac stared and then shook his head. "No."

"Everyone in town should know what she got up to down in the city. She comes back here pretending to be pure as the driven snow, paints Darrell as a monster when she was opening up her legs to anyone who offered. Maybe that's why Darrell left her. She was doing the dirty to him before the wedding."

Jace was going to freak the fuck out when these rumors—ones Mac was sure his father had planted—got to him. And that made everything so much harder than it had to be.

"You know that's a lie. As does everyone in this town. You pulled this right after Darrell ran off and left Katie Faith. Remember how that turned out? This isn't going to get you reelected. It's only going to get the Dooleys all worked up and pissed off in defense of their Patron. And they'd be right to do so. You gain absolutely nothing from this so stop it now. Do you hear me? No more rumormongering. This is going to blow up in your face and I'm not going to be able to save you. No one will."

Dwayne sighed. "Why are you always trying to argue me out of doing what I need to?"

"Because you think you need to do stupid crap like start rumors about the Patron of another pack. You asked me for help with this campaign. You promised to take my advice. Play your strengths. You have the experience to get Diablo Lake back on track." Mac had only been running this campaign for his father for a week and it felt like five years. He was past hoping that if he just repeated it enough times his dad would finally hear it and listen. All he could hope was that his dad's loss wasn't so crushing it affected the pack negatively.

His dad's gaze narrowed a moment as he leaned in and sniffed at Mac. "You're still going with that Benton girl. You got Nan all in a lather over it."

Mac said, "Nan likes Aimee. She's just a little over-enthusiastic about the speed of the relationship. Back to the forum—"

"What's her strategy tonight then?" his dad demanded.

Mac gave him a hard, incredulous look. "Really? It's a question-and-answer format with people you know and have worked with for decades. You've done this many times before. There's *no strategy other than being prepared*. And," he added, "she and I don't talk about the campaign, especially anything about strategy." He was damned if he was going to let his father question his loyalty again.

Which he did nearly immediately. "You're choosing this witch over this pack."

Mac's mother sighed. "Don't be an idiot, Dwayne. That girl can bring a lot of power into *this pack*. Lord knows I hate to agree with your mother, but in this thing I surely do. Them Dooleys have Katie Faith, why shouldn't we be encouraging Mac and Aimee?"

Mac held his hands up. "Nope. We're not discussing this." He faced his dad. "Don't question my allegiance again." He turned his back and stalked away.

A long table sat in the middle of the room, down where the chairs for the audience normally were. The only spectators invited that night were the candidates, two guests and the city council members, along with the editor of the town paper.

It sounded pretty grand, but really it was a dozen people. If his dad couldn't manage this, he didn't deserve to be mayor. Which, naturally, was becoming apparent to pretty much everyone.

But before Mac could think about that any further, a ruckus caught his attention.

Darrell stood at the side of the room, arguing with Carl about why he should be allowed inside.

With an annoyed grunt, he headed over before Darrell could cause an even bigger scene.

"Go on home, Darrell," he told his brother. "I told you we'd call you when this was over."

"You're in here! I should be in here too. Carl gets to be in here!"

Carl's magic rose, steely and more menacing than Mac usually saw from the man. He pointed a finger at Darrell. "I will haul your ass out this door myself if you don't get out of here."

"Sheriff, please allow me to handle this. I apologize for the delay." Mac picked his brother up bodily and hauled him through the door back out into the small grassy area out front.

"Get the fuck out of here. Dad needs calm right now

if he's going to be effective. You're acting like an ass-hole," Mac told him. "I'm inside because I'm Prime of this pack. Because he named me as one of his two guests and because I'm not prone to acting like a tan-truming toddler in front of the newspaper whose en-dorsement we want."

Darrell's face reddened with fury. "He didn't an-nounce you Prime. That's my place, not yours! You abandoned this pack when you left."

Mac had known this would come and probably that it would come at the least opportune time.

"He didn't *have* to announce me. I'm Prime and every wolf in this pack knew it without anyone having to say a word. That's why it's *always* been my place and never yours." Brutal words designed to bring his brother to heel. "I was sent away to be trained to run this pack. You're *not capable* of this job. You're out of shape. You're close-minded. You're envious and petty and lazy. Dad gets up at five every single day to get ahead of any potential issue the pack might need him to handle. Since I've been back, it's been *me* who pro-vides him with daily reports about everything going on in Diablo Lake. You have no curiosity. No ambition. Running this pack would be a job every single minute of every single day. It doesn't make you weak to admit you don't have the desire, or the skill set to do it."

"He's been training me since we was kids." But his yelling had subsided. Sadly, his shitty attitude remained.

It hurt to have to deliver the blow to his brother's pride. But he needed to get a clue so he could turn him-self around and enjoy who and what he was without try-ing to tear the pack apart.

And Mac wasn't going to allow that.

"You're old enough to know the difference between a wistful fucking fantasy and real life. If not, consider this your lesson. *Go home to your family.*"

Mac turned and went back inside, closing the door behind himself.

Aimee had settled at the table so he angled his chair to watch her and his father better. She'd changed into a pretty blue suit and looked smart and able and adorable. Though he wouldn't tell her the last bit because she'd punch his nuts.

Katie Faith sat with Carl, Aimee's plus-two apparently, and waved at him with a goofy smile.

Mac tipped his chin at her.

Beside him, his mother shifted, the annoyance and anxiety coming off her in waves. Becoming Prime had amped up his emotional connection with all the wolves in the pack.

She'd just essentially thrown her lot behind Mac dating Aimee, so it couldn't be that. He'd asked her several times, but she continued to insist nothing was wrong but the same usual, tired attacks on Katie Faith.

At the table, the rules were being explained and the first question was asked. His father turned on the genial-mayor bit, laying on the condescension a bit thick. If he thought he could get to Aimee that way, his dad was mistaken.

She never lost her cool. She wasn't a shark—or a werewolf—but she wasn't a doormat either. An alpha in her own right, Aimee never let him shake her as she answered the questions in a thoughtful manner. She didn't let his father talk over her—though he tried repeatedly—and held her own. On the issues she was informed and forward thinking. But she managed to speak in terms even the older folks could hear and not be offended or threatened by.

She was, he realized, perfect.

His father was used to being in charge and he'd gotten lazy. His grasp of the issues was borne of holding the job, which was a big point in his favor. But it was outdated in many ways and when that was brought up he got defensive and closed-off to the point of being rude to the person who'd asked the question.

Not a winning strategy.

Worse, his father was a complete patronizing asshole to Aimee, and through her, all the witches, including the ones who'd married into the Pembry pack. They didn't have to be there to hear about this. In a town like Diablo Lake, the gossip tree was far more efficient than the emergency broadcast system.

He was dismissive of her magic. Of magic in general, but especially nurturing magic. He had no idea the kind of power Aimee could wield and Mac feared it would be his father's undoing in the end.

Thank heavens Dwayne didn't bring up the rumors about Katie Faith. Mac had thought a lot about how to get out in front of the situation. He sent texts to Huston, having him poke around to see how far the rumors had gotten and who'd been passing them along.

Hopefully it was something they could clean up quickly. Then Mac would deal with that person himself. And he'd let Jace know it had happened. Otherwise there'd be another bloody, gaping wound between Dooley and Pembry that'd take a lot more than a bit of pack discipline to fix.

At the table, the forum was winding down. His dad's vanity and ego would be the death knell of his career as mayor of Diablo Lake. And Mac wanted it to go that way. Though he had a soft spot for the woman challenging his dad, Mac thought of the pack and the town as well. She'd win anyway.

Dwayne shouldn't be mayor, but if he had a way to leave that allowed him some pride, it'd be better for the town and the Pembry pack.

At the end of the ninety minutes the forum broke up. He smiled Aimee's way before following his parents back to his dad's office.

"She kept interrupting me," his dad snarled as they got the door closed.

Already looking for excuses.

"No, she didn't." He held up the pad of paper he'd been using. "I timed each of you to see if they were being fair. You actually got two and a half minutes more than she did." He'd also interrupted Aimee twelve times while she'd interrupted him three. "You got plenty of time to answer the questions." Mac phrased it like a positive, not wanting to trip down some lane where all he did was complain.

"Sure felt like it."

Well, feelings weren't reality and he wasn't sure why his father needed that said.

"Let's look forward to the town hall next week and not get worked up over nothing."

"That girl can't be perfect," his father said.

"Surely not," Mac said, suppressing his snort. "Everyone has their weak spots. Hers is her inexperience. Which is great, because your strength is your years of experience."

"We need to find out what those weaknesses of hers are so we can take her out."

Sharp, cold anger slid down Mac's spine.

"She's too cozy with those Dooleys. Mac, you need to talk to her about that," his mother told him.

"You don't need to *take her out*, for God's sake. I wouldn't take kindly to something like that, Dad. Are we clear?"

His father sneered but didn't argue.

"Take this as an opportunity to show all the people in town that you support them. Not just Pembry wolves, but witches too. And Dooleys."

"Dooley or not, I expect the wolves to stick with their own on this," his dad said. "Some of 'em will go with that Katie Faith, of course, and I wager she'll stick with her friend. The cats, well they're tricky, but I'll talk with the Ruizes next week. They're shifters too, after all."

"Except you've been dropping rumors about the Patron of the Dooley pack, potentially throwing away any support you might get from them. Even if they do vote for you, you can't just play the numbers. You need to convince the witches you're not going to let the magic here die off. They're worried and if you don't allay their fears they'll only redouble their efforts to take your seat."

"I've done this a time or two before, you know." His father shot him a look.

"I'm aware. And it bit you in the ass a time or two before as well. Attacking her will be your weakness and something I will not tolerate—professionally or personally. *Don't do it.* People like her. She takes care of a lot of folks in town. You go in on her and you'll lose even more support."

"Not if I expose whatever she's hiding. Let me do

what I do best, boy." His father gathered his things and headed out the door, his mother right behind him.

She cast a look over her shoulder at Mac and he wanted to hug her and demand she just tell him what the hell was going on with her.

"Being a jerk isn't doing what you do best, Dad," he called out.

"You're Prime now, act like it," his father replied before he got into the car and left.

"Okay then. You asked for it," Mac said.

Chapter Seventeen

Mac woke up with his woman draped over him, warm and delicious—despite the drool on his arm. Want rose slowly as he woke up little by little.

She had on flannel pajamas old enough to be soft against his skin. Old enough he knew the heat of his palms on her ass would have registered through the thinned material.

Her eyes opened slowly and she sighed happily at the sight of him before closing her eyes again and snuggling against him with a little extra squirm to let him know she was just as happy to get up to something dirty as he was.

Aimee was the best thing in his universe. Even as the mayoral race had kept heating up, things between the two of them had only strengthened.

At first he thought the knocking at the front door was his heart pounding after she'd grabbed his cock at the base. Enough that he got a little annoyed when she stopped and sat up.

Then he noted the annoyance in her sigh as she got out of bed and pulled a robe on and realized someone was at the damned door.

"I'm going to kill whoever it is, okay?" He growled

as he managed to get some sweats and a T-shirt on and followed her out. "Let me go see who it is, for fuck's sake." The day before she'd received a threat note everyone in the pack had denied knowing anything about. But his brother had certainly seemed mighty pleased to hear it upset her.

"I already told you that I enlarged my wards of protection all the way to the sidewalk. Whoever it is, they're recognized as friendly by my magic. Gonna be a Pembry I'll wager."

He moved in front of her anyway. "I can take a lot more physical damage than you can. I don't know why you argue so much."

She snorted. "Yeah, well, it looks like it's Huston. So I'm going to start some coffee and something for breakfast. Come in when you're done whispering about how much you adore me."

Mac grabbed her, pulling her back for a quick kiss and a hug, drawing in the scent of her a moment. "Good morning. Don't forget where we left off in there, okay?"

"I'm pretty sure you'll know how to get back on track the moment you can," she called back over her shoulder as she walked away.

He wiped the grin off his face as he opened the screen door to admit his cousin. "This better be important. Like someone bleeding or on fire important."

But Huston's expression told him it was, indeed, very important.

"Fuck. Okay, come in the other room and tell me what's going on." As he'd sort of taken up residence with Aimee, she'd given him one of her spare rooms as an office so that's where he took Huston, having him take a seat once they'd closed the door.

"Your mom is the one who started the rumors about Katie Faith."

"Wow, no easing me in on that, huh?" Mac scrubbed his hands over his face.

"Figured it was one of those 'shove you into the freezing-cold water to get it out of the way' sort of things."

"I can't say I'm surprised. I did find out about this from my dad. I just thought he'd be smart enough not to leave breadcrumbs right straight back to himself or my mom. How did you find out?"

"The wolves supporting your father to that degree are a very small number. I think you don't really get that. The pool of possibles was pretty easy to go through. I started with Darrell and his little followers and sure enough I found someone who bragged about what he'd heard after I bought him a few beers. From there it was only one more person until I found your momma as the source."

"Do we know if this has gone any further than these numbskulls my brother lets fetch his water?"

"I don't know. I've got my ear to the ground. The dipshit I bought beers for says he talked about it at the bar, but it's so damned loud in there, even with shifter hearing I'm not sure anyone could have overheard unless they were very close. I don't want to poke around so much I actually create a problem where there is none."

"I'll go talk with her now. I expect she got it right straight from my dad. I'll just handle them both at once."

"I'll go with you," Huston told him.

"You don't need to be in the middle of this mess."

"I'm *already* in the middle of this mess, Mac. I'm your lieutenant. It's my job to be with you when you deal with this sort of thing. And this is my pack too. My family too."

"Aimee is in there making us coffee and breakfast. Come on through and visit with us. I have to figure out how much to tell her. Some of it is about the campaign and we've said we weren't going to talk about that. So far she's respected that and kept her distance. But this involves her personally."

"And she'll be Patron with you someday soon enough. This mayoral race has only sped up the process for you to take over. You know that. Your dad loses more of his grip on his control every day. He's letting this get personal. Your momma? I don't know what is going on with her, but she's gone from salty to bitter. And they're letting Darrell run riot all over town stirring up his buddies and causing trouble. At some point you're going to have to share this with her."

"It's the when and how much that I'm struggling with. She's intuitive. Good with people. Wolves keep telling me what an asset she is. Like I'm buying a piece of art or some property."

Huston laughed. "She'll handle herself just fine. Aimee isn't one for letting herself get talked over. She's quiet, surely. But a quiet force. Tell her all you can, as soon as you can. That's my advice. Now let's go eat. I smell bacon and coffee."

Aimee gave them both the once-over when they joined her in the kitchen. She'd gotten dressed and put her hair back with a headband and looked fresh and pretty.

"Coffee is done so help yourselves. I'd say something like I hope y'all like pancakes but whether you do or not, that's what I'm making."

Huston just shook his head as he poured himself a cup of coffee. "I never would have pegged you for so much sass. Mac needs more sass in his life. He's too used to getting his own way."

"On account of being so smart and handsome and accomplished? Yeah, it sucks." Mac snagged the butter from the fridge, along with some preserves and syrup.

"He's got low self-esteem, Huston. Give him a break."

Laughing, she reached over to grab her phone, which had started to ring.

"Hey, Mom, how are you today?"

He and Huston took over the pancake flipping as she dealt with her mom's call, but about three minutes in Aimee said, "What?" with so much alarm he knew the rumors about Katie Faith had to have gotten out.

Aimee cut her eyes to him and set her mouth in a hard line as she listened to whatever TeeFaye was telling her. Finally, she said her goodbyes and with one hand on her hip, she said, "Something you want to talk to me about?"

Huston, the traitor, jumped a little. "I'm just going to, uh…not be here. Sorry, Mac, but you're on your own. Call me later if you're still alive." He grabbed his freshly buttered pancakes, rolled them up and scampered from the house lickety-split.

"Let's have breakfast while we talk," he said, taking the platter of pancakes to the table, where she'd already settled.

"I take it your mom had something to tell you that upset you. Why don't we start there."

"Don't do that. It won't end well for you."

"What?"

"Don't fucking patronize me. Or try to handle me.

I'm empathic! I felt it when I was talking to my mom. You *knew* what it was about. You weren't surprised when I confronted you and Huston ran out of here so fast he left burn marks so he knew too."

"Will you please tell me what your mom said? I'm not going to lie to you, I just want to know what happened."

She frowned at him. "My momma and Nadine were at the market when they overheard a Pembry wolf telling another that my best friend had been a total whore and that's why Darrell left her at the altar. As you might imagine, Nadine was none too happy to hear such things being said about her daughter and she threw a jumbo can of peaches at the wolf saying it. Surprise surprise, it was Ronnie who, according to my mother, cried like a baby when the can hit him square in the goolies."

Mac winced.

"Before Nadine could grab him though, he ran out of the store along with some other Pembry wolf he was with. What is going on? And is that why Huston was just here? They reported Nadine's can to the junk like a bunch of crybabies?"

Aimee was *pissed off* and his wolf responded, wanting to fix it. Needing to make her feel better.

"Because if you all think we're going to sit idly by while our reputations are being torn down by *your fucking family* yet again, you have another think coming and you all better watch out for *your* goolies. You catch my meaning?"

Damn, she was scary. And that was really hot. Something he wasn't going to pass on at that moment.

"I do catch your meaning, yes. And in the interest and well-being of goolies everywhere, I'll let you know, yes,

I was aware of the rumors and Huston has been doing his best to track down where they came from." Ronnie had been sent away from town and he'd just been allowed back the day before for this sort of shit. When he ran that fucker to ground it would be to grind him into a greasy spot and then kick him out of Pembry for good.

She raised her brows at him and the room got colder. "How long have you known and not mentioned it to me? Because I've got a problem with that, Mac."

"I only found out two days ago and got right on handling it because I didn't want it getting out and upsetting you or Katie Faith."

His New Year's Eve plans of sex and champagne at midnight were quickly fading.

Because of his damned family. Again.

Sometimes being the only adult in a room full of people supposed to be adults really fucking sucked.

"This isn't going to help your dad in the polls. I know we're not supposed to talk about this election, but there's *no* way I can see this as anything but a pitiable last gasp of your dad's as he's losing his ass."

Mac thought about it. Didn't want to harm the pack, and despite what his father said, would never do anything to damage it, even if it meant not telling Aimee anything right then and possibly damaging their relationship.

But he didn't think he had to do that. Because she was right, it was totally out of line.

"I know it won't help him in the polls. Rumors like that never do. Especially when he's done Katie Faith wrong, as has my brother. And my mother. She's who's to blame for this. That's what Huston came over to tell me."

"And?"

"What do you mean?"

"Really? Are you that sure you're fast enough to escape me when I leap across this table and use that wooden spoon on your head?"

He barely withheld his surprised laughter, and was glad he had because she wasn't in the mood to be teased.

"No, ma'am. I understand a woman as pissed off as you are can move very fast indeed. I'm only relying on the truth here. I *am* trying to fix this. This is not a pack thing. Some members of the pack did it. And they will be dealt with. Ronnie had been exiled after the shit at the market with you. He just violated the terms of his return to Diablo Lake. When I find him this will be handled."

He had to go to his mother and talk this over with her.

"He's too tight with your brother. He knows he can get away with stuff."

Mac shook his head. "He did get away with stuff. Now I'm Prime. Like I said, when I find him, this will be handled. I'm asking you to trust me, even though you don't have a lot of reason to trust my family right now."

She gave him a long look and then sighed. "I do trust you, Mac. That's why I'm not kicking you out and using the hose on you. Nadine would have called Katie Faith by this point. And I'm guessing it was a long call or she'd be lighting my phone up already. I'm going over there. She's my best friend and this is happening to her because of me."

"It's not because of you. It's totally on Ronnie, Darrell and my parents. I wish you'd wait for me. We could go over there together. Then I'll have something concrete to tell Jace as to how my wolves were dealt with."

"I'm not about to make your job easier right now, Mac. If the situation was reversed she'd come to me too. I'm going over there in an hour. You can deal with your business and go there to meet me, or come when you've taken care of it. I don't care which. As to the rest. The next campaign event is in three days. I need this to be dealt with by then or I'll have to deal with it myself and I'm quite sure your daddy won't like that one bit."

"After breakfast I'm headed out to do just that." He looked across the table at her, his beautiful woman. "I promise you."

"I'm trusting you. Don't make me regret that."

"I do my best, Aimee. I truly do."

But when he stopped by his parents' place, no one was there. He even used his key to let himself inside just in case they were ducking him. Annoyed, he headed over to his aunt and uncle's place.

Huston was there, but he hadn't told anyone else what was up. A very good quality in a lieutenant, Mac believed.

But this was the core of his new administration, so to speak. His cousins, aunt and uncle and a few trusted insiders, so he gave them a quick update.

"This is a waste of time and energy. Why all this focus on Katie Faith? She hasn't done a damned thing to Pembry. She's over at Dooley, being a Patron and not causing us any grief. But let me tell you right now, those rumors? Ronnie and whoever it was with him got Nadine and TeeFaye all worked up, and then they called Aimee. My woman is beyond angry. And she has the right to be. Which means the witches are going to be angry at us. Again. And for what?"

"You're preaching to the choir." His uncle Bern got himself another cup of coffee. "What are you going to do about it? We moving the timeline?"

They'd planned to challenge Dwayne after the election. To get the decks cleared so all the effort necessary would be far more easily used with no other distractions. "I wish he could keep himself under control so we could have an easy transition once he loses."

His aunt gave him a stern look. "Boohoo. I want to be twenty-five again. I want a million dollars. Wanting's just a wish. Stop whining, boy. I know this is hard. We know you love your momma and daddy and want to do the right thing by everyone. That's impossible and this still needs to be done. You're the only one who can do it. You have the support of the bulk of this pack. You're strong and smart and you're Prime. You can hide all that before the election, maybe if you can keep him from doing something else stupid. But that's a lot of maybe and hope."

"He's been challenged halfway through his term because he's doing such a piss-poor job of being this pack's Patron and the mayor. Your daddy has had a lot of good fortune in his life and he used to know how to make the most of it. When I challenged him, he got lucky and he won and I respected those results. I stood behind him when he took over as Patron. And all these years as he's been training you to run this pack, he's done it at your expense over that dumbo brother of yours. And at the expense of the Pembry wolves as he's gone and let your momma and your brother's little friends turn the town against us."

"We can't keep on with this uncertainty," his aunt said.

A pack needed a real leader or leader couple and it

needed a clear line of hierarchy and governance. They were always at risk in a world where their numbers were far lower than humans. If they couldn't trust one another, they went a little feral. Diablo Lake would get dragged into the whole mess and eventually, the town would lose its magic as people left to seek safety elsewhere.

Uncertainty was death to a pack.

Mac sucked in a breath. "I'll tell you, honestly, what my concern is. If I move on him before the election, I'm messing with the democratic process in this town. For my pack. Aimee's ahead in the polls by a pretty fair margin. And she'll continue to widen that lead because this town likes her. Hell, she's taken care of most of us at one time or another, shifter and witch alike. When he loses it'll be a natural time for me to take over as Patron and we'll have respected the election for the rest of the people who live here."

"Your daddy's a terrible loser. And there's something really deep and personal between your momma and Katie Faith. Neither of your parents is going to let go. And your brother can't deny you're going to lead Pembry anymore. Makes him dangerous because he's so entitled and stupid."

"Josiah," his uncle said to his aunt. "That's what's between them."

Mac stilled as everyone turned to his uncle.

"What do you mean? And how could Katie Faith have anything to do with Jace's dead father?" Mac asked with a wince. They weren't supposed to even say his name.

"I don't know the story. Your momma and I were never close or even part of the same circle. I just know there was some talk back when Josiah was repudiated and her name was part of it."

"Why does no one tell me any of this?"

"Because of the rules. He was repudiated. His name to never be repeated. His story never to be told. That's the point of the punishment," his aunt said. "But I'm not a Dooley wolf. I don't have to put their rules before my need to help you out. This is about our pack. Our wolves."

Mac blew out a breath. "Okay. Okay. I'll ask her directly." He hoped it wasn't something like she had an affair with Josiah Dooley. He shuddered at having to have *that* conversation with his mom.

"I'm going to discipline Ronnie—again—for shit stirring. He needs to be shunned from the pack. He's not obeying and we've got plenty of disobedience as it is. And then of course, Darrell will cry about it and run to my parents. He better hope he gets to them before I find him. Because he needs to be disciplined too. He's most assuredly part of this and he's been warned before. Then, of course I'm going to have to deal with a very pissed-off Patron of Dooley who's going to want to know why his wife is being spoken about like that by our wolves."

"Which is one of the many reasons why I'm doubtful you'll make it until after the election to deal with pack leadership. I wish I was wrong but I don't think I am."

His uncle was most likely right.

"We've got wolves in place, if you're right," Mac told him. They'd been planning this carefully enough over the last few weeks and now that he'd become Prime, he had even more strength to draw on.

Things were precarious, but he'd steer the pack

through the worst of it. No matter what came, in whichever order.

"Huston, Everett, you're with me. Let's go pay Ronnie a visit."

With a nod of thanks and a request that he be called or texted if his parents returned or showed their presence, he and his cousins headed out.

"Stop by Darrell's place," Mac told Huston.

His sister-in-law was home, along with their kids, who all came running at the sight of Mac. He may have thought his brother was a dumb asshole, but he loved his nieces and nephews.

"Darrell around?" he asked Sharon as he kissed the top of one of his niece's head before putting her back down on her feet. She skidded off after the rest of her older siblings.

He sat, pulling James Royce into his lap. The toddler started telling him a very long, involved story about something or other that may or may not have involved a cat of some type.

Sharon sighed deeply. "Don't put me in the middle of this."

"I have done everything possible to do this in ways no one gets put in the middle of it. But the truth is, I can't anymore. Darrell is his own worst enemy. Where is he? This is pack business and he's got some things to explain to me."

"He isn't here. Honest!" Sharon held a hand out a moment. "He left about an hour ago. Didn't say where he was going. Just that he'd be back in time for the party we're going to later. We have a babysitter and everything." She looked at him, her eyes begging him to let her have this moment, not to spoil this fragile fantasy that her life wasn't about to change.

He hated that she was going to be hurt because his brother was so weak.

"Did he go with someone?"

"Ronnie and, uh, that tall one, buck-teeth, Jay, yeah, that's him. I don't know him very well."

"Jay's one of my cousins on my mom's side." And easily swayed because he wanted to be liked. "Where do you think he went? If something happened and you needed to find him, where would you look first?" At her hesitation, he added, "It's way better for him that I find him before a Dooley does."

She cursed and James Royce cheerfully repeated it in a singsong voice. Mac laughed and then the baby laughed and sang curse words. He wished it could be like this instead of what he had to do next.

"I'd look at Ronnie's place. If he isn't there, maybe he's getting a drink? Stop laughing at him or he's just going to keep saying that," she scolded Mac.

Mac stood, handing the foul-mouthed toddler to his mother. "I'm trying to help him before he does something I can't save him from. I know he doesn't believe that, but I hope you do." In this case, help might mean sending his brother's dumb ass far away to start a new life in another pack.

"He means well in his own way. He's just very committed to only seeing his own way sometimes. Okay, a lot of the time. But he's a good dad and mostly he's not a bad husband," Sharon said.

He headed out after more kisses and hugs and hoped he could look them all in the face the next time he saw them after whatever he had to do to their father.

"Ronnie and Jay came by to get him an hour or so ago," Mac explained as he returned to the car. They'd already gone by Ronnie's, but no one was there.

"Jay Twombley? Your mom's sister's boy?" Everett asked.

"Apparently he's been hanging out with Darrell and Ronnie a lot. Jay lives out on Marsh."

They headed over and he tried his mom's cell once more. When it came time to leave a voice mail he said, "I'm acting in my position as Prime to handle the pack discipline regarding member wolves who have been causing dissension by spreading gossip about the Patron of the Dooley pack. Gossip I know they got from you. And Dwayne. If you want to save his ass, you better call me back, Momma."

Everett cleared his throat. "Ten bucks she calls back in less than three minutes."

Mac laughed, relieved that he still could. Grateful for these two dumbasses he could always count on.

Just as they turned onto Marsh, heading to Jay's, Mac's phone rang.

Huston handed Everett a ten.

"Where are you, Mom? We need to talk," Mac said as he answered.

"Your dad and I are off on a trip for a few days. Going to find us a little hotel that strikes our fancy. We'll be back by the town hall on Wednesday. We can all talk then, including how to deal with whatever you imagine your brother has done."

"That's not how this is going to work. If Dad's away from Diablo Lake, I'm in charge as Prime. I'm duly appointed to mete out justice and punishment." And it had been long enough that his father had neglected his job.

"You'll do no such thing," she told him, her voice sour.

She was the damned reason he was out there right then!

"I know you're the source of those rumors about Katie Faith. And I know Darrell ran off with Ronnie earlier, coincidentally not too long after Nadine Grady nailed Ronnie in the stones with a can of peaches in the grocery store when she overheard him calling her daughter a whore. Imagine that. Now imagine that Darrell is a momma's boy and he's awful close with the same wolf who keeps turning up every time there's a problem. You want to run off because you can't face what you've done? Do it knowing *I'm* having to deal with the discipline of these wolves because you two are turning tail and leaving them to it."

He disconnected the call and shoved the phone back into his pocket.

Chapter Eighteen

Aimee knocked on Katie Faith's back door and waited until her friend called out for her to come in. The last thing she wanted was to walk in on kitchen nookie. She'd learned after the first time. Also that Jace had a really great back.

"Hey, Katie Faith, it's Aimee."

Her friend whipped the door open. "I keep telling you to come on in. You're not a guest who has to knock."

"And I told you that since the last time I came in before knocking I can never see a can of whipped cream again without snickering."

Katie Faith waggled her brows. "My husband is very creative. Come on through. We're in the living room."

She'd called over after Mac had left and gotten an earful before she said she'd be over in an hour and that Mac would also be coming by at some point.

Aimee took her hand, stopping Katie Faith in her tracks. "I'm so sorry about this. I know how hard it was before and I'm sorry you have to endure it again."

Katie Faith hugged her tight. "You don't have to apologize to me for this. This has nothing to do with you or even this campaign. This is all Scarlett and Dwayne."

In the living room, her mom waited, along with Nadine. Jace was on the phone out on the back deck, the lines of his back broadcasting anger.

She hoped Mac wasn't going to get hurt, or hurt Jace. She knew sometimes wolves would punch each other through a disagreement. So totally weird, in her opinion. But this was all his parents, so if anyone deserved a pop in the nose it was them, not Mac.

"He's really mad. To be honest with you I don't even care what Ronnie has to say. If I had sex with every single person living in the state it still wouldn't be any of Ronnie's business. Or Dwayne's business. But this has *Scarlett* written all over it. Enough about that. Come on. Eat dip. Momma brought it over."

"Oh, eat-my-feelings day, huh?" She insinuated herself between her mom and the food, helping herself, feeling much better now that she knew Katie Faith wasn't upset with her.

Aimee felt Mac's approach before there was a knock on the door.

"What's he doing here?" one of Jace's newer lieutenants asked.

"He's with me." Aimee got up and went to Mac to stand at his side. That's when she noted the blood on his clothes.

He didn't look as if most of it came from him though.

"He's here because he's a friend and I expect he's going to let us know how he dealt with a wayward wolf," Katie Faith said.

Mac tipped his chin at Katie Faith. Jace seemed to materialize out of thin air, so quiet was his approach.

"Why is it, Pembry, that your wolves have my wife's name on their lips again?" Jace's voice was little more than a growling snarl.

"Pembry seeks pardon for the words spoken by three of its pack members. They've all been disciplined by the Prime who made sure they understood their transgressions and would not be repeating them, or idle gossip, again. They have shamed my pack, and for that, they've been sent out for a thirty-day suspension."

Aimee made a mental note to ask what a suspension was. This werewolf stuff was so intricate.

"This isn't the first time, Mac," Jace said, features less furious, but still concerned.

"I know. I wasn't here the other times. But I am now. I'm working on it."

"Thing is, none of that is my problem. I've got plenty of my *own* over here in Dooley. But when this stuff happens, it *becomes* my problem and then I get cranky. And what is my problem in a major way is that my wife is unhappy. I don't like that. Not at all."

Mac looked to Aimee a moment. "I understand. Which is why my discipline was severe and immediate. Ronnie's already gone from town, along with Jay Twombley, who was the other numbskull with him down at the market. Don't expect to see either back."

"What about Darrell?"

Mac's mouth hardened. "He's hiding. He better hope he's better at it now than he was as a kid. I found him every time. I will this time too. And when I do, he'll be disciplined as well."

"And the source of this here little bit of gossip?" Nadine asked, and Katie Faith made a face.

"Momma, this is werewolf stuff. Hang on a second."

"Don't you tell me to hang on, child. I'm your mother and I have a right to know what is going on."

Jace gave a look to Mac, who nodded very slightly.

Aimee knew what was happening there. One of those "see what you'll have to look forward to soon enough" looks dudes gave one another.

To their credit, the men waited until Katie Faith soothed her mom enough to get back to speaking.

Jace and Mac moved away from everyone else to finish talking while Katie Faith shooed all the rest of the wolves from the room, along with mothers and best friends.

"It was said about me. I don't know why it has to be all hush-hush now," Katie Faith said. "It doesn't matter anyway. Who cares what Ronnie and Darrell think?"

"This is about way more than you. Not that you aren't totally awesome to make up rumors about, naturally. But this is flailing. It's like Dwayne has lost his mind and is panicking and throwing stuff out the window. Like in a cartoon chase. Scarlett did this to protect him in her own weird way. And it served whatever obsession she's got with you and Jace."

"She used to be nice to me! She's going to be your mother-in-law. Bummer," Katie Faith stage whispered.

Aimee flicked her ear. "That's Mac's momma. Stop." Not that Scarlett had some hidden soft and wonderful side. Or if she did, it didn't matter to Aimee. What mattered was getting things stabilized and she didn't want to hurt Mac to do it.

"You love him," Katie Faith said, and this time her whisper wasn't so loud. "Oh my goodness. I know, it's shocking. But it's too late. Once you love one of these goofy wolves, they won't go away."

Mac was easy to love. It was his family she struggled with, but that happened to other couples too.

"Can I squeal a little that we both love werewolves

and you'll be Patron of the other pack? It's sort of like we always planned." Katie Faith grinned like a loon.

Mac and Jace turned to take them in, both men looking a little wary.

"I like it that he's scared of me sometimes. Keeps him on his toes," Katie Faith murmured.

Aimee snickered.

After an hour or so, long after the two wolves had worked out whatever it was they'd been whispering about in the corner, Aimee wanted to get Mac home where she could clean him up, snuggle him and figure out what happened to him that morning after the call came in from her mom.

She grabbed his hand and tugged. "We're going now. I'll see y'all later."

"I'll walk out with you," TeeFaye said.

At the car, her mom hugged her tight and then, surprising Aimee, she hugged Mac too, holding his cheeks in her palms. "You're a good boy, Macrae. Do what you know is right."

His features softened and he hugged her once more. "Thank you, Mrs. Benton. I'm trying. I'll keep Aimee safe, I promise you that."

TeeFaye's smile was quick. "Oh, I know you will, boy. Because my friend Nadine is a whiz at throwing cans of fruit at a man's pecker if he gets out of line. Just remember that and we'll be okay." She winked.

"Uh," Mac managed, "okay then. Well. Say hello to Carl and send my apologies about the gossip."

"He went fishing with Avery today. Ha. They think we don't know they're just hanging out in the fishing cabin talking sports and drinking beer. It kept them both out of the fray, so that was good. You two head on home. I love you," she added to Aimee, stepping back and rapping the top of the car twice for good luck.

"Are you all right?" she asked as he drove away.

"Been a long day, baby. A very long day."

She took his hand, careful of the knuckles, which were healing but still looked pretty bad. "Want to tell me about it?"

"Do you mind a drive?"

"Nope, that sounds nice. As long as you're okay."

"I broke Ronnie's nose," he said quietly. "On purpose because, damn it, he won't fucking listen any other way. Beat him severely enough that he couldn't stand at the end. And then I sent him away. I banished him."

Aimee wanted to soothe and take away his upset. But he needed to get it out, work it through. She could tell the way he spit the words out.

So she simply sat with him and let him unburden himself.

"Thing is? It had to be done and I don't feel guilty about it. He deserved it for fucking up over and over and making me have to fix yet one more thing. I have enough on my plate and that asshole pulls me away from something important, like rare time with my woman, to instruct him on how to act. Pack discipline has been not only lax, but it also ends up with wolves acting out. They need a Patron. They need to be guided. My dad has barely paid them any mind and when he does, it's to allow this kind of shit. This won't be the last time I have to mete out discipline. If some of them fear me and that's what keeps them in line, so be it. Idiots."

She liked that he didn't make excuses for the violence he had to use. Trusted that she understood the differences in his world and accepted them. And in doing so she accepted him.

And one thing Aimee knew for sure was that Mac needed to know who accepted him. Who found him worthy and good, even the dark edges.

He pulled off onto a barely visible logging road that ended at an overlook. When he turned the car off, she unbuckled and turned herself to face him better, taking his hand again.

"I'd left about a dozen voice mails for my parents after leaving our place and finally my mother calls me back after I lay out exactly what I'm going to do to Ronnie and the others. She didn't deny anything. Says she and him are off on some last-minute trip away from town and the stresses of the campaign. Naturally they're staying *wherever strikes their fancy* so they can't give me any details yet. Tells me I have to wait to discipline anyone."

Her eyes widened at that. The nerve of that woman to cause this whole mess, run off and then tell the only responsible person he shouldn't act. Unbelievable.

He leaned forward to steal a quick kiss. "Thank you for reacting that way. I let her know how things were and hung up and had to discipline wolves who'd gotten that gossip from my mother in the first place. That's what gets me. She did all this! I have no fucking idea why. The rumors aren't even about you. How does she think this will turn out? It's so fucking senseless I'd punch something if my knuckles weren't sore already."

"Her energy is very chaotic. Normally she's a big character. She's got a lot to say, most of it negative. But her sense of self is usually pretty good. But since Katie Faith came back, and her ending up in the Dooley part of town and then turning up to be Jace's sweetie, something else is happening with her. I don't know what it is. But it's not always aimed at Katie Faith. Usually it's—I can't explain it well enough—but it's about Jace. Sort of. In that area. Anyway, I'm not even sure this gossip was about the election. If it was your dad doing it I'd think differently, but that's just what I'm picking up."

Mac blew out a long breath. "My uncle mentioned Josiah today. That back in the day when he was…when he left, my mom's name came up. But none of them knew exactly why."

"Hmm. Interesting. You guys have pretty much acted like Jace's dad never existed so I guess it never occurred to me that her issue might be with Jace's daddy instead of Jace or his grandpa. Though JJ Dooley could aggravate a saint."

"That was his punishment. To have his name never repeated again. To have his presence erased."

"Oh my God, did you just tell me some sort of state werewolf secret?"

He laughed and this time it reached his eyes. "I can't tell you much because I don't know much. Whatever Dooley did, whatever Josiah did to merit his punishment has been sealed. I can make some educated guesses, given Josiah's reputation and all. But I'm going to ask my mother, since hers is the name that keeps popping up."

"I'm sure that'll go over well."

He snorted. "She's not an easy woman. There's something happening that I'm not seeing or understanding. Hopefully, we can get through it. As for my dad? He's going to make me fight for every inch of the Patron seat."

Mac was going to have to challenge his own father.

What a terrible thing that must be to have to face. Sure, it was how packs worked, and even Jace'd had to bloody his grandfather to take over. But according to Katie Faith, it was more ceremonial than him actually harming his grandpa.

This sounded like Dwayne being a jerk.

"You should just say it all," Mac told her. "Honey, you'd lose at poker so badly. You have no ability to hide your reactions."

"I can if I need to. Usually. It's just, I hate that you're going to have to beat up your daddy to take over his job. And I hate that he's making you do it. And I hate that he keeps stringing Darrell along, making him think he could take over when everyone else knows that would never happen. It's mean. And I don't like it when people are mean to you."

"You defending my honor?" He brushed the pad of his thumb over her bottom lip.

"Someone needs to, may as well be me. I'm fearsome, don't you know? If I could challenge your daddy in your stead I would just so I could kick him in the balls."

"I've had entirely enough talk of ball kicking and can throwing at balls for one day, thank you. And thank you for being you."

"We're a team. Which works out for me because it means I rarely have to lift heavy stuff or deal with hard physical labor. But I know people. People who'd happily serve up some much needed justice to your parents. Usually I like people. Your parents and that dumbass brother of yours, I really don't."

"I wish you could feel the way about my family the way I feel about yours."

"Well, your cousins are nice to me. I like Everett and Huston just fine. And your aunt and uncle, though I don't know them awfully well, they've been very nice when I've interacted with them."

"I'm supposed to invite you around more often. I should have told you that. My aunt will kick my butt for not saying it sooner."

"You've been a little busy, it's okay. Right now it's just me and you. Let that be."

Overhead, though the clouds were out, the full moon hung, calling to his wolf.

But it was the understanding in the gaze of the woman next to him that brought him to his knees.

She leaned close then and he heard the gallop of her heart, scented the heat of her skin and the desire coming from between her thighs.

"You know what?" she murmured as she brushed her lips across his ear, combing his hair back.

"I knew a lot of stuff but all the blood in my body has settled in my cock. I'm at my dumbest just now."

He felt the change of her mouth, her smile as she continued to drop kisses over his ear and neck.

"I was thinking I've never actually had sex in a car before."

"Darlin', your daddy's the law," he managed to say around a pretty useless tongue.

She sat back to give him a look. "I heard stories about you back in the day." Her grin—*dear God, her grin*—sent a shiver through him.

"That so?"

She nodded as she went up on her knees and whipped her sweater off. "Males, be they fifteen or a hundred and fifty, think they're the only ones who talk about sex among themselves."

Mac sat suspended there, as always, utterly fascinated by her. *This* was what his wolf had imprinted on. The way she made every part of him perk up and pay attention. He never knew what to expect from her but when she inevitably surprised him, it had been the good kind of surprise.

The way she spoke and moved created its own sort of magic, a magic that seemed to always draw his own. There was no sound but the occasional ping of the cooling engine and the wind through the high treetops.

He paid attention to her skin and the way she held herself, assuring man and wolf she wasn't cold. On the contrary, she was rosy, a pretty blush on her chest and up her neck as she teased him.

"Girls you dated shared pertinent details that had us all swooning. Don't you notice how we all look at you when you're around?"

Silently, Mac eased himself over the seat to her side, sliding it back to give them both a little more space. A decision he was doubly glad for when she straddled his lap to face him, settling in over his cock with her heat.

He had to let out a slow breath but he couldn't erase all evidence of a little quaver at how insanely good it felt.

Her grin changed as the knowledge hit her. As she realized the power she held over him. Satisfaction settled in his bones.

He traced his fingers and palms up over her chest, across the curves and hollows of her collarbone until he grasped her slightly, the whole of his right hand wrapped around her throat to hold her still.

Her heart thundered, her skin heated and her pupils swallowed most of the color of her eyes.

"My weird little witch, when you're in a room I don't see anything but you." He pulled her in gently for a kiss, letting go of her neck to draw down the skin of her spine.

Her taste seemed to pour into him, fill him with sensation as she took over, leaving a series of slow kisses across his face.

"You make me feel that way. Like there's no one else for you in the world but me," she said, her lips against his.

"Certainly no one else as important to me," he told her as he popped the catch of her bra, releasing her breasts into his hands.

She arched into his touch, his name on her lips.

Around them, the night seemed to take a deep breath and then hold it. Anticipation hung as heavy as the moon. Something was coming that would change Diablo Lake and everyone in it.

"Do you feel that?" she asked him as she eased his shirt open, button by button.

Mac wanted to tease that he was feeling a lot of things, but he knew it wasn't the time.

He nodded. "Is it harder for you, do you think? Because you're empathic you get an extrahard dose of all the tension in town?" Mac worried about her in another way as he realized that must be true.

Aimee pressed a hand to her belly. "There's a special kind of magic between you and me," she said at last. "An old, elemental kind of magic."

She got to her knees as he helped her shimmy from her jeans and panties, leaving her naked and gleaming in the wintry moonlight.

Her words, the way she said them, pulled him in like an embrace. Drew him in tight to her.

Like armor.

"It's New Year's Eve. A time between old and new. Here we are, you and me with our chemistry swirling all around, our magics making my head spin. There's potential here." Aimee placed a kiss over his heart. "It's just... I want to pass from the old to the new out here under the moon with you. It'll help, as we face whatever's coming."

How could he refuse that when his entire being seemed to nod in agreement? He needed that reassurance, the talismanic magic of that coming together would be his shield to face what was to come.

She freed his cock as he pulled out a blanket he'd just tucked in his truck earlier that day because he liked to go deep into the middle of nowhere and run and he'd planned to ask her along that night.

He held her, slowing her down. "I want to take my time. I've got a beautiful naked witch on my lap just waiting for me to pleasure. Let me marvel over my good fortune a moment."

Which he'd intended to be stern about until she undulated, rolling her hips as she ground her pussy against him, slick, scalding heat surrounding his cock. Mac's eyes may have rolled up into the back of his head for a moment at that slap of sensation.

Her laughter brought his attention back as he went in close, hugging her tight.

"You're a temptation, Aimee."

"Thank goodness. Otherwise you'd have moved on by now and I like you too much for that."

"In case you haven't noticed, I've kind of moved into

your house. What makes you think I'd go anywhere but wherever you are?" He pinched one of her nipples to underline that.

She hummed, clearly liking it so he did it again and once more until he moved to the other one.

Mac teased, moving from nipple to nipple, drawing out her pleasure, guiding her along that line between pleasure and pain. She let him know what she liked, and definitely what she didn't.

Demanded more. Seduced him heart and soul. Gave herself as she took everything he gave.

They'd fogged the windows up, sealing them into their own world. He stretched a little, luxuriating in her weight in his lap.

She kissed across his neck, pulling his shirt away from as much skin as possible.

What a fucking thrill it was to have a woman like this touching him, worshipping him, giving him her whole self. There was nothing, no speech or guidebook, that could have prepared him for the entirety of what he felt right there with her.

As she'd said, they created magic, a mixing and marrying of hers and his, sewing them closer.

"You're so damned beautiful it hurts to breathe sometimes when I look at you," he told her, quite happy her response was to do that undulating thing again.

"Please fuck me already!" she cried and he pretended it was a chore to angle his cock with one hand while he guided her hip with the other.

"Fine." He thrust up and yanked her down at the same time.

"Yes! That's the way," she shouted and he laughed.

"You know I love you, right?" he asked her, teasing with short, shallow strokes.

Her smile went very satisfied and a little feline. His wolf stirred at the sight. Pleased.

Proud.

"Well. I'd certainly hoped you did, as I love you back and that would have been so awkward if you just wanted to be friends after we banged awhile. Then I'd have had to get really mad at you for going and making me fall for your navy SEAL romance-novel-cover good looks, the giant dingle and your talent at making me come."

He frowned, holding her from speeding his pace. "I was in the army."

"Really? Right now that's what your response is? You tell me you love me. Which is a good thing to say, I'll grant you that. Then I tell you I love you too and how you're all pretty to look at and have sexy times with and you get all pissy because I meant navy SEAL in a generic sense and you were in the army?"

He thrust deep and stilled, both of them gone silent but for an intake of breath. "Well, you put it that way and I do apologize."

"You can make it up to me by getting down to business. You know how I like it. I know how you like it. And it turns out, hard and fast is the answer to all those questions."

He had a beautiful woman fucking him and demanding more. Whatever he did to deserve this turn of good fortune, he'd be eternally grateful for.

"Brace your hands then," he told her.

She made a little sound as her pussy tightened and heated even more. Then she braced her palms on the roof of the truck.

What a picture she made, bathed in winter moonlight, her magic seeming to sparkle around her here and there. Her position brought her tits right to his face, a very clever choice on her part to put them there.

Teasing slowly, he nibbled and licked around each nipple, making sure each time he came back, the edge of his teeth was harder.

And each time she grew wetter and hotter, her inner muscles clamping around his cock to the place where he only held back from climax by sheer force of will because he wanted her to come first.

Her clit under the pads of his fingers was hard and slick as he touched her, circling in just the right way.

She held back too, a challenge in her eyes.

But he knew exactly how she loved to be touched and when he began that slow squeeze and release of her clit, she only lasted two more thrusts, climaxing so hard there was simply no way he could stop himself from following her.

He fucked her as deep as he dared, she took and gave herself right back, demanding. A warrior in every way, even if she didn't give herself the credit for it.

And the woman he loved.

She curled up against him and he covered her better with the blanket.

"Dingle?" he said at last and the ferocity of the happiness he made her feel brought a full-throated laugh from Aimee's lips.

Lips still swollen from his kisses.

Her heart swelled with love. *Right. On.* Who knew how awesome such a thing could feel when it was absolutely right?

"I can say the other words. Cock, dick, prick, penis,

rod, thunderstick, doodle, dingle, meat, jingle-jangle, Johnson, salami, all the good ones. I like to mix it up."

"Jingle-jangle?"

"I made that up, I think. I like it though. So I'll be using it in the future. Just so you know."

"Okay, thanks for the warning."

She needed to move and, uh, clean up her business because it'd be getting messier very soon in the position she was in.

Wiggling to the side—after he was a little grumpy to have her move, she loved the wolf part of him that loved to cuddle—she got herself back to rights as best she could.

"Happy New Year," she told him as she settled against his body once more.

He turned, kissing her senseless right as she was just getting all her damned motor skills back. So sneaky.

"Happy New Year. Let's go back home. Break out the champagne, have some snacks and hide from everyone in this town."

As he unlocked the back door and held it open for her, she also sensed how much her house and the magic there had welcomed his. More than that, it had stamped him in a sense. Claimed.

"I like that you call it home." Of course she'd noticed he'd moved in. Their coming together had been quick and intense, but despite that speed there was a deep intimacy and sense of comfort between them.

He followed her to their bedroom, undressing in that very shifter way—unashamed of nudity—and catching her attention for a few moments.

"This feels like home to me. You're a big part of that.

But this house gives me a sense of peace and safety. My wolf likes it. Likes the way you smell and the way our things carry a scent unique to just you and me."

She gulped, snapping out of it long enough to change into flannel pants and a long sleeved shirt. He kept her house cooler than she did before, but as he was a giant, gorgeous furnace, she made do without complaint.

He knew she used the movements, the space to get changed, to think over her reply.

And how did one reply to her perfect male saying such amazing things to her and about her?

There weren't words that could do it justice. So she settled on "Thank you. So, I guess I should tell you that you've got my magic all over you."

Naked, tawny and gorgeous, he prowled from the bedroom and out to the kitchen. Naturally, as he was the aforementioned naked, tawny and gorgeous, she followed him out.

"Like how is your magic all over me? Tell me how it works?" he asked as he grabbed the champagne from the fridge.

"I think my magic is a lot like your wolf. Part of who you are. A life force that is *of* me, energy I can manipulate and shape to my will. But also I'm part of it. I need to nourish and respect my magic or it could fail me. Grow weak. It happens sometimes." Aimee shuddered to imagine reaching out to connect with her magic and it not responding.

She grabbed some cheese and crackers and a few trays of appetizers she'd made earlier in the day before everything had gone to shit and ferried them to the big bed they so often spent their time in.

"So when I was upset and you touched my arm, you

obviously used your magic to calm me down. How did that work?"

He poured them both a glass and they toasted.

"It's more like my magic helped you clear your head long enough to think about it. So I didn't calm you as much as I helped you focus. That's the key to you."

After she said it, she realized how creepy he might find such a thing to hear.

But instead he smiled in that soft, boyish way that made her heart go all gooey and then want to punch his momma. Like he did not hear how special he was often enough.

She needed to always remember that. She held the key to his most vulnerable side and that was a responsibility.

"The key, huh?"

"You're a natural leader. I mean, obviously because you're Prime and soon to be Patron and those things don't happen to lazy wolves who only feel, or weak wolves who're afraid to own what they are. At one time even your daddy had the guts to look himself in the mirror and lead Pembry."

That was such a "Katie Faith" thing to do she stunned herself silent for long moments.

He wasn't offended though. Something like pride seemed to flow from him.

"Usually it's Katie Faith who blurts and speaks before she thinks. You've made me more like that. I'm sorry. I don't mean to insult your dad. I mean, not at this very moment anyway."

Mac rolled his eyes. "You didn't insult either one of us. You were telling me about your magic and the key to me."

She sent him a pretend-censorious look before going along. "You have a huge, passionate heart. The heart of a leader who does not expect anything less than total commitment from those under their command. But you're also a trained thinker. You're strategic. You see problems and immediately begin to break them down to figure out how to fix them. In a situation like the one you brought up, my magic helped you think because that's what you needed to do."

The wonder on his face was a gift. So rarely could she really talk about her magic like this. Other witches understood, as they had their own gifts but it was old hat after a while. And when she dated a human, she didn't discuss it at all.

Opening up this part of herself to him mattered to her. Like it mattered that he wanted to know. Wanted to understand her.

"That's pretty cool. So if someone else needed to feel more, your magic might work differently on them?"

Aimee nodded. "The better I know someone, the more intuitive my magic is. It's why I chose this sort of work originally. It gives me the opportunity to develop years-long relationships with the people I see. My empathic ability is different with each person I encounter so that plays into it as well. Sometimes people just need a freak-out, you know?"

He paused, thinking about it. If anyone needed a little loss of control it was Mac. She doubted he even knew that.

"Do you think? What about my mom?"

"I'm fairly sure your mother gives in to her need to flip her shit on the regular. However, in general she's a very guarded individual. She holds herself close and, look, lots of people do." Aimee shrugged.

"Like she's hiding something?"

"I can't read minds," she reminded him.

"I know you can't. And I know we're stepping over the line where we don't talk about my family and the election. But I can't imagine how we can continue to pretend to ignore the problem. And it appears the biggest problem is my dad and mom and I'm trying hard to figure out what the fuck to do. So any help would be appreciated."

"As we talked about earlier before you sullied me in your truck, Scarlett Pembry is an angry person." Maybe if she used *Scarlett* instead of *your mom* it would soften the blow a little. "She's fearful, which is sometimes an indicator of harboring secrets. Sometimes those secrets are things that have happened to that person. They've been victimized and then buried it for self-preservation or it was part of the abuse and they're silent out of fear, humiliation, pain, confusion, that sort of thing. And sometimes it's secrets about things someone has done or knows about that bring a great deal of anxiety."

"Which is she?"

Aimee sighed and ate some more. "She's the latter. She's done something, or someone close to her has, and she's terrified someone will find out." God, she really hoped none of those brothers of Mac's were actually Josiah's. That would be so weird and horrible for everyone.

"But I have to find out," Mac said. The sadness was clear in his tone.

Scarlett was a grumpy old bitch who'd made Aimee's best friend's life hell, but she was Mac's mom.

"I'm sorry. I don't want to hurt you. I could be wrong. I could be reading her wrong. It's not an exact science."

He gave her a look. "Aimee. Darlin', I love you for trying to make me feel better right now. But you're rarely wrong about people. I know that."

Except for that whole "dating a married man on and off for a few years" thing. That big, glaring mistake.

She should tell Mac about Bob.

After the election, or at the very least, after Mac dealt with his parents and the whole future of the pack, she'd tell him.

Yep, total hypocrite because now *she* had a secret. And like most people with secrets, she told herself it was for the best if she just kept quiet.

Chapter Nineteen

Aimee got up before Mac to make him a big breakfast. He'd been working himself to the point of dropping into bed, totally exhausted as he tried to rein in his parents who'd still been avoiding him.

What. Assholes.

It pissed her off to no end because it made him responsible for the mess Scarlett and Dwayne made but they'd still complain about whatever he did while they were gone.

How dare they order him not to do anything to the wolves who'd broken pack law? They put him in a place that no matter what he did he couldn't win.

He stumbled out of their bedroom about ten minutes later, drawn by the scent of freshly brewed coffee and biscuits in the oven.

Naturally, she stopped what she was doing to take in the sight of him.

"Morning. Long day today so I figured you might like more food than usual to start off right," she said as he pulled her to him for a kiss.

The anxiety and worry seemed to cling to his skin, even as his power dominated it.

"You nervous?" he asked.

That night was a town hall debate where she and Dwayne would take questions from the audience and the panel. She'd done all she could to prepare by that point. Spent a lot of time reading up on the basics of the town budget. Came up with some ideas as to how to make some improvements, save some money, spend it on the crumbling infrastructure like giant potholes on Diablo Lake Avenue and the sidewalk around the park with big cracks people kept tripping over.

"At least I'll know where to find my mom and dad tonight. I'm going to stake out city hall and have this out once and for all. Ducking me for three days. Bullshit."

She shoved him toward the table. "Get us both some coffee and I'll deal with everything else."

Huston came to the back door, knocking to be let in, along with Everett. Thank goodness she'd put on clothes when she got up, and made extra food. Some of Mac's wolves had begun to show up there at the house on a regular basis for advice or reassurance, so Aimee had learned to put on pants and a bra before doing anything that let Pembrys know they were home and ready to receive visitors.

"Huston and Everett are here," she called out. "I'm up to my elbows in sausage gravy so you need to answer it."

"Your momma raised you right," she told them when they dropped a heavenly smelling brown paper bag containing some sort of hot, doughy delight on the table.

"Why are you here?" Mac asked them and she swatted his adorable butt.

"Stop being grumpy," Aimee told him.

"We were about to have breakfast," he told her.

"I've noticed most of our meals here at home will

have an extra guest or two. There's plenty and now we have something sweet and warm for dessert."

"There's no such thing as dessert after breakfast."

Aimee made a face and looked around him to his cousins. "Please tell me you all weren't brought up so sad."

"No, ma'am. I'm a big proponent of dessert after every meal. Or even every meal being dessert."

"I like you." She pointed at Huston. "You got some sense. For a Pembry." She winked at Mac as she went back to her gravy. "G'wan now. You're Prime and they need you."

"We don't really. It just smelled good and we like to look at you." Huston kissed her cheek as he passed on his way to get a cup of coffee.

"See, if you make them feel at home, they'll take you up on it and make themselves at home. I keep telling you that," Mac said.

"You did not."

His adorable little pout nearly tipped into a smile. "Well. I *thought* about it. I was going to during breakfast this very morning."

Aimee snorted. "You're going to hell for lying, Macrae."

Everett laughed. "I'll have you know these are Nan's cinnamon-and-sugar doughnuts. She showed up about ten minutes ago to the house. Tossed us this bag and ordered us to share."

"She told us to make sure Aimee got at least two because the 'nasty-tasting junk' you gave her for her headaches seems to be working," Huston added.

Mac shoved past them all, opening the bag and shoving an entire doughnut in his mouth.

"I guess all the good ones are taken, huh?" she teased Huston.

They settled at the table and began to eat not too long after that. Aimee had a doughnut as a breakfast appetizer and was quite glad of that choice.

"These are amazing. I knew she could bake like nobody's business, but I had no idea she made doughnuts that God probably has at Sunday after-church mixers."

Mac snickered. "I'm going to tell her you said that."

"She already loves Aimee, that'll only raise her stature to Nan," Everett said.

Mac nodded. "Yeah, it would." He turned back to her. "She only makes these for birthdays."

"And *only* if she likes you at the time your birthday comes around. Sometimes you'll just get cake, even if your favorite is doughnuts and she made them for you before. She holds a grudge," Huston said. "Apparently she likes your girlfriend."

"Right now," Mac said.

"Right now is all we're assured in the world," Aimee said as she peppered her gravy.

"She's steely like that too. Probably why you rate doughnuts for no special reason of any sort and definitely *not* to say *hey, good luck debating against my son tonight*." Everett added lots of emphasis so they got that it probably was, indeed saying that very thing.

Mac just stared at Everett, shaking his head. "You need to work on your subtlety."

Aimee couldn't hold back her laughter. "Imagine what the world will be like when we get her together with TeeFaye and Nadine, huh?"

"I'm not sure space and time could handle the three

of them in one place. Maybe we shouldn't cross the streams on that," Mac said.

"As long as it's not aimed at you, it could be fun to watch."

She eyed Everett carefully. "I bet."

They finished breakfast up and when Everett and Huston told Aimee to go on and get to work and that they'd clean up after breakfast, Mac knew they had some official business to relate and didn't want to do it in front of an outsider.

She didn't need the added stress of whatever it was they were going to tell him anyway.

"Okay, she's in the shower. Spill." Mac tipped his chin at Huston.

"Sam called Nan and told her he wants to talk to you about something privately."

Mac's youngest brother, Samuel, had a checkered past and had only just gotten out of jail the year before. But for the first time since Mac had left home, Sam was truly trying to change his life.

He worked in the freight warehouse the Pembry family owned and by all accounts, showed up on time, worked hard, was respectful and had a good attitude.

They weren't exactly close; in fact he'd only seen his brother twice in the months that he'd been back home. But he'd been cheering his brother on in this effort to turn his life around, including buying him the clothes he worked in, which his brother had been repaying slowly but regularly.

"Why Nan and why didn't *she* just call me herself instead of sending you two over here with doughnuts?"

That old woman was up to something. Multiple some-
things.

"Yeah, well if you want to know that, I'll let *you* do
the asking. Because I like having her make doughnuts
for *my* birthday," Everett said with a shrug. "Call her
to set up a meet with him. This clandestine crap means
he's got some dirt he wants to make sure your dad and
brother don't know he's telling you."

Mac knew she had bigger and more complicated
plans for whatever she was up to, but he also knew she
was smart and a well-respected elder who had his best
interests, and the best interests of the pack, at heart.

And though he had reluctance at letting his grandmother act like she was making some sort of secret spy
drop, he'd do what she and Sammy asked because it was
most likely important, as Everett had just pointed out.

Once Aimee got out the door to work, he showered,
got dressed and then called his grandmother, who told
him to get his butt over to her house within the hour
because it was already after nine in the morning, and
why wasn't he at work anyway?

He drove out to his grandparents' place. It sat out at the
edge of the forest, up on a rise. A den his grandfather
felt could be defended and that served as the heart of the
pack. Pembry wolves were encouraged to spend time
there. They hosted many seasonal events—bonfires in
the autumn, summer picnics. The land all around the
house meant an abundance of hunting both two and
four legged, as well as plenty of fish to be caught in the
nearby stream or at the far edge of the lake.

Growing up, Mac and the other kids in the pack had
slept in the giant bunkhouse that still stood to this day.

Mainly it was older wolves now who spent the night out there on a regular basis. His grandfather had died and when Dwayne had won the challenge to be Patron, he'd chosen to live in town, shifting the social heart of the pack along with him.

Except wolves didn't really hang out in his parents' large yard or in the house unless it was a special pack event. Sure, Darrell and his buddies did, mainly to mooch food off their mother. Mac found himself taking runs as his wolf on his aunt and uncle's land far more often than his parents'.

There needed to be a reestablishment of the heart of the Pembry pack. Be it here once more, or in town. Their wolves needed that camaraderie and connection. Needed a place to come and go, just to be around one another in whichever form they chose. They'd let go of some of the important rituals to keep them close.

And it showed.

With that niggling the back of his mind, he paused to breathe in the crisp air, full of home and family.

His grandfather had been dead for just over thirty years and the scent of his magic still permeated the air. It made Mac relax a little every single time he came out here.

Rebecca Pembry opened her front door and he marveled that her hair was perfectly done. Her lipstick matched the flowers on the flirty scarf tied jauntily— and perched perfectly—on her shoulders.

He hugged her once he climbed up to her. "Morning, Nan. What are you up to?"

She patted her hair and then waited a few beats.

"Oh! New hair. I like it. Suits you." He had no idea what exactly she'd done to change it, but "new hair" would encompass a lot of things and he'd complimented her like he was supposed to and they could get down to business.

"Thank you, honey. Come on through to the kitchen. I was just making a pot of coffee. Your brother is here already."

He followed her down the hall to the back of the house and the kitchen that took up half the entire first floor, including a huge table that could easily seat at least ten.

Sam stood when Mac entered, his eyes going down to Mac's toes. Immediately submissive.

That out of the way, Mac clapped his brother's shoulder and then pulled him into a hug. His grandmother nodded her approval behind Sam's back.

"Sorry to bring you all the way out here but I had the morning off and I wanted to talk to you," Sam said.

"And you didn't want to risk being seen by someone who'd tell Mom and Dad? Or Darrell? Something like that?" Mac asked, nodding his thanks at the cup of coffee Nan placed near his right hand.

More doughnuts appeared on a plate and the brothers shared a brief, gleeful look before taking one.

"Your girlfriend is a nice person." Sam stirred sugar into his cup. "When I got out of jail, she came by my place to make sure I was okay. Heck, even before that when I didn't much care about being a better person she was nice to me. She *believed* me when I told her I wanted to get my act together. Lots of people, hell most people, don't believe me. And I know why because I said it before and screwed up."

Mac listened, knowing his brother had to get this all off his chest and a big part of being a brother, and a Prime or Patron, was listening to your brothers' troubles.

"Dad and Darrell hired a private investigator to find dirt on Aimee and I think they found something. I overheard Darrell talking to Dad yesterday. It sounded like they were going to toss it at her tonight. I've been trying to figure out how to tell you or even if I should, but in the end, you're Prime and she's too kind to get whatever it is thrown at her without any warning."

His dad knew he and Aimee were together. His mother had been encouraging it! But now they were going to do something that would hurt her, and for what? It hurt that his father had gone to Darrell—a wolf his father knew Mac had been looking for to punish. It hurt that his dad was willing to do something so underhanded it would possibly break up his relationship with Aimee.

Worse, whatever it was—and what could it be really? Aimee was a nice person—wouldn't be that bad and the revelation of whatever it was would make his dad look abusive. He'd end up getting tossed out of office anyway and leave a huge, steaming mess in the process.

His grandmother spoke. "That girl of yours'll bring some magic and class along with her into this pack when you two finally get yourselves married." She gave him a raised brow. "I mean, Macrae, really. You're living with her in her house and you're not married. What if she gets pregnant? What then?"

"Nan, I'm going as fast as I can without scaring her. It'll happen eventually."

She waved a lily-of-the-valley-scented hand. Her nails were done up a glossy pale pink that managed to survive runs as her wolf. He had no idea why they could other than that she wanted it.

"She goes out of her way for people and I won't have

your father and his wife trying to hurt that child. And you should know her parents most assuredly won't take kindly to whatever dirt they dig up on her being tossed out in public."

"Why don't you like our mom?" he asked Nan.

"Your mother and I have our own business that will stay private. No need to perpetuate this another damned generation. And it's just a small part of what's happening. This election business has driven your father over the edge at last. And she's got her own mess that complicates everything."

As much as he wanted to challenge her and make her tell him the truth, he knew once she said her piece she wasn't going to say more on it unless and until she wanted to.

"Just tell me if it has anything to do with Josiah Dooley."

The flattening of her mouth gave him her answer.

"Did they have an affair?"

Her look of incredulity made Mac feel a tiny bit better at least. "No. Now, I'm not talking about this any further. What are you going to do about your daddy and that brother of yours trying to hurt our witch?"

"Our?" he asked his grandmother.

"Of course our. Macrae!" She thunked him in the head. "Are you listening to me? Aimee is a witch. We all knew that. She's got more power than most in this town gave her credit for until recently."

The defense rose to his lips quickly. "It takes a strong person to do so quietly. Easy enough to yell out about whatever you've done and want credit for. Aimee does what she does because that's part of her gift and why she's so powerful. She's driven to heal and soothe and help because that's part of who she is right down to her toes." Mac couldn't stop a smile at that.

"And when you and she imprinted and began to grow those roots of relationship, her magic began to settle into the heart of this pack. Especially the part of the pack that is the most closely tied to you. I'm told Katie Faith is much the same with the Dooleys. You're an alpha, a leader and you'll be Patron. That means she's got that in her too. She's part of our future. A stronger future where the pack is led with discipline instead of petty revenge or greed. She already ministers to people in town like a Patron should. Like your momma never has. Your Aimee has tamed my brother, Jeph, for goodness' sake. She delivers food and clothing and medicine, hell even for my headaches. I love your daddy, but he's selfish and he's made a mess here. You're going to have to undo it and I know you'll have to shed some blood. Don't hesitate or you'll lose the pack and maybe her too."

Mac looked across to his brother. "Okay then, Sammy. Tell me everything you know and let's see if we can't put a stop to this before it hurts her."

Chapter Twenty

Katie Faith stepped back to look over Aimee's shoulder into the mirror so she could check out the outfit she'd just helped zip up.

"Huh. Do I look mayoral?" she asked Katie Faith. Aimee had chosen a navy blue dress with some white piping along the edges of the seams. Classic but with a little flair.

Her hair she'd just had trimmed a few days prior so it gleamed, lying perfectly around her face. Aimee felt like she maybe exuded some solid steadfast energy.

"You look pretty and competent, which is always nice. Nothing too tight or loose. Your knockers aren't out. Cute shoes but if anyone messes with you, whip one off and start toward them like my momma does," Katie Faith advised.

Aimee snickered at the thought of doing that to Dwayne. "I'm going to have dreams about that. What fun I'd have."

"Have you heard from Mac?"

"Nothing since that text this afternoon. He went off on some errand with Huston and Everett I think. They were all here when I left for work this morning."

"Something pack related, most likely."

For the first time ever, Aimee wasn't sure what to share with Katie Faith. She wanted to talk about some of this pack stuff, but in a way, Katie Faith wasn't so much the enemy, but her pack was at odds with Mac's and Aimee didn't want to betray either one of them.

She settled on "Probably."

"I can't believe they've been avoiding him this whole time. How's he supposed to run Pembry if the Patron couple aren't even around and won't say where they are? I mean, tacky. So tacky," Katie Faith said.

"He's got to come back tonight so Mac will be able to connect then." And the Pembry wolves had already begun to shift their fidelity to Mac. Every time they were in town together, she felt it, that tug at the power Mac carried as Prime. Each wolf that showed up at their back door needing a hug or a pep talk, everyone who looked to Mac instead of Dwayne or Scarlett, had added power to Mac's.

Even just in the few days the Patrons had been gone, the weight had clearly shifted to Mac and she wondered how Dwayne would take it. Worse, how Darrell would take it because he was still living in a dream world even though his father knew what was coming and was about to toss him out an airlock without warning.

If Darrell hadn't been such a turd, she'd feel sorry for him. But since he'd been on the run, hiding from whatever punishment Mac was going to administer, she wasn't going to let herself feel bad.

"I'll drive you over. Your mom and mine will meet us there with the dads and most of the rest of the Consort. You're going to do amazing. You look very leadery and cute and you're so smart Dwayne doesn't have a chance. He's just ego and hairspray."

"I'm going to keep that in mind every time I look at him tonight." That'd be the trick to keeping him out of her head in a negative way.

"Let's get moving then. Grab your coat. Just because a hot-blooded shifter keeps your bed warm doesn't mean it's not cold outside."

Aimee rolled her eyes at Katie Faith. "Okay, Mom. I think I got it."

"Don't get an attitude with me, young lady," Katie Faith teased back as they headed out. "Are you okay that he's not here? In your place I might be panicking. Then again, in your place I'd have me, so then I'd stop because duh."

"I wouldn't have chosen this even six months ago. I'd have been nervous then too. But at this point I feel like *I got this*. He said he'd be back for the town hall and so he will but I admit it might make me *more* nervous if he was with me at every moment. Tonight he's still Pembry."

Katie Faith ended up having to park way down the street. She offered to let Aimee out in front of city hall, but she preferred to go in with her friend at her side so they walked together, raising a hand in greeting here and there as they went.

"Sure he's Pembry. Like I'm Dooley. But he's about you. You're the best person for the job, even if it is against his dad. He's a wolf, but he's not blindly supporting Dwayne. Jace says he's got a good head on his shoulders."

"He was horrified by those rumors, you know." Gutted that his damned parents had put him in that position and then ran off.

They didn't deserve to be Patrons of the pack. Worthless as a tit on a boar, as her grandpa used to say.

"We've all got those people in our family. Granted, there are a lot more on the Pembry front porch just now. But none of us can say a whole lot on that." Katie Faith snickered.

As they entered the city council chambers, Aimee couldn't help but smile when she noted how packed it already was.

Though she was leading in the polls—which was to say the forty or so people asked in a call-in poll they'd conducted two days before—she really wanted the people in Diablo Lake to realize the town and the health of the magic protecting them all was something everyone was responsible for and a part of.

Wanted neighbors talking about what was best for everyone, not just their family or their group, be they witches or shifters. And that's what had happened, despite the trouble she knew Scarlett kept trying to cause.

No matter, because this was about Diablo Lake and it felt like a majority of her citizens were paying attention for the right reasons.

The steady hum of conversation was laced with some raised voices here and there, a little tension, but so far it seemed to just be neighbors chatting and discussing things without getting too heated.

One of the council staff saw her and waved her back to be fitted with her microphone so Katie Faith hugged her tight and said she'd be right there in the front row to cheer her on.

"Where's Mayor Dumbass?" Sherry, Dwayne's assistant, asked quietly. "He's been completely out of contact for days."

Surprised and totally delighted enough to relax a little, Aimee laughed. "I figured you'd know. I'd tell you to ask Mac, but he's not here either. I say if he doesn't show up I automatically win by default and I'll take office tomorrow."

Sherry gave her a keen look and then laughed. "I like you, girl. We're going to work well together once you take over. Because whether he shows up or not, he's not going to win. His time is over in a lot of ways."

But on that very mysterious note, Mayor Dumbass—and she needed to stop thinking that because she'd end up using it to his face and it'd be bad—came in through to the antechamber where they'd been putting on Aimee's microphone and testing the sound system.

At her side, Sherry made a sound that hit Aimee right as she got a snootful of Dwayne's expression and his energy.

"That pissant is up to something. Watch your back," Sherry whispered before she headed over to her boss.

Her heart raced as worry began to ease back into her belly. The energy he bled off was mean and dark. Darrell strolled in, making things even worse.

Her mom came through the doors and upon catching sight of her, rushed over with a smile.

"You look so pretty. I do love that dress so much." She enfolded Aimee into a fierce hug. "What's wrong?"

Aimee shook it off. Whatever he had up his sleeve, she'd deal with it. Wasn't much like she could stop it. The man looked bound and determined to cause a ruckus of some sort.

"Did he say something to you? Because I have had *more* than enough bullshit from that man. I will take him out." As she said it, she turned to Dwayne who'd just finished up.

"Lordamighty, Momma. What are you thinking?" Aimee stepped between them, breaking the eye contact.

And when she did, the land at her feet, the magic that lived in and fed Diablo Lake responded like a shield, snapping around her and deflecting Dwayne's energy.

Cool!

Her mom's eyes went wide. "Did you just do that?"

Aimee mouthed, "I think so!"

"You won't be so high and mighty after tonight," Darrell said under his breath as he escorted Dwayne out.

"Aren't you still on the run from your punishment? I'll let Mac know you've popped out from under that rock you've been hiding, shall I?" she called out, not feeling very professional.

Still, since she'd actually wanted to say, "Bitch, I'm motherfucking high and mighty because you're a fucking tool," she felt she'd done the better of the two options.

No matter how appealing the idea of knocking Dwayne Pembry and his son on their asses was.

"He needs to take it down a notch or I will be coming for him. This has gone on entirely too long and I am over it, as you kids say," her mother told her. "That man was part of rumors about Katie Faith years back and he's at it again, using his wife to do his dirty work." She shook her head, disgusted. "So if he makes it his goal in life to mess with you that way, I will make it my goal in life to make him sorry for it. That's my job as your mother and I won't hear anything else about it."

Her mom was about a million times scarier than

her dad but a lot of people didn't know that until they crossed her and it was too late.

"I get it. And I appreciate the support. Let's just get this done, okay? Without fuss if possible. The election is next week. We can make it if we don't let those jerks get under our skin."

Her mother's harrumph of annoyance told Aimee she'd gotten all she was going to by that point.

She walked out, her mom at her side, and realized the room had filled up even more.

Darrell had disappeared but Scarlett sat in the front row with Samuel, who smiled at Aimee and waved.

She knew a lot of people in town didn't trust Sam Pembry, but despite his mistakes—and he'd made a lot—Aimee really believed he was trying to change. And if you can't get support when you're trying to do the right thing, doing the right thing might get so difficult people quit and go back to the easy path of making bad choices.

He wasn't the sum of the dumb crap he'd been up to since he was a teenager. Not at twenty-five. He had plenty of life in him, plenty of time to do better and that's what she'd told him. And then wanted to cry because she could tell not a lot of people believed in him and his promises of reform. She understood that too. And gently reminded him that his best revenge was to make good choices and that eventually the right people would trust him again.

She really hoped that was true.

Mac wasn't anywhere to be found, which made her frown a little. But her parents were there, with Katie Faith, Jace, a bunch of her wolves and Nadine and Avery. Witches and their magic had taken up chairs and lean space against the walls, their magic coursing through the room.

She drew strength from that. Her people there to support her at an anxious and important time.

Right as they finished up the introductions and launched into the first question, Darrell came in with a woman she knew wasn't from Diablo Lake. Then Mac barreled in after them and a tense interchange took place at the back of the room.

But she kept answering, hoping it was nothing, but knowing it was something terrible. The energy of it seemed to creep ever closer to the stage and when Aimee finished and turned to Dwayne, he was still smirking at her with a mean light in his eyes.

"Before I answer your question," Dwayne started, "I have something the folks in this town should know about my opponent." He snapped his fingers, interrupting Darrell and Mac's argument. "Boy, bring her up here and introduce her to the folks of Diablo Lake."

The city council members and the moderator all started arguing, yelling that this was irregular and not in the rules but Dwayne ignored them as the woman finally approached the dais and turned a look at Aimee so full of hatred she realized right then who the stranger was.

"Aimee Benton had an affair with this woman's husband for three years," Darrell said into the mic he'd grabbed.

"You whore!" someone sounding an awful lot like one of Darrell's friends yelled out.

The slap of it stunned her for long moments as everything swirled around her. Naked humiliation washed over her. Her *parents* were there! Miz Rose. Nadine and Avery. And Mac. Oh dear God, what would he think?

Despite the horror of the situation, Aimee, as she looked back toward Bob's wife, nearly drowned in the maelstrom of anxiety and upset rushing from her. The woman was on the very edge of losing her sanity and looking for something, *anything* to blame for it.

Aimee made a convenient target and no one who'd brought her there had even given a thought to what it would be like for Bob's wife. Only how it would hurt Aimee.

The carelessness of it sent rage through her like nothing else in the campaign had done thus far and had her rushing down the steps toward the other woman, her magic seeking to soothe and calm. After this business was concluded though, she'd do everything she could to be sure Dwayne Pembry never held office again.

She let her magic trickle out slowly, siphoning out the anxiety, letting in the calm soothing energy in its place. Holding a hand, palm out, she said softly, gently, "I know you must be upset and feeling betrayed and confused. Would you like to sit down? You're looking a little pale."

"I don't want anything from you people!"

In a regular town this sort of public display would be disturbing, but to an outsider the sight of shoving and posturing that the shifters got into and the magic that'd heated and grown sharp and barbed around the witches had been a nearly physical thing.

Her confusion seeped from her pores and broke Aimee's heart.

Behind her there was a scuffle until Dwayne stood

at her side, crowing about her scandals and how it made her unfit to be mayor.

That was the final straw.

Aimee spun to face him. "This woman has been horribly used already by her husband. And you and your son go and victimize her all over again. Just more men using her up to suit your motives. And for what? A job you sucked at and barely seemed to want until I showed interest."

He pointed at her. "You're a damned whore just like your friend and you think you can come in with your holier-than-thou attitude while you open your legs to married men? You think you can take my job and my son when you're not worthy of either. You need to be knocked down a few pegs."

Before she could do anything, it was Mac's fist that shot out, popping his father smack in the jaw, sending him stumbling back several feet as people began to push and shove. There was yelling and punching and all that shifter nonsense. Blood already hung in the air, the greedy darkness of her power rose to echo it.

"Knock it off this instant!" Miz Rose waded in and got knocked aside in the scuffle.

Everything went silent for a moment until the gasps started at the sight of a little old woman getting sent reeling by a bunch of giant shifters who'd become a knot of fists and snarling.

Witches, determined to protect Miz Rose, waded into the fray to grab for her before she really got hurt.

Her dad had gone into cop mode and was shouting orders and using the force of his personal magic to push groups of shifters back, away from the stage.

God only knew where her mother was, but Dwayne

better be hoping someone had gotten her out of there and out of striking distance until she cooled down.

At the double doors leading to the front walk, Jace hauled his wolves outside, though Aimee didn't fail to notice the elbow he shot to Darrell's head as he got close enough.

The utter chaos and violence of it was enough to snap her out of it. She turned and calmly but firmly took Bob's wife's elbow before steering her out of the main room. The other woman was stunned enough to let it happen, but the tumult of emotions still churned around her like a storm.

Aimee paused once they'd gotten to the back-hallway waiting room leading to the city administrative offices. She kept her voice as calm as possible. "I'm sorry. I know what you think. But you're wrong. I had no idea he was married until long after I'd stopped seeing him. If I'd have known I never would have gone near him."

"Why did you apologize then?"

"Because you're a person and I'm a person too. I'm so sorry he betrayed you and I'm even sorrier you got dragged into something like this. *You* did nothing wrong."

Bob's wife sighed out on a sob. "They, the father and son, came to my house and told me, *in front of my kids*. There are pictures of him with other women. He told me you were one of them and they'd bring me to you to confront you."

Oh, those assholes were going down. She'd find a spell to make Dwayne's left nut swell up to the size of a softball and turn orange. Yeah. That would do it. He could suffer while he thought about how he had nothing left because he was such a spectacular dick he'd brought it all on himself.

"I can't speak for Darrell and Dwayne. They're also totally in the wrong here. But I didn't know and maybe none of those other women did either."

Katie Faith popped in, watching Bob's wife warily. "I'm sorry you were used this way, ma'am, but Aimee did not know he was married. He's a pig. I'm sorry about that too. The guy who brought you here? He cheated on me and stood me up at the altar, so I know from jerks, I tell you. But I also know the blame for this falls on your husband's head, not hers. He has an apartment in the city. Did you know that?"

"Katie Faith!" Aimee exclaimed. "Not the time for that."

"I knew it! He told me that apartment was something he and some of the people at his work paid for so if they needed a temporary shelter space for a client, they used it." Her sobs turned into wails.

Seriously, how on earth did she miss what a spectacular garbage can Bob was?

Miz Rose entered, heading over, her gaze assessing Aimee's emotional state first and then she turned her attention to Bob's wife.

She pointed and said something under her breath and fortunately, the chair was close enough for them to drop Bob's wife into, propping her so she wouldn't fall off. Given the strength of Miz Rose's knock-'em-out spell, Bob's wife would be out awhile.

"I honestly don't know why you won't tell me that spell," Aimee said. She'd been after it for years, but Miz Rose had told her she wasn't ready for it.

"I think it might be time to share it with you. Not this

moment though. Right now you need to tell me just what in the hell is going on here," Miz Rose asked calmly.

Aimee told her, red faced and humiliated.

But by the end, Miz Rose shook her head, clucking her tongue. "How could they do this to you? They've just turned the town upside down, torn apart families. Quite possibly their own. Scarlett looks hopping mad *at* Dwayne so I don't think she knew about this stunt."

"That's the least of the problems with this," Katie Faith said. "Dwayne and Darrell violated the town rules. They sure as heck didn't get permission to bring an outsider to town. She doesn't know what we are, but she knows we're not normal humans. Tomorrow she'll have started to piece it all together and then what?"

Miz Rose nodded. "I'll be making the charge on behalf of the Consort shortly. He's unfit to hold office one more day and he's most certainly unfit to hold governance over a pack of werewolves when he has no discipline at all. The magic in this town doesn't much want to succor and nurture Dwayne Pembry. That could easily bleed down to the rest of the wolves in the pack and then what?"

"I feel kind of bad for the rest of the Pembrys though," Aimee said. "Aside from a few, they're all pretty nice." And she most definitely felt bad for Mac, who'd either have to fall under his father's rule after this terrible breach of the law, or challenge him immediately.

Neither thing would be easy for him.

"What if Mac doesn't love me anymore?" she asked quietly.

"Mac punched his father in the face when he called you a whore. He still loves you. And he'll know you well enough to talk to you before making any judgments."

Katie Faith frowned before hugging her tight. "Things are going to get harder before they get easier on that, though. Jace says all sorts of pack law stuff is about to happen as well. And in the end, if Mac is somehow so stupid and selfish he doesn't love you, well, we'll have to hate him forever then like his dumb brother Darrell."

Nadine and TeeFaye barreled in and held up at the sight of the unconscious woman in the chair and the rest either crying or comforting the crier.

Her mother pulled her into a very tight hug. "We know the truth. I already told your dad about this so he knew as well. Even if the truth had been that you slept with a married man for years I'd still love you even as I kicked your butt for making bad choices. Luckily for us both you did the right thing."

Aimee took a deep breath, letting these women make her feel better, and once she got herself centered again, she looked around them at the chair.

"What are we going to do about her?" she asked, tipping her chin toward the still unconscious Bob's wife. "And we need a name because I can't keep calling her Bob's wife in my head."

"She didn't know." Jace caught up to Mac as they stood on the grassy patch in front of city hall. "Did you? Were you part of this?"

Mac turned to Jace, wanting so much to punch someone else he could taste how good it would be to watch Dooley's head snap back as blood spurted from his nose.

"You think I'd do that to her? Or to that sad woman they dragged into town? I found out this morning that he'd hired a private detective and that they'd dug something up on Aimee. I've been out all day trying to track them down and stop whatever it was they'd planned."

Her face… He'd watched her composure slide and then crumble. Knew she'd felt the blow his father and brother had so calculatedly tossed at her. Knew too, that no matter the truth of it, he'd love Aimee Benton until the day he died.

Because her instinct was to help the woman who'd been tossed into the situation without any warning. That was the heart of his woman. Kindness. Compassion. Not malice.

Jace cleared his throat. "Okay. That's what I figured, but I wanted to be sure. She's got a tender heart, but I expect you know that and will go out of your way to reassure her that you still love her."

Mac sighed. "I got this. Thanks though."

Jace nodded and melted away, off to deal with his own pack problems.

His uncle approached with Huston at his side. "We'll be meeting at my parents' place. Your Nan wants it that way," he added before Mac could ask.

Better out there than in town. Better away from his father's house. Because he planned to strip all the power from Dwayne Pembry and take it, along with the rest of the pack, for himself, and he wanted it done on ground that celebrated all Pembrys, not just a few.

"Okay. He knows that?" Mac asked, meaning his father.

"Your grandmother told him herself. Mac—" his uncle lowered his voice "—you know the witches are going to file an official complaint. Ray Ruiz said to expect one from the cats too."

Mac was going to have to take over the pack and

discipline his father and brother and it would be painful and something he'd never be able to take back, and he needed to do it pretty soon.

"I need to find Aimee first. Then I'll meet you out there."

"No more being on your own, Mac," Huston said. "You're going to be Patron, you need security. That's the way things go. We'll wait for you right here and drive over together. Tell Aimee I said hey and to not sweat the small stuff. We know her heart and I hope she finds it in her to forgive the Pembry wolves for this mess."

Of course his cousin wouldn't turn on Aimee. But hearing it for sure made Mac straighten his spine and head out in search of his woman.

Chapter Twenty-One

He found her in an intense discussion with Miz Rose and a bunch of elder magic users. Bob's wife, Nancy he'd learned her name was, lay sprawled in a chair but someone had tucked a coat around her and she was breathing, so he'd just leave that be.

Her gaze found his and he saw it, the fear, and it broke his heart a little. Instead, he smiled. "So about my family, huh?"

"I didn't know. I swear to you," she said, coming toward him.

He pulled her to his body, hugging her long enough to assure man and wolf that she was all right. That *they* were all right.

"I love a weirdo witch who's a badass but not malicious about it. That's what matters to me. I'm sorry I couldn't stop it. I found out just hours ago and I've been trying to track my dad down ever since. I didn't know about it before today, I swear to you. I wouldn't have allowed it."

"Never even occurred to me to think you were part of this mess." She rested her forehead on his chest for a moment.

"Okay, so we got an unconscious human who was

brought here without sanction," Miz Rose said, moving Aimee to the side to poke the spot her head had been.

"Yes, ma'am, I know and I apologize on behalf of the Pembry pack."

Her face went very serious then. "You know we have to file an official complaint. Your father and brother have broken our most important law. I'm going to have to use magic on this woman's memories. But her children know about the cheating so we can't take that away. That's a lot of messing around in her head. We have rules too and you make us bend them to protect everyone else in town. I don't like having my back up against the wall like this. Especially because your daddy and brother made this very big mess to start with."

Damn, she was scary for such a sweet-looking old lady.

Fortunately for Mac, he was used to sweet-looking women being totally strong and in charge so he'd managed to get himself maneuvered to jump away if she decided to get mean.

Mac said, "You can fix it, right? Even if it takes a lot of magic, you can wipe her memories of this place enough to keep us all safe? And the kids? Do I need to get them?"

"Jeez-a-lou, no! Leave the children wherever they are. At least if they're with their daddy, he can't be out with one of his girlfriends. We've been working out just how to do this so we can accommodate as much of her actual memories as possible. A memory alteration will be better than a total wipe of what happened. She'll have to live knowing her husband is a total moron and her kids will too. I'll do what I can about making sure she doesn't remember Diablo Lake, but I can't erase

Dwayne and Darrell though I'll do my best to make it fuzzy. One of the cats will help us get her back to where her car is parked so we've got the heavy lifting and sneaking covered. It should work, because who in their right mind believes there are towns in the mountains where werewolves run city hall?"

TeeFaye jumped in, "Not for long. The city council will be voting tonight to use an emergency order to suspend him from office. The election will go as planned next week and my daughter will be mayor in this town. And if your parents know what's good for them they won't show their faces in town for a good long time," she said. "I like you, Mac. And I know my daughter loves you. But no one will be allowed to do this to my child without punishment. You can do it, or I can do it. But it'll be done. Are we clear?"

"Don't you think he's got it hard enough?" Aimee asked her mother as she came to stand at his side, taking his hand. "Imagine if you had to go and punish me and maybe even kick me out of town?"

TeeFaye was unrepentant. "I don't need to worry about his feelings. I'm worried about *you*. That's my job and I can't help it if his parents don't do theirs."

Mac wrapped an arm around Aimee's shoulders and squeezed. "It's okay. She's right to be mad. I'm mad too. And I *will* handle it for the pack and then for me. Because your daughter is everything to me and what Dad and Darrell did, just on that level, means they've pretty much destroyed our family."

"Let's get moving on Nancy over there. I want her back home before she's gone long enough for anyone to call the authorities," Miz Rose said, snapping out orders and getting people moving.

Leaving him alone with Aimee.

"Thanks for defending me," he told her.

She took his hand in hers, kissing his knuckles. "Thanks for defending me. I'm sorry you have to do this with your family. What can I do to make it better? How can I help?"

He took her face in his palms and kissed her. "You already do make it better. This is Pembry business. It'll be ugly and I don't want you to see it. Call me selfish. Are you going to get Nancy home?"

"No. I'll stay here. I need to help get the witches calm and get everyone home before too long. Miz Rose will take Nancy to her car, which is in a mall parking lot somewhere. I want to check on a few of the older folks in town who were here tonight. Lots of excitement and I don't want anyone having a heart attack if I can help it."

"You do realize everything you just said was about you taking care of everyone else. Like my brother, Samuel. I hadn't known you'd been so good to him but I wasn't surprised. Thank you. He's the one who tipped me off today."

Her expression brightened. "He did? I knew he meant it when he said he wanted to turn his life around. He idolizes you, you know. Oh, and hey, I guess I should leave off checking in on any Pembrys? Will you all be out at your pack meeting?"

"Just the elders tonight so pack wolves will be home. But…if you go visiting anyone, will you take a friend along?"

"You don't think anyone would hurt me?"

He shook his head. The ones he didn't trust would be the ones getting punished. But he couldn't be everywhere at once and he didn't know the extent of this plan between his dad and brother. If something happened to her, he'd never forgive himself or his wolves.

"I don't, no. But things are unsettled. Wolves are upset and you know our control is at its lowest when we're worked up." It had just been a full moon a few days prior as well. No use tempting fate. "If you want to go tomorrow and check on Pembrys, I'll come with you."

She looked up at him and he knew she understood. Knew he'd been warring with the need to take over and the knowledge that it was something that'd change his relationship with his parents forever.

"I'm sorry you have to do this. But I'm proud of you. It's not often easy to do the right thing."

Knowing she understood what it would take from him to do this next part was enough to bolster his choice. It had needed to be done for some time and he was the one to do it. Like it or not, the wolves were his to lead and sometimes that meant making really tough decisions.

"I'm going to be pretty late tonight. Maybe I'll just sleep over at Huston's."

"I'll be so pissed if you don't come home. I don't advise you try that. Not if you want to walk without a limp." Her bright smile made him snort.

He gave up on arguing because he hated the idea of not being able to see her after the next ordeal was finished. "I like you in that dress. I'll see you when I get home. I'll try to keep you updated as I go. Don't forget I love you, all right?"

"Only if you do the same. I love you too. Come home to me. I'll be there."

"Don't make me worry. Lock the doors. I'm not joking around."

"I don't like this new tone. And I don't like the worry on your face. So I'll remind you my magic will protect me better than a lock ever could."

"I could break into your house in under five minutes," he said, trying not to patronize her.

And failing, given the slow rise of one brow that made his cock pretty happy. "You *think* you could. That's part of the magic. But you can't. You come inside because I allow you to. If I didn't, you wouldn't get over my threshold. In any way."

"And I do like getting over your threshold," he murmured as he hugged her.

"If you need me, I'll be there. My phone will be on."

He kissed her forehead and left, keeping that close to his heart.

"He's going to have to punish his daddy," she said as her mom came up behind her. "I hate that."

"Me too, baby. Well, not that his daddy will get his. But that our boy has to do it. But Dwayne is so far out of line there's nothing to be done but punish him. And Darrell."

Aimee knew it. Understood it. Still hated it.

"Honey, come on over here," Miz Rose called out. "I need you to keep her nice and calm while we finish up here."

Aimee headed over, kneeling on the floor next to the chair. Nancy looked so sad, even unconscious. She wished she could take that away. Wished she could spare her the pain of discovering this terrible secret life her husband had. Wished even more that it hadn't been someone from their town who'd done it.

She opened up to her magic, to the land and the connection between witch and earth. Opened up and let the power pour out through the hands she held Nancy's in. Soothing. Calming.

The heat of it coursed through Aimee's veins, leaving her sleepy and no small amount calmer herself as her magic swirled through Nancy, picking up and collecting all those bits and barbs. Anxiety. Guilt. Self-doubt. Bob had planted those seeds and Aimee did her best to respect what had to be a grieving process, while also helping just a little by clearing away the worst of it that had kept her looking the other way over the years.

At her side, she knew Miz Rose's magic eased its way into Nancy's memories as Nadine spoke softly, using her own magic to help. Katie Faith stood nearby, feeding the three of them more power as needed.

It took a while, but at last, Miz Rose tapped Aimee's shoulder and she pulled back enough to realize they'd finished.

"I think this is the best it'll get. Robbie Ruiz is here to help load her in and out of the car we take her back in. You stay here and away from any of the rest of this," Miz Rose told Aimee. "You did good tonight. I know there's still so much to deal with, but you held yourself together and I'm proud."

TeeFaye grinned. "She did great!" Then to Aimee, "I think you need food though. Come home and I'll make you a plate of something. We'll wait for the all-clear from the crew taking Nancy here back home to her cheating pig of a husband."

"I should check on some of the older folks. Just to make sure they're all okay."

"You're off duty as of right now. Everyone will know where you are anyway so if you're needed, they'll contact you. They know you'll help." Her mom pushed her into her dad's hug.

"I'm going to get this town locked down for the night and I'll meet you back home shortly." He kissed the top of Aimee's head.

"Come on." Aimee slung her arm through her mom's. "Katie Faith drove over with me and we've got wine in the trunk."

On the way out, there were several knots of shifters and witches, some arguing, most of them puzzled and hurting. Aimee started to blush, but Katie Faith pinched her arm really hard.

"What the hell did you do that for?" Aimee hissed at her friend.

"You will not feel bad about this. You didn't do it. This is all Bob, Dwayne and Darrell," Katie Faith said loud enough for everyone to hear. "Jace is telling Dooley wolves that right now."

"The cats are always in your corner," Bonita Ruiz said before she and her husband faded away down the street.

Not all cat shifters kept to themselves, but most in their part of the country did, much like their wild cousins. They weren't secretive or hostile. Just cautious and private.

Aimee had made plenty of visits out to the area of town the cats had settled in and even within their neighborhoods, they kept to themselves with their houses dotting the land but never close together.

"That's as good as a full-throated 'I love you, Aimee' from a cat," Katie Faith said seriously.

It was *nice* that they'd noticed. That they'd understood her visits had been out of genuine concern and affection. Nice that not everyone in town thought she was a homewrecker.

They drove over to Aimee's parents' house and by the time they arrived, four cars were already parked outside.

"Just be aware there are several pissed-off, overprotective mommas in there. And that your most overprotective, pissed-off bestie is so close to knocking some Pembrys out Jace sent me to you because he knew you'd keep me out of trouble." Katie Faith grabbed the wine.

"He's a keeper."

"I'm sorry this happened to you. My God, you were going to kick Dwayne's ass and he knew it and so he did that to Nancy and to you! What a jagoff."

"Okay, sis, let's go inside before they send a search party or before you scamper off to try to start a fight with an old guy." Aimee tugged Katie Faith up the walk and into the house.

Chapter Twenty-Two

When they pulled up at their grandparents' land, Mac noted that Huston took a different, less-used back road and parked at the edge of the old barn.

"No use being flashy," Huston told him as he got out. He left the keys in the ignition. If they transformed they lost their clothing, which tended to rip and then money or keys got lost.

Long ago they'd learned to leave the keys in the car so even if they lost everything, including their clothes, they still could get in the car and go home.

"Dad's in the bunkhouse," Everett said quietly.

The moment hung there. This was it. If he went to see his uncle before he showed up at the house to discipline his father and brother, he'd be drawing that line that'd separate him from them for good. He'd be taking up the leadership his father had simply let fall from his hands.

He turned toward the bunkhouse instead of staying on the path to the main house.

Inside, Bern waited with six of the ten elders.

Huston and Everett settled at either side of Mac as he nodded his greeting to the others gathered there.

"We're all here to pledge, openly and without hesitation, our fealty to you as Patron," Bern said. "The rest of the elders will wait to see what you do next."

Then they went to one knee, fist and forearm over their hearts.

The weight of it, of their loyalty and strength, fit right into spaces he hadn't known he possessed. All just waiting for this moment.

"I humbly accept, proud to lead," Mac told them as he indicated they stand once more.

These men and women were the strongest in Pembry. The most respected. With this group on his side going in, the coming trial would be easier. He'd still have to play everything exactly right to survive; agitated wolves who didn't have a clear leader would tear one another apart after a while. Mac would be fighting against that and he'd have to tap into their greater need to belong. The need of pack, fraternity and community.

"Full house tonight," Bern told him as they approached the wall of glass beyond. The kitchen was full, as was the table, where his father sat, unrepentant, with Darrell at his side.

His mother perched on a couch in the family room, staring off into space. He wished for Aimee just then. Knowing she'd help, even after how terrible his parents had been to her and her loved ones.

"Yeah, I see some cronies around. I imagine Nan let them in for a reason so I'll let it go." His father's crew, a bunch of friends since high school so he figured they should know better, were derogatively known as the cronies. Good enough guys. Or they used to be, but like him, they'd gone lazy and entitled.

Bern snorted.

"You took your sweet time," his father said, standing and sending the chair back a few feet.

"Shut up and sit down." Mac kept walking, not stopping until he'd gone to his grandmother and showed his respect.

She smiled at him, pride clear. "You got this, punkin."

He knew he did. Which was scary enough in its own right.

"You don't tell me to shut up," his dad challenged.

"For fuck's sake, Dwayne, you've done enough. Rein it in before we lose everything," his mother said from across the room.

"Don't you talk that way in my house," Nan told her and his mom flipped her off.

He didn't really blame his mom for that. His grandmother could be such a self-righteous person for someone who smoked weed when she thought no one knew.

"Enough. This is not why we're all here. Mom, I need you over here now." Mac sat at the head of the table opposite his father. In his grandfather's old seat. His mom settled in at the middle and Samuel came to sit just behind Mac.

"You don't get to decide that. You're not Patron yet," his father said after his gaze flicked over to Samuel. The eldest, Billy, sat next to their mother at the table, but on Mac's side, which given his brother's extreme avoidance of any kind of conflict, was a statement in Mac's favor.

"I get to decide *everything* right now. You brought an outsider into Diablo Lake without sanction."

"It had to be done. She's a lying whore."

"We're going to pause a moment right here." Mac folded his hands on the tabletop in front of him, his knuckles red from where he'd given his father the swollen nose and developing black eye.

His grandmother put a cup of cocoa with little marshmallows at his right hand. The absurdity of it nearly made him laugh. He thanked her because he liked doughnuts on his birthday too much not to.

"Right now this is just you and me. Mac to Dwayne. If you speak that way about her again I will knock out your teeth. And when they grow back I'll knock them out again. And so on."

He sipped his cocoa, noting that she'd put in some cinnamon, his favorite.

"Now, we're back to our situation as Pembry wolves. Because you violated the most sacred rule. You endangered us all and for what? None of them are going to vote for you now. Well fucking done."

Nan tutted at him but he didn't flip her off.

"The Consort has filed a complaint, as have the Dooleys and the cats. They had to use magic on the human to keep her from exposing us all. What were you thinking other than what a thin-skinned sore loser you are?"

"That b—girl," he corrected himself before he called Aimee a name and got his teeth knocked out. Subtly, more energy in the room shifted to Mac as his father's support dwindled. "She had to be exposed."

"*You broke the law.* You brought that human woman here unsanctioned. You exposed us all. And on a side note, you destroyed that human's family and told her kids. What right do you have to act like that?"

"What about the witch trying to shove me out of my job? No one cares about that?"

"He doesn't because he's nailing that witch."

Mac got up, stalked over to his brother and yanked him up, out of the chair.

"You and me got some talking to do when this official pack business is over," Mac snarled as he got in his brother's face.

"You think."

Mac sneered. "That's your response? It's going to feel so good to beat the hell out of you. Again. Sit down now and let the adults talk." He turned his back and headed to his place once more.

"I know Darrell and Dwayne Pembry were part of this action. The question remains as to who else was involved." Mac looked to his mother.

"If I'd known this was what they were up to I'd have stopped it. These two have no idea what they've done. I wanted you to end up with the witch! I wanted her in the pack to make us stronger. I don't know if I want some homewrecker in this family though."

"As Darrell and Dad know, the human male had an elaborate second life. His mistresses had no idea he was married, including Aimee." Several people had told him independent of one another, and Carl Benton had been one of them. He'd given Mac a brief overview, including the way Aimee'd found out not too long before she and Mac started dating. Long after she'd broken things off with the jerk.

"Your mother didn't know." At least his dad had some honor left and wasn't going to let his wife be punished for his misdeeds. "This was part and parcel of the election. I had a right to expose the witch. Even if she claims she didn't know, it just goes to show her bad judgment."

"You brought a human to Diablo Lake unsanctioned," Mac repeated. "The why might have been a mitigating factor in your discipline, but it doesn't erase the law breaking. And in your case, it does the opposite. You do understand that, right?"

"I don't have to sit here and take this. We run this town. We don't need to be beholden to any of them. The witches fixed it up, didn't they? It was a misunderstanding."

"Dwayne Pembry, I find you guilty of breaking the law of sanction. Darrell Pembry, I find you guilty of the same. You will be sent up for twelve months, after which time you may petition to return. You have an hour to get what you need," Mac said after looking at the wall clock.

His dad stood again, sputtering with rage. Darrell came at Mac, who nodded and jerked his head, indicating they take it outside.

Their mother yelled at them both to stop.

"You're the one who started all them rumors about Katie Faith and now you're going to call me out for this?" Darrell bellowed at her.

"No one's gonna fight. We're gonna calm down and think before this gets out of hand," his dad said, struggling to sound reasonable.

"I challenge you for Patron," Mac said then.

Nan chuckled at his back and the energy, all that swirling, forest loam and fertile earth began to pour into him as Pembry wolves settled their allegiance with him over his father. One by one.

"You think you're ready for that?" his father asked.

"Let this be the physical part of your discipline," he said to his dad, feeling like a stranger in his own body. "Huston, Everett, make sure Darrell sticks around. Since he's been hiding from me, I made it public knowledge that he'd be punished and he's violated the pack rules. Again."

"You didn't hand that down in person. I didn't even know there was a problem until today," Darrell lied.

"You knew enough to hide for two days. Stop lying. You're crappy at it and I'm good at knowing when people don't tell the truth, Darrell." Mac looked at his dad. "So?"

"Dwayne, don't do this," his mother said quietly. "This is the way of things. He's meant to take over."

She didn't say that he was old and slow compared to Mac, who'd had Special Forces training. Mac was the sharpest blade possible and they ought to know because they sent him away from home to be made into their weapon.

Except he was no one's weapon but his own and only in service of his pack. He'd learned that too. Learned it while falling in love with Aimee. Realizing he had so many reasons to be proud and confident in his path and ability.

He waited, staring his father down.

He came in bloody.

Took his shoes off at the back door, stripping off dirty, torn clothes, tossing some in the wash basket and the others into the trash.

She stood there in the kitchen, watching him. The sadness clung to his skin, but there was pride too. He'd taken on the Patron position; she could see the power around him like a cloak.

All his wolves, their needs and wants, on his shoulders.

Despite the blood, dirt and sadness, there was a satisfaction to him. He'd made a choice and there was no regret.

He looked up, catching her gaze. She wanted to move, to close the distance between them and pull him close. Wanted to use her magic to soothe all the anxiety and sadness away.

But she knew him. Knew this male she loved needed that distance for a while until he'd finished picking things over in his head. As much as she hated it, she respected the way he had to work through something pack or family related.

They said nothing, but in that look she told him how she felt. That nothing had changed, despite the blood tracked into her mudroom.

What had changed was the fact that she could no longer pretend away that she'd be Patron with him at his side. His wolves would be hers too. She hoped she could do as good a job as Katie Faith had.

Then again, Katie Faith's in-laws were a walk in the park compared to what hers would be.

"I'm going to shower," he said at last, once he'd stripped down.

She nodded. "I'll get you a towel."

He smiled. It wasn't a big smile. Or even a happy smile. But it was for her. *To her.* His way of reiterating what she'd just told him. That nothing had changed between them.

His spine was straight and he stood tall as he took his adorably naked butt down the hall to the bathroom.

Two in the morning. She heated a towel in the dryer and then left it for him, folded up on the counter in the bathroom.

After a quick text to Katie Faith to say he'd come

home and was all right, Aimee snuggled down in their bed to wait for him, pretending to read but really just staring at the screen until the letters swam into soup.

He prowled in some minutes later and she lay back against the pillows to stare. So masculine and powerful. Sexy.

A few bruises marked his torso and his hands were a mess, but otherwise, he didn't seem to be injured too badly. Not physically anyway.

He climbed into bed and pulled her to him, holding her close. She let down the walls she kept her magic behind and let it free, let it slowly blanket him. Protective.

"Tell me," she said at last.

"I'm Patron. Everyone knows you weren't at fault for that debacle at city hall."

She kept waiting.

"I exiled Darrell and my father for a year for breaking the law of sanction. Darrell unfortunately needed a beating to get that fact through his head and I added another year to his sentence after that to underline just how serious I am. Wherever he goes, he might need some medical attention. No, you're not going anywhere." He tightened his hold. "He'll get the help he needs but you won't be the one to do it. I don't want him near you or this town."

Shifters did have healers, so it wasn't like she was the only person who could help. And frankly, fuck Darrell Pembry.

"I didn't want to have to physically challenge my father. But he wouldn't listen. Not to my mom or anyone else."

He shuddered and she had to fight her instinct to ask more questions. Fight her instinct to run out there and beat these wolves for hurting Mac's heart the way they did.

"I had to really hurt him. He just kept coming. Over and over. I wanted him to keep down, to just fucking let it be over. It wasn't as if he ever could have won. But…"

"Sometimes only the very painful lessons stick with some people."

"He couldn't stand anymore." The emotion in his voice tore at her. "By the end, he was lying there on the grass under the moon and I felt good. I felt right. I beat the hell out of my father and all the wolves there howled and celebrated it. Including me. What is wrong with me?"

She let go then and poured her magic out, sheltering and comforting. He sighed, snuggling tighter to her.

He could always be vulnerable with her and she'd never betray him.

"There's nothing wrong with you, Macrae. You did what you were born to do. What you had no choice but to do."

"People don't just beat their father nearly to death when they take over the family business."

"Shut up about that. You're not human. You tell me that all the time. Usually to talk me into something involving sex, but still."

He snorted and she felt a little better.

"You're a werewolf. Beating your daddy nearly to death when you take over a pack is sort of your jam. I mean, he could have avoided it if he'd passed it to you like JJ did, or like other Patrons when it's time for a younger wolf to take over. He made his choice and because he made that one, you had to make yours. You did what you had to for the good of Pembry."

"I know that in my head. My heart is another matter."

She understood that very well.

"I think that just means you have a very big heart. What's going to happen now? You exile them for a year, hell two for Darrell. What happens to Scarlett and Sharon and their kids?"

"Sharon and the kids will stay here in town. She's got a job and the kids are in school. It's not necessary to punish them any further for being related to my brother. Maybe Sharon will find her spine while he's gone. Maybe he'll figure out he needs to be a better man. Who knows?

"As for my mom, she's a retired Patron like JJ and Patty are. Dad and Darrell claim she had nothing to do with the thing with Nancy at the town hall. She wants you in the pack, so I'm inclined to believe that. She's got other secrets, as we both know, but I can't punish her for that. Not unless I know more. She did start those rumors about Katie Faith so I fined her and made her donate the money to the Dooley recovery fund. She gave over her seat as Patron without blood so at least I didn't have to leave her unable to walk, bleeding on the grass."

Thank heavens, because though *she'd* love to punch Scarlett's lights out, she knew Mac didn't want to.

"She'll remain in Diablo Lake. Billy offered to have her stay with him, but I think it'll be the other way around. She'll still make trouble, I can taste it."

Aimee didn't hide her growl. He had enough to deal with! His mother should be *helping*, not making things worse. And, her trouble seemed aimed at Katie Faith and Jace, which wasn't something Aimee was prepared to tolerate.

But right then, it was about Mac. And about Scarlett

being his mom and not the meddling, busybody bitch Aimee wanted to punch. There'd be time to handle that cow and Aimee would be the one to do it because she was done letting the former Patrons of Pembry hurt those she loved. Especially as the new Patron was Mac and she knew one day she'd be at his side.

It had been easier for Katie Faith when she took over with Jace, but Aimee saw the difference in their situations. As much as she loved Mac and most of his pack, she wasn't ready to go get hitched and start running a pack at his side. At least not for a few months. Let them have a Valentine's Day as a couple first!

She'd help. She'd nurture and love and do her very best. And as she did, she'd be preparing herself for the job. She didn't want to reflect on Mac poorly, didn't want to walk in without knowing a whole lot about pack culture and rules.

She'd been the instrument to hurt Mac and that needed to be in the rearview awhile for the other wolves in Pembry. If she pushed now, some would reject her out of hand simply because it was too much change.

Mac needed to make his way as Patron. Let his wolves see his leadership and commitment first.

"Go to sleep. It's been a spectacularly awful day. I love you. You did the right thing and you'll keep on doing the right thing. It's who you are."

He squeezed her, laying his head on her shoulder so she could comb through his hair as he fell asleep.

Chapter Twenty-Three

Mac woke up to the scent of chocolate. He remained in their bed, eyes closed, the warmth of the room and the smell of brownies baking the sweetest wake up in the world after the nightmare of the day before.

Her side of the bed still bore her fragrance and the slight indentation of her weight but her heat had evaporated so she'd been up at least an hour or so.

After a few moments he heard her moving around out in the kitchen. He listened a little while longer, assuring himself they didn't already have a house full of wolves. Once he'd ascertained they were alone, he opened his eyes because brownies, Aimee and *alone* could lead to a very good morning indeed.

He sat, sucking in a deep breath as he continued to listen to her putter. Drawers opened and closed. The fridge opening up. Her footfalls as she moved through the kitchen and dining room.

As much as he loved his grandparents' place and the part of town his parents and aunt and uncle lived in, he preferred this side of Diablo Lake where the edges of several communities met. Magic swirled around with shifter energy here. A few blocks in either direction and there were Dooleys as well as Pembrys. Lots of witches.

It smelled better here. Usually because Aimee was baking, but he'd take that any day. And his wolves already knew where he was and had been coming to visit.

Perhaps the shift to Aimee's house would help his wolves step into this new reality. Leave behind some of the traditions they'd had under Scarlett and Dwayne and make new ones.

What he'd done the night before still lived in his memory. But the sleep and being able to unload all that on Aimee when he'd gotten home meant he was pretty much okay with it. It was, as she'd said, what he'd needed to do.

She popped her head in, smiling at the sight of him, and he'd never been happier. "Morning. I've been baking. Plus we've had a few visitors already today."

He stood, finding a pair of sleep pants to pull on. "Why didn't you wake me?"

"Because you were sleeping and they were here very early. I told them all you'd get back to them when you got up but if there were problems to talk to Huston. He's been by a few times too and I'm pretty sure Everett has driven past at least twice."

Patrolling around the Patron's home was a pretty common thing. "That'll be happening regularly from now on. Huston and Everett are my lieutenants."

He'd need to think about the logistics of that. Maybe purchase a pack house nearer to this one so they could sleep there and trade off guarding him. And Aimee, though he'd save that for another day.

"So right now we're all alone and there are fresh-baked brownies," he said.

She nodded, one brow rising. "And a lot of other food.

Is it common for werewolves to bring casseroles after a challenge is won?"

"We're in the South. Everyone makes casseroles for any old occasion. But if you told me my aunt dropped off her ham-and-potato soup, I'd be very grateful."

"She didn't. But Huston did."

"Bring me brownies and let me fuck you," he told her.

"That's an offer I can't refuse." She darted away, and he pulled the just-put-on sleep pants off and tossed them aside right as she returned with two pans. "They were still cooling, but I've honestly never let that stop me. I made a batch with walnuts and chocolate chips and one without in case you're a weirdo who hates nuts and chocolate chips."

"What if I was allergic?"

She tossed her robe and quickly got naked and he sort of forgot his question until she said, "But you're not allergic to either. I don't want to poison you! I like your dick too much for that."

He reached out and grabbed her hand, pulling her down to the mattress as she laughed.

"I'm glad. I think." He kissed her and she wrapped her arms around his neck. "Thank you for being such a good listener last night."

"Part of the service I provide. I will be here for you. Always."

"Even though my family is loopy?"

"My mom's best friend nailed a dude in the cans for talking shit about her kid. It's not like my family is shy and retiring."

Mac flipped her to her back, reaching out to grab a fork, scooping up some of the chocolaty goodness.

With nuts and chocolate chips, of course, and she was right, they were so fucking good. Could have been that he hand fed them to a naked, willing witch, but whatever, he was blessed in many ways.

He kissed her, chocolate only spicing her elemental taste. Her hum of pleasure shocked along his spine, settling at the base of his cock where it tightened.

That slap of desire, of deep want of this woman he loved to his very core, should have left him unsettled. It was big and bold and had the power to take him to his knees.

And yet, he embraced it because it was her. Because he knew he couldn't resist her and didn't want to. Knew too, that she'd protect him as much as he protected her. Sure, they'd fight. He was bossy and so was she in her own way. She was independent and had her own mind. He found that remarkably sexy even as he also sometimes found it infuriating.

But she'd never misuse his heart.

He spread her out, taking his time kissing and nibbling from the fingertips of her right hand, across her body to the fingertips of her left. He licked across her nipples until she writhed, a pleading tone entering the sounds she made.

She attempted to grab the dick she claimed to love so much but once she touched him, it would be over, so he avoided her move, taking her hands and putting them above her head.

He kissed over the velvet skin of each of her ribs, across the hollow of her belly and the curve at her hips. The happy sigh she made when he pushed her thighs open and looked his fill at her pussy only pummeled his self-control.

And that was before he took a lick and was lost in her. Her taste, the way she responded to his touch, the magic that surged the closer she got to climax seemed to stick to his tongue.

All of it ensorcelled him. Willingly.

He traced his fingers over her inner thighs as he ate her pussy like he'd been starving. Knew when she was getting close and pulled back over and over until he deemed her ready.

When she climaxed, her back bowed as she nearly roared his name, one of her hands tangled in his hair, pulling to get him where she wanted.

And when she was nothing more than a bunch of jumping muscles, he moved back up her body and entered her slow but deep.

Those beautiful eyes opened and she smiled, catlike as he began to thrust, keeping that slow, deep rhythm that drove them both crazy.

There was no need for words. Everything she felt was clear in her gaze. Clear in the way she opened to him, heart and body. Clear in the trust she gave him when she was soft and vulnerable.

As always he was torn between letting go deep within her and dragging things out as long as he could.

Which wasn't much longer, because she wrapped her thighs around his waist, changing her angle and bringing him impossibly deeper. Where she was impossibly hotter and even tighter.

The grin on her face told him she knew it too. Minx.

He held off, sweat beading on his brow, his control a sheer, thin thing as orgasm took up space in every single cell until there was nothing but pleasure and he came, hard, still so deep in her it was like their hearts pounded in time.

"Ms. Mayor, that was pretty astonishing," he managed to say.

"I haven't won yet, so don't count your chickens. But you can call me Ms. Mayor when we're alone." She giggled and he leaned over to kiss her quickly.

"My father wrote a letter to the city council last night, resigning his seat. They're meeting today I imagine. Whether they appoint you now, or wait for the election next week, we both know the outcome. Gonna be a lot busier around here between your promotion and mine."

"Second jobs more like," she said without any acrimony. "But I figure we can try something new around Diablo Lake. More decisions made as a community. That'll spread out the work and also bring people together. And we need it just now."

"Has the magic changed since last night?"

"It doesn't quite work that way, but I know what you mean. I think everyone will be holding their breath a few days to see if banishing your daddy and Darrell sticks. I think once we know it will, things will ease up and we can get back to normal. Or, normal for Diablo Lake anyway. Until the next thing happens."

His mother still had secrets. His father would be away from town twelve months, along with his brother and some of their allies. If they came back and they weren't chastened, he'd have to beat down some more wolves. And do it over and over until the lesson finally got learned.

Until then he had a woman who made him sex brownies, listened to his troubles and accepted the fact that werewolves came to their house all hours of the day and night. And when he thought about it, it was a pretty damned good turn of events. They'd make it through because she was tough and smart and magic and he loved her. The miracle of it was that she loved him back and he made a pledge to never forget what a blessing that was.

* * * * *

Acknowledgments

Because no author gets to this point on her own, I am forever grateful to:

The Carina Press team from stem to stern especially Kerri Buckley—you're all fantastic and amazing.

My husband—2016 was my least favorite year of all time and without his support through it all, I'm not sure I'd be here today.

About the Author

Lauren Dane is the *USA TODAY* and *New York Times* bestselling author of over seventy-five novels and novellas in the romance and urban fantasy genre. She lives in the Pacific Northwest among the trees with her spouse and children.

You can check out her latest releases, backlist and upcoming books at her website: www.LaurenDane.com or you can write her at LaurenDane@LaurenDane.com or via her PO Box: Po Box 45175, Seattle, WA 98145

And don't miss the next book in New York Times *bestselling author Lauren Dane's Diablo Lake series:* Diablo Lake: Awakened.

After a long six years away, Ruby Thorne is home. Her connection to Diablo Lake and its magic has snapped back into place, strengthening her already powerful abilities and bringing her a much-needed sense of peace. But this Diablo Lake is a far cry from what she left behind. Relations between the magical residents have deteriorated, threatening the sacred balance of magic.

Chapter One

Ruby pushed her buggy down the produce aisle. She'd been so smug about avoiding the one with the rickety front wheel, but the one she'd chosen instead would randomly lurch to the right and Ruby had only narrowly avoided colliding with an end cap of canned green beans.

She came to a stop at the display of oranges, piled high. They were so brilliantly orange they nearly glowed. How she'd missed the produce grown in Diablo Lake! Nothing like it anywhere else. The magic in the soil created something truly special.

Happiness spread through her as she grabbed several, bringing them to her nose to take in the gorgeous scent.

Home.

Being back in the place she'd been born and raised had filled Ruby with a sense of purpose and rightness. The magic embraced her, filled her with pleasure and comfort.

The woman at her side, chattering like a dingdong, was one of her oldest and dearest friends, Aimee. "That last time I was pretty sure you were going to take out the potato chip pyramid. Not gonna lie, I'd have pretended not to know you. But I'd have laughed about it with you later."

Ruby snorted a laugh as she tucked oranges into one of the produce bags she'd brought along. "True friendship."

"Obviously." Aimee pointed at the muslin bag Ruby had just filled. "Hey! Those are so cute! Where did you get them?"

"I made them. They're super easy. I can show you if you want."

"You did?" Aimee asked, one brow rising.

Ruby nodded, grinning at her friend's disbelief. "Right? I wasn't the craftiest growing up other than candles and my tinctures. But I got talked into a sewing class. I'd been away from Diablo Lake six months and I had a lot of school but I needed to do something else. Something more creative and there I was, absolutely in love with this craft I'd sort of only perfunctorily engaged in for most of my life."

"Oooh, *perfunctorily*. Lookit you all smart and stuff." Aimee bumped her hip to Ruby's. "What's the coolest is how as a grown-up, you're as amazing as you were when you were a kid and a teenager. I love that you're into sewing now and I'm totally up for learning how to make those little sacks. Easy is my speed. You can show me at the next Sip, Stitch and Bitch night. I bet Katie Faith would want to know how too."

Every other week, they had a standing date to hang out, drink, do some sort of craft—obviously one safe to do while drinking—and watch reality shows while talking terrible shit about all the casts. In the years she'd been gone, Ruby had been envious of the time they'd set aside so she was very much excited to be part of them at last.

Ruby leaned over to hug Aimee quickly because that made her happy. "Damn I missed your silly ass."

Aimee grinned. "My silly ass missed you too."

The small town grocery store was busy as she and her friend did their shopping. Ruby had to pause every few feet to say hello and accept welcome back wishes from friends and neighbors she'd known all her life—and keep her buggy from maiming anyone.

"When I was seventeen and dreaming of life as an adult I honestly never considered making a date with a friend over grocery shopping," Aimee said as they perused the jars of spaghetti sauce. "Yet here I am on a Wednesday night because you and I are so busy it was this or wait a few more days to hang out."

"Adulting involves far more time being awake and doing things I'd rather not like clean toilets and pay bills than I ever imagined," Ruby said.

"The only real consolation is the sex and the freedom to eat peach cobbler for breakfast if and when you might want."

"You're a sage." Ruby snickered, thinking of the cherry pie she'd had after finishing her eggs that morning. And that she'd shared that pie with her mom as they stood at the kitchen counter and watched through the window as the dogs played in the yard. "But that's totally true." She grabbed a few cans of chickpeas to make hummus and some Greek olives to add to the pasta sauce she and her mom planned to put up over the weekend. There were so many tomatoes waiting to be made into salsa and pasta sauce she probably wouldn't need to buy any until near time to can more the following year.

"I totally am. Mac says I'm a *chatterbox stuck on shuffle* but I'm sure he just misunderstands what the words mean. Maybe he didn't pay attention in his classes at the London School of Economics." Aimee waved a hand airily. "Clearly I'm fucking brilliant."

"I probably wouldn't challenge him at figuring out percentages or gross national product and what have you. But you *are* the brilliantest," Ruby agreed as they turned the corner and headed into the bakery section. Her favorite. The scent of fresh bread and all the best carbs greeted her.

"Right? God I love bread so much," Aimee said as she picked up a pretty French loaf with a leaf pattern cut into the crust. "Ever since Merilee took over the bakery here, I've probably eaten my weight in baked goods. All is right in the world."

Merilee was a witch in town whose skills with bread and pastry were very well known. Her magic hands made crusts perfectly chewy and crisp, the cinnamon seductive, and her cherry thumbprint cookies were so good, Ruby's mom used to send her a box wherever in the world she was living. A little bit of magic from home.

"I wish there was a way to bottle this smell," Ruby said, beginning to think on how she might actually make that happen. A candle that scented a room like fresh baked goods would be pretty cool. She grabbed a few loaves knowing that her parents' kitchen was nearly always full of hungry family and sandwiches made an excellent snack.

She paused to look over the selection of breakfast bars to check the ingredients lists. "I'm working on a recipe for these. I can make them fresh for half the price and never come across a raisin unless I put it there myself. And I never would."

"Chocolate is good for you. Don't forget to put some in the recipe," Aimee added.

"You have good ideas. A great reason to keep you around. Walnuts for sure since my dad is allergic to hazelnuts. In case you're not following along, I've switched topics. I promised a bunch of baked goods in payment for help moving when I find a place. I got off pretty easy I think. I didn't even attempt to pay anyone with actual money. No one wants an offended Anita Thorne."

"Goodness no." Aimee shuddered at the thought. Ruby's mom, Anita, was, pretty much like Aimee's mom, a force of nature. She didn't get where she was in her life without a lot of kicking down doors and demanding her due. She was one of Ruby's idols. A compass in a chaotic world.

"As for your way of floating around on the wind of a conversation?" Aimee waved a hand. "Please. You and Katie Faith both have that stream of consciousness thing. So since she was here when you were gone, I never fell out of practice following your sentences into new and exciting topics at a moment's notice. Like a roller coaster and I don't even need to stand in line."

Ruby snickered. "One of the things that made it easier when Nichole and Greg moved back here was knowing she'd have you and Katie Faith to keep her company until I got here."

Aimee bumped her hip to Ruby's. "Well, as much as we love her and she's definitely fitting in just fine, I missed you too. You were out in the world doing important stuff and I was here. Katie Faith was away for years too and it was just me and Lara. And now she's off in Scotland for however many years." Their friend had gone to England and Scotland to see some family and had found love when her car had broken down and the tow driver was now her husband. Life had its own plans.

"And now the three of us are living within two miles of one another for the first time in six years. You're *mayor*! And you're getting married in two months. Katie Faith is happy and married and at Jace's side to lead the Dooley wolves. These are hopeful, powerful days."

Aimee breathed out slowly and then quickly hugged Ruby. "Oh my god, I needed to hear all that. There's so much happening and we really do need to catch up but in private because everyone here is listening and watching everything we're doing."

"That part of small town life I didn't miss that much. Come on. I promised I'd grab a few gallons of milk for my mom. I'll be sure to keep the bread up here in the purse holder thing. Nobody ever wanted smushed bread," Ruby said.

"Says you. I'd still eat it that way. I mean if it was necessary like after the apocalypse or smushed by a can of soup. It's still bread. Some things are worth lowering your standards for, Ruby."

Before she could stop snickering and reply, Aimee came to a sudden halt and Ruby only barely managed to swerve the recalcitrant buggy at the last minute to save her friend's ankles from dreaded grocery buggy injury.

"Yikes! I nearly maimed you," she said but Aimee's attention was on the woman coming their way, lodging her cart catawampus so that they couldn't get around her.

"Perfect," Aimee said under her breath.

"There you are. I need you to tell my son to return my calls." Scarlett Pembry attempted to loom over

Aimee but Aimee was an alpha too and didn't show her throat.

"You need to leave a message when you call," Aimee told her soon-to-be mother-in-law with patience that frayed at the edges.

Scarlett Pembry was a striking woman. Not exceptionally tall, but she had a big presence. Light brown hair, cut well to flatter the slightly heart shaped face. Always made up and dressed well and that day was no exception. If she hadn't been such a spiteful, mean person, she'd be beautiful.

Regardless of the fact that she was no longer in charge of the Pembry pack, Scarlett would always be an alpha wolf. A dangerous predator with decades of political experience under her belt. Ruby knew a threat when she saw one. And Scarlett Pembry was a threat.

"I don't have to leave a message! He can see his mother has called. It says so on his phone. That's all he needs to understand he should call me back. He's a very smart boy but sometimes he misses the details. That's *your* job." Scarlett jabbed a long pink fingernail at Aimee for emphasis.

"My actual job is mayor of the Township of Diablo Lake. And I also have a stake in the town medical practice. Nowhere in the job description for either is being Macrae's personal assistant. First, he's a grown man. And he's already got a personal assistant as you well know. You can contact him if you like. But leave a message so he knows what you need."

Scarlett's mouth flattened and her eyes narrowed. "Don't play games with me. You know what I mean. I surely don't need to be calling in outsiders to get my child to return a phone call."

At that point Ruby knew her features showed her shock but Scarlett didn't deserve the effort to hide it.

"He's your nephew. Hardly an outsider. He's eaten pancakes at your table on Sunday mornings for years of his life," Aimee said quietly of Everett, Mac's cousin who Ruby figured was his personal assistant or whatever the packs called that person.

Scarlett had the dignity not to argue that point. Everett was more than just a guy who kept Mac's calendar. He grew up at Mac's side as a guard as well, Ruby knew that much. She was really proud of Aimee for keeping her composure but setting her boundaries. It was very badass.

"Your generation might be keen on airing your family business to all and sundry for the drama of it, but mine knows how to act. Everett is my nephew, but *you* are Mac's soon-to-be wife. You will lead the pack at his side once you're married. It is your *duty*. I know there are those who doubt your ability to lead with Mac. Because you're not one of us." Scarlett paused, looking Aimee up and down, grabbing the cart to hold her in place. "But I'm not one of them. I tell them you're a powerful witch who has already begun to bring Pembry strength. I know you can do a good job. But you have to let go of your modern ways and remember this is Pembry. We don't act out like Dooley does. The wolves look to you to lead by example. You must be worthy of this place in the world, Aimee."

Ruby slid her gaze over to Aimee, whose eyebrows had risen up her forehead. *Oh no.* This was not going the way Ms. Pembry thought it was. "Worthy?" Aimee asked, scorn in her tone.

"Ma'am. What the ever-loving heck are you talking about?" Ruby didn't say a curse word because her grandmother would have lectured her for three hours about how she needed to know how to *act in public*. But no one attacked her friend like that.

Scarlett looked around and finally noticed Ruby. "Oh. You." Scarlett's lip curled ever so slightly that Ruby hated her for it while also admiring the skill. "Why are you eavesdropping? This is not your business."

"*Eavesdropping?* You're in the grocery store at six thirty on a Wednesday night. Pretty much half the town is here listening to *you* air your business on aisle five," Ruby said. "If you don't want your private business aired out, you're in control of that."

"Be on your way," Scarlett hissed, waving her hand at Ruby.

At her side Aimee actually guffawed. "We're on a date so it's us who'll be on our way to the checkout line. Call your son, who is a *grown-up*. If he doesn't answer, leave him a message and tell him what you need after the beep. I'm not part of this in any way, nor will I be. I've made my stance clear about the Rule of Silence but the rest is up to the wolves. As you know." She pulled her cart free and they strolled past.

Ruby wasn't going to discuss any of what just happened with Aimee. Not while they were in the store with everyone watching. And they were watching and barely pretending not to. But there was clearly more to the story than she knew. So she'd make small talk until they could get out of there and speak in private.

"You should contact Damon. He and Major do most of the real estate stuff around here so he'd know what's available to rent and would have access. And you already know him so that's a plus." Aimee smirked but did not mention Ruby's knowledge included exactly four dates and some of the best kisses she'd ever shared in the short time they'd dated six years prior, right before she left Diablo Lake.

"Apparently you're still a shit stirrer," Ruby murmured.

Aimee laughed aloud at that and Ruby was glad she'd said it. She knew her friend had to be under an intense amount of pressure from all directions. Marrying the person you loved was wonderful. If you were fortunate enough to get good in-laws that was even better. But when you were getting some really bad ones, well that had to be a real damper on happiness.

It made Ruby even more protective of Aimee.

"I plan to give him a call to set up an appointment." It wasn't like they broke up and hated one another and as Aimee had said, Damon was the source of the service she needed and there was no reason not to contact him.

Chances were he'd still smell really good, look even better and that slow Southern drawl wouldn't fail to make her a little tingly. And she wasn't going to lie to herself. She wanted to show him what he'd been missing all those years.

Aimee said nothing but the smirk remained in place.

Once they got to the parking lot after checkout, Ruby paused at Aimee's car.

"Thank you for defending me like that. Oh god her face." Aimee hugged Ruby tight. "She's being a pest right now about wedding stuff. More than usual. And there's the Rule of Silence stuff that she's getting everyone worked up over." She looked down at her watch. "I can't talk more right now as I'm due to meet Mac in less than an hour for wedding stuff and I need to drop the groceries home first. I'll text you later. Love you."

"Love you too."

The news about that little scene in the market meant Ruby had to get home—her parents' house—to let them know what happened before the first phone call or text happened. There weren't many secrets in a town as isolated and small as Diablo Lake. Mainly because the gossip network was lightning fast.

Hell, the wolves had decided to claim it was part of being a wolf shifter to be bold and nosy as you please. It worked because they were generally harmless and tended to be charming too, which eased the nosiness. Usually.

As she drove away from town, she cranked the window down, her music up and let herself just be as the scents of her hometown flowed into the car.

Fall crept in through the bite in the air and the first burst of orange and gold had begun to dress the trees. Soon signs of the biggest holidays of the year would show up in town. First Halloween, then Samhain and Collins Hill Days. Which launched into Thanksgiving, and all the winter holidays. Her absolute favorite season and she was home for good, making the difference she'd spent years dreaming of and working toward.

She'd venture back out into the world again. Travel to get more training. Travel because she loved it. But not much could compete with the magic of Diablo Lake all dressed up for some shindig or other. No, this was home in a way she understood would not be true of any other place. She'd always return.

Nothing compared with the way she felt as she saw the lights burning inside the house she'd grown up in casting a glow on the spot Ruby parked her car. She faced the shed where her dad stored all the lawn junk in the shadow of a huge, gnarled oak that still held the swing she and countless other kids had played on.

Her dad had taught her how to ride a bike on the sidewalk out front. She'd learned to drive on their slow poke street. And now Nichole and Greg's car was there, parked in front of the garage their apartment was above. Her mom's youngest sister Ruby's aunt Rehema's Jeep was in front of the main house.

So many of her favorite people all in one place.

Before she went into the house though, she called Damon to leave a message about wanting his help, but he answered instead.

"Ruby Jean Thorne," he said. "What can I do for you?"

She couldn't help the smile at the sound of his voice and then naturally the tingles came right along. It was a great voice.

"Hey, Damon. I'm back in Diablo Lake now and I need a place to live. I hear you're the person to call. Do you have any time to show me what's available? House or apartment, though I prefer a house."

"I heard you were back. And I was glad to hear it. Yep, I've got some rentals available to look at. A few you'd have to wait a month or so to move into, most of them you'd be able to get within a few days at the longest. If you've got about ninety minutes I can show them all to you."

"That would be perfect. Thank you."

"How about tomorrow? Two or three? We get after-noon help at the Mercantile so I'll have the time then."

"Three works well. I'll be at the clinic. We're nearly ready to open up but there are last-minute details to finish. I can meet you at the Mercantile."

"I'll pick you up at the clinic. I'm nosy," he admitted. "I want to check it out."

Nosy, he most definitely was. She laughed and he

joined her. That rhythm they'd had before seemed to *click* back into place. "Fine. I'll see you tomorrow at three."

Grinning, Damon updated his calendar before stepping back into what was three quarters of a laundry room. Pretty much every night after closing up the Mercantile, he headed up to the house he was building to work on it.

Winter was coming and he really wasn't relishing the idea of living in that trailer once it started snowing so he wanted to get enough finished that he could move in and complete the rest into the spring.

And then on to getting Major's house finished. Damon and his twin had bought the land over the summer and while Major was still working on his house plans, Damon had been ready to go first.

Major had been helping finish off the framing of the mudroom slash laundry room that would lead from the back of the house into the main living area. As dirty as he could get either working or running as wolf, he needed a place to dump his dirty stuff so he didn't bring it in.

"You sure took your time," Major groused without any real heat. He just wanted to complain.

"That's why it's my time. I do with it what I want."

His brother said some stuff their grandmother would have cut a peach tree switch over, but he just laughed and flipped Major off.

"I've got an appointment tomorrow afternoon at three. I'm showing Ruby Thorne some properties. She's looking to move out of her parents' house."

Major snorted. "I've seen her around town over the last two weeks. She's looking real good."

Damon had thought very much the same thing when

he'd seen her across the street just a few days prior. But while it was okay when *he* thought so, Major didn't have those rights. When he came back to himself, Major stared at him, one brow raised.

"Interestin'. Just what are you up to?" Major didn't meet Damon's gaze straight on, instead focusing just to the left. Avoiding a fight.

How quickly had he shifted into that space where his wolf rose to a perceived challenge over Ruby? Damon shook his head and held up a hand, palm open. "That was unexpected. I apologize."

Major nodded and then rolled his eyes. "Apologize for what? Being a wolf shifter? Fuck off. You two had chemistry back then, seems only right you'd have it now." His brother went back to work without saying another thing.

Damon remembered having a very similar moment with his oldest brother, Jace, back when Jace and Katie Faith had first come together again. She'd been away from Diablo Lake for a few years and had returned home, all grown up. Just like Ruby had.

The similarities bore some thinking on, so he figured there was no harm in thinking while working.

Ruby heard laughter before she'd even reached the steps leading up to the back door. Her dogs, Kenneth the Magnificent and Biscuit, ran around in the large yard just outside the kitchen along with her parents' dog, Pipes—so named because she had no problem using hers to bark and yodel any time she felt a need.

"Hey there, babies," Ruby called out and they all three turned and galloped her way. Pipes was a leftover casserole of a rescue. Probably some Lab and maybe a German shepherd. A collie perhaps. Whatever she was, she was on the large side of a medium-sized dog with blue eyes and splotches of white and dark brown on her fur. She yodeled and crooned and barked and talked back and fit into their family just fine. She also kept an eye on the boys, busy, curious little Cairn terriers, like a responsible older sister.

After Ruby gave pets and compliments about general goodness and beauty, they all headed up into the house.

A chorus of hellos greeted her when she got into the kitchen. "There are some groceries in my backseat," she told her brother Greg. "Can you please bring them in?"

"Sure thing," he said, pausing to kiss her cheek on his way past.

Nichole rolled into the room with a big smile. "Hey there, gorgeous."

There were lots of hugs and smooches and the like once Ruby put her things in her old bedroom and changed into a far more comfortable outfit.

They ran things from the kitchen to the table, adding a few more settings as two more cousins showed up. But before long, they were all seated at the big, scarred wooden table in the dining room, passing around platters of food as a pleasant murmur of conversation settled in.

"Before the phone calls start, I need to tell y'all about what happened at the grocery store tonight," she said after the edge of hunger had been taken off.

Her mother put her fork down and clasped her hands, waiting.

"It's not a big deal," Ruby hastened to add before anyone got worried. She told them all about the scene at the grocery store and her mom rolled her eyes.

"That woman. She just can't help herself. It's like she's got a compulsion to embarrass her momma every chance she gets." Anita Thorne waved a hand. "I'm glad you spoke up and let her know you weren't the one. I'll be sure to underline that with a look if I see her around town." Her mother made a sound, like a hum, but with threat. Scarlett better run the other way if she caught sight of Anita.

Ruby hoped so because she didn't have the time or inclination to play clownish games with Scarlett Pembry. And if Scarlett started something with Anita, well, it'd be a whole different sort of problem.

"And I have an appointment tomorrow afternoon with Damon Dooley. He's gonna show me available rentals in town."

Her mother's dark look regarding Scarlett washed away, replaced with an arch smile at Ruby. "You make sure you like the feel of whatever place. You understand? You don't need to rush. It's important to feel right in your home. And I know you. You're going to need a big garden space. We're in no hurry to have you leave though. So don't choose some dark little place in a terrible neighborhood."

Ruby couldn't help but laugh at that. "Bad neighborhood? Oh that one with the house with the curtains drawn all the time?"

"I still say that's suspicious," her mom replied, setting off another wave of laughter. "What are they hiding?"

"Or, they're all freaked out by that witch in the thirty-year-old Buick who keeps driving by trying to peek in their front window," Ruby teased. "Ow!" She drew back the hand her mom had just whacked with the back of her spoon, trying not to laugh anymore. "Okay! I promise not to move into some dark little hovel in any bad neighborhood that may or may not exist. I can't live here forever, Mom. I do really appreciate being here until I find the right place though. And I'll most definitely use all the offers of help to move when it's time."

Her mom's mouth flattened into a line but it was really more a matter of her trying not to smile at being ribbed by her children.

"You didn't get all sad like this when I moved away," Greg said, grinning.

"Well. You brought back Nichole. So that saved me from being too sad about it."

Ruby snickered. "She likes me best," she told her brother in an exaggerated stage whisper. "But your wife is a close second."

Greg tapped the side of his nose, their childhood shorthand for a middle finger and wow, Ruby was simply joyous at having this back in her life regularly.

"Stop hogging the potatoes," she told her brother.

Don't miss Diablo Lake: Awakened *by Lauren Dane available now wherever ebooks are sold.*
www.carinapress.com